Never VACATION WITH Your Ex

Never VACATION WITH Your Ex

EMILY WIBBERLEY & AUSTIN SIEGEMUND-BROKA

VIKING

VIKING
An imprint of Penguin Random House LLC, New York

First published in the United States of America by Viking,
an imprint of Penguin Random House LLC, 2023

Visit us online at penguinrandomhouse.com.

Library of Congress Cataloging-in-Publication Data is available.

Printed in the United States of America

ISBN 9780593326909

1st Printing

LSCH

Design by Kate Renner
Text set in Elysium Std

Never VACATION WITH Your Ex

PROLOGUE

Two Years Ago

THIS ONE WILL BE perfect.

I hold the volleyball out in front of me, visualizing the impeccable form I want for my serve. The precise height I have to jump, the spin I need to put on the ball by tucking my hand over the top, the curve I want to capture to send the shot down onto Malibu's pearl-white sand.

There's so much to remember. So much to get right.

I breathe in, preparing to exhale with the movement as I toss the ball up, and—

"I knew I'd find you here."

I smile despite the distraction, letting the volleyball drop in front of me. It's instinctive whenever I hear his voice, this flicker of warmth in my chest. Facing the direction of his words, I find Dean walking down the sand.

The night wind plays gently with his dark hair. His shirt hangs loosely on him, his pants cuffed. Where other guys in our grade haven't *quite* gotten used to teenagerhood—unshaven, gangly from their growth spurts—Dean is uncommonly graceful. The moonlight over the ocean makes his face glow, or maybe it's just the smirk lighting up his features.

"Now"—he comes up to me, playfully scrunching his expression, pretending to unearth something deep from the recesses of his memory—"was I confused, or did we just spend pretty much the entire day, including dinner, at *someone's* favorite sushi restaurant, celebrating the news *someone* is going into her sophomore year the cocaptain of the varsity volleyball team, the youngest in her school's history?"

In my sheepish silence, the wind whispers over the peaceful water. Nighttime in Southern California is unimaginably serene. Except for me swatting volleyballs on the sand, of course.

Dean comes up next to me. "Kaylee," he says, sincere now. "It's nine p.m. on our summer vacation. Everyone's relaxing in the house. There's *no possible reason* you need to be out here training right now. I'm no . . . sports person, but I'm pretty sure you've just proven you're the number-one volleyball player in our grade. Probably our entire school."

"Yes, exactly!" I reply, half-indignant. He doesn't realize he's hit right on what compelled me to haul my volleyball bag dutifully onto the sand to hone my serve while our families play Pictionary in the house.

I *wish* I felt like I could just be proud of myself instead of ever-fixated on proving more, on being everything, but I don't. Not with the spotlight I feel following me every day. I love the warmth of it, the light, I do. But some days I wish I could escape the searing way it exposes every corner of my life, every choice, every uncertainty. Every insecurity.

"Everyone's going to doubt whether I'm good enough," I say. "Or if I only got the title because of . . . my mom," I finish.

When Dean doesn't reply, I pick up the volleyball, preparing to change myself into rhythm in motion, interlocking every detail of my form honed over practices since I could walk. Pulling my hand back, I bend my knees, preparing to jump—

He catches my fingers in his.

Instantly, I still. He's just stopping me from serving, I rationalize. Yet—for the first time since we were kindergartners crossing the street with our parents—Dean, my best friend, is holding my hand.

"No one could ever doubt how incredible you are," he says.

He drops my hand, nodding to the ball like he understands my mind is made up.

I hear his compliment echoing over the sea, but I straighten my posture, preparing to begin again. Out of the corner of my eye, I see Dean grin, then hold up his phone. "Can I photograph you?" he asks.

I feel my cheeks flush. Dean doesn't realize just how many people at our school would go weak in the knees at that question from him. But I know he's not flirting with me. Or not *just* flirting with me. He's gotten really into photography and is working on convincing his parents to buy him a real camera.

"I'd like that," I tell him. He raises his phone's lens.

With the memory of his hand lingering on my skin, I can't stop smiling.

One

I FROWN INTO MY fries.

Brianna picks over the remains of the wraps we got for dinner while I flick through the photos she took on the beach earlier today. Me, serving the ball while wearing one of the sweatshirts a local sustainable clothing company sent me to promote to my Instagram's half a million followers.

I quickly hide the stress beginning to stretch over my face, because this isn't Brianna's fault. She's not a photographer. She's my current sand volleyball partner—soon to be *former* sand volleyball partner since I'm a junior and she's a senior, about to graduate high school and move for college, which I can barely bring myself to think about. She'll be playing for Stanford next year instead of being my teammate.

We've been friends since I started on our school's varsity team in my freshman year. Though only in her sophomore year herself, Brianna was one of the strongest players. It meant the world to me when she instantly embraced her youngest teammate. Since, she's been the kind of world-class friend who would drop everything to be my photographer for the day despite having no experience whatsoever. I didn't really expect her to pull off the perfect shot.

Still, I need something to post. People have expectations of sports photography, even unconscious ones. If I'm in the middle of crouching instead of springing up with sharp form for the serve, I'll look off-balance, ungainly, contorted. No one likes to see every frame of the effort involved. Just the perfect moments.

On instinct, I start mentally rehearsing my expressions of enthusiasm for Brianna, who is impatiently fiddling with the charm on the necklace her boyfriend got her, the garnet winking against the deep-brown skin of her collarbone. There's still some sand from the beach in one of her black braids. I press on through my camera roll, evaluating the photos with the eye I've trained over years of developing my social media presence.

They're . . . fine.

Swipe. Fine. *Swipe.* Fine.

Just okay. *Swipe.*

My head starts to hurt, pressure making my pulse race. I'm no longer very hungry for my fries, despite the small, cottagey Sun Spot Café near Easton's Beach being our favorite spot. The truth is, none of these photos are up to the caliber of my account.

Brianna must read the disappointment on my face. "I told you. You know what you have to do," she says dryly.

I look up, starting to see schedules, blocks of time shifting on my precarious calendar. "Try again after practice tomorrow?"

Bri rolls her eyes. "Call Dean," she says.

I feel my whole body stiffen. My schedules disappear, the calendar blocks vanishing under the wave of ridiculousness of what Bri's suggesting. Frustration pounds in my flushed cheeks. "*No*," I say.

Bri fixes me with a wordless stare.

"I *dumped* him," I go on incredulously. "Like, dropped him with hardly an explanation not three weeks ago, and you want me to ask him to photograph me in bikini bottoms as a favor?"

My friend just shrugs. "He's a great photographer," she says, like it's justification enough. Which it is not.

I frown—grimace, more like. Yes, he *is* a great photographer. My account saw huge growth when he started helping me with my content. It wasn't why we were dating, obviously. It wasn't why we broke up, either.

Honestly, I didn't give Dean a reason for why I ended our two-month relationship because I knew I couldn't explain this . . . feeling I get. This wound-up, suffocating spiral. In every relationship, it happens. The clenching cold fills me up, spreading from my chest into my fingertips, up past my eyes, until the only thing I see whenever I'm with the guy I'm dating is how I want out. It's kind of horrible, honestly. But it's the way it is.

Could I have done a better job of breaking up with Dean? Definitely. Have I done a better job of dumping guys in the past? On numerous notable occasions. But Dean was different.

Which was the problem. Is there a nice way to dump your childhood best friend after two months?

It's not like breaking up with people is easy. In media, you only see the pain of being dumped. But where's my breakup song from the perspective of the dumper? It's its own special sort of heartache to hurt a nice, cute boy who did nothing wrong. I'm usually not one for excuses, for cheap outs like *It was hard* or *I didn't know.*

But . . . it *was* hard.

It's over now, though, and it's time to move on.

Brianna shrugs without remorse.

Studying the photos with every ounce of concentration I can muster, I feel a migraine coming on in the fuzziness of my phone screen. It's one of the early signs, the warping of the small, intensely colorized display. *Well, great.*

Deep down, I'm not entirely surprised. Between practicing nearly every day to set myself up to qualify for the Olympics after high school, growing my social media in order to attract sponsorships, and doing passably well in my classes, it's *possible* I'm taking on too much. Factor in the breakup with Dean, and "too much" is far behind me.

I pull my aspirin out of my sweatshirt pocket. While Brianna watches, I swallow them down with my Diet Coke. "I'm driving you home," she declares.

Grateful, I nod. I've had chronic migraines for the past few years, brought on by stress and my cycle. This isn't the first time Bri's been here to help when one knocks me out. "Let me choose the photo first," I say, restarting my review while the medicine begins to ease the pounding in my head.

It would be easy to pick something impulsively, to decide one post in thousands didn't matter much. I don't, though. I force myself to evaluate each of Brianna's shots until finally I decide on one where I'm running back from the net, volley-ball in hand. The sunset shines off the top of my dark blond ponytail, which is overdue for a color appointment to return it to a shiny yellow-gold I look tan, which is good—studying for finals turned my skin pale beige, but thanks to my mom's genes, one or two days outside returned me to bronze. In the photo, I'm mid-laugh, my expression offering no hint of the effort these photos took. I look casual. Carefree.

Which people respond to, I've noticed. While they engage with my sports content, they love the unguarded humanness, the reminders I'm a person. It's one principle I've learned on Instagram and found extends into real life—no one loves a princess who doesn't make it look easy.

"This one," I say. I hold out the phone to show Bri.

She doesn't look to see the photo I've chosen. "You really don't want to call Dean," she comments, her brown eyes on me.

Just like I did in the photos, I put on a smile as I begin editing. "Thanks to your excellent photo taking, I don't have to," I say, willing my headache to remain manageable until I get home. I work steadily, warming up the muscles I've developed from years of doing this. First, I change the contrast, then play with the saturation to keep this photo consistent with the color profile on the rest of my feed. I write my caption, tagging the local clothing company.

When I'm about to hit post, my phone buzzes. It's a text from my dad.

> Remember we have to book flights
> for California tonight. I need to know
> what days you have practice.

Unexpectedly, the logistical reminder is exactly what I need right now. I let out a breath, immersing myself momentarily in the thought of Malibu, where my family goes for summer vacation every year.

The memory is enough to ease the pressure in my head. *Crystal water. Soft sand. California sun.* The trip coming up—three weeks in Malibu, between training and tournaments—will be my chance to unwind after the busiest year of my life.

I can't wait.

Feeling renewed, I post the photo. I set my phone on the table, then reach for a fry, finally ready to enjoy my dinner.

My phone vibrates to life once more.

When I look down, my heart stops. It's my dad. I read his message once, then over several times. Fighting past the zigzags in my vision, I start to hope the headache is making me see things.

> The Freeman-Yus are getting into LA
> a day before us, so the earlier we can
> fly out the better.

"Crap," I say quietly.

Bri pauses expectantly, fry midway to the ketchup. I show her my phone, which she reads expressionlessly.

"Kaylee," she says calmly. "Tell me your dad means different Freeman-Yus."

I wish I could.

I thought it would go without saying. I thought it was obvious our vacation plans would change this year from the tradition of our California trip every summer with my parents' closest friends. Friends who they've known since college, who they settled down on the shore of Newport, Rhode Island, in part to be near—the Freeman-Yus: Terry Freeman, Darren Yu, their daughters, Jessie and Lucy, and their son, Dean.

Dean Freeman-Yu. Dean, who I've known and vacationed with in Malibu since we were in diapers.

Dean, my *very* recent ex-boyfriend.

"Tell me you're not going on vacation with the guy you just dumped," Bri prompts me.

I feel like I'm watching my Malibu escape go up in flames, their devouring heat licking my face. I shove my phone into my sweatshirt pocket.

"I absolutely am not," I say.

Two

MY HEAD IS FULLY pounding by the time Brianna drops me off in front of my house, but it's just bearable enough to get through what I have to do next.

Storing my volleyball bag in the hall closet, I walk through the entryway of the home where I've lived since seventh grade. While the Victorian-inspired design took me years to feel comfortable in, I eventually inscribed memories into the ornate banisters, the dark-wood furniture, the Newport coastline waiting outside.

In the living room, I pass the framed photo of my mom on her knees in the sand after winning her third consecutive Olympic gold medal. The shot is stunning. It never fails to pull complicated emotions from me, mostly good ones. I remember being there in the stands nearly a decade ago. It's her only Olympics I can remember. I was full of pride, inspired in a way I never forgot. It was one of the coolest days of my life.

I find my parents in the kitchen, seated on the barstools,

eating takeout. My dad is in slacks and a crisp blue button-down, which means he spent the day showing a house. He's one of the top Realtors in the state, the square-jawed face of John Jordan plastered out in front of the city's priciest historic coastal homes. In person, he looks just like his posters, with perfectly white teeth and no hint of gray in his chestnut hair.

I speak before they can turn to greet me. "You weren't serious," I say. "Right? Just one of your hilarious jokes? The Freeman-Yus aren't coming to California with us this summer because that would be an awful, terrible idea—*right*?"

My parents face me, eyes wide.

"Why wouldn't they come, hon?" my mom asks in honest confusion. She's fresh out of the shower, sun-bleached hair dripping down her shoulders, which show her intense sports bra tan lines, the streaks of pale white between golden brown. She retired from professional volleyball after her last Olympic win and has run a volleyball clinic here ever since.

I literally gape, met only with earnest, empty stares. "Because I, like, *just* broke up with Dean?" I remind my parents. "Did you forget?"

My dad laughs without sarcasm or spite. His charming good cheer never feels forced despite how often he reproduces laughter just like this for clients. "Of course we didn't forget," he says, prodding his salad.

I fold my arms in defiance of his easygoing amusement. I don't understand what game they're playing.

With my parents' perfect relationship and professional

lives—Judy and John Jordan, the Olympian married to the enthusiastic and entrepreneurial real estate king—it's easy to imagine they would change behind closed doors into ruthless, judgmental people. Instead, I'm fortunate to have the great relationship I do with my parents, free of the pressures and petty judgments I know my friends get from their families. Being their only child, I'm used to it being just the three of us, doing everything together. When I took up volleyball, it made them so proud. They've been friends, inspirations, mentors to me my whole life.

It's why I'm caught up short standing in my kitchen, looking from my pressed and polished dad to my tanned, limber mother, struggling to figure out why they're cheerfully conscripting me into the worst vacation plan in history.

"Okay," I say slowly, fighting my headache. "Then *why*?"

"We go to Malibu with the F-Ys every year," my mom explains gently, starting to look like she's worried I'm suffering from some sort of head injury. I'm suffering, but not from memory loss. "It's the whole point of the trip," Mom goes on.

I match her incredulous stare. Their confusion is starting to confuse me. I mean, I understand how traditions work. We *have* gone with the Freeman-Yus every year to California for two or three heavenly weeks in the house my parents own in Malibu right on the beach, except for the summer when we were ten and they visited Dean's grandparents in Taiwan instead. I've played countless games of cards with Dean's family in the living room and pickup volleyball with the parents on the sand in the shade of the cliffs. Dean's sisters feel like they could be my own. I even suffered memorable humiliation in front of his whole family when I face-planted during the group surfing lesson we all did one year.

Still.

"Surely an exception could be made," I say sternly, "for, I repeat, the summer *right after* I broke up with Dean. Have you even thought about how awkward it's going to be? He's my *ex-boyfriend*."

My mom's face softens only slightly. "Kaylee," she says delicately. "Maybe you should have thought of this before you and Dean started dating?"

Despite her reassuring voice, I know there's no sympathy in her words. They close in on me like pillowed prison walls with my migraine pounding on them outside.

"In fact." My dad speaks up, squinting like he's recalling hazy historical details. I'm in no mood for his playful posturing. "*I* think I remember specifically warning you this would happen when you got together," he goes on. "I said, *Kaylee, don't date Dean because you're just going to dump him in two months and then Malibu will be awkward.* And what did you say?"

I frown. There is, unfortunately, no way I'm getting out of replying.

Mom looks down into her salad like she's letting me save face.

I sigh.

"I said, *You don't* know *we'll break up*," I grind out.

It hurts to remember in ways I don't think my parents understand. I'd reassured them not just because I'd wanted to chase my romantic whims without considering the family consequences. It was because I believed it myself, because I really, *really* wanted it to be true.

I'd wondered if Dean would be different. With our family histories, with how long we've been friends—with the years, nearly the decades of memories I have of him growing from the bookish kid whose bar mitzvah party was Lord of the Rings–themed into my tall, leather-loafer- and beige-cardigan-wearing classmate never without his chunky black camera and over-the-ear headphones—I thought he might. He knew my likes, my dislikes, my secrets. I felt completely comfortable with him. He was my best friend.

I didn't set out to ruin our relationship. I *didn't*.

In fact, I wondered if maybe Dean could be my escape from my worst quality. I know I have a reputation as a heartbreaker. My unfortunate habit of dumping guys after a few months is well established at school, even on my social media. I play it off in public and in my head, pretending it's not the one ugly stain that separates me from the image of myself I want to live up to. What celebrity breakup ever made the stars *less* famous, right?

No matter how much I deny it, though, I can't hide from what it really means. There is something wrong with me.

I shouldn't get the suffocated feeling months into every relationship. With Dean, I'd started to convince myself I wouldn't. Maybe I was being impulsive. Maybe I was being rash. Maybe I was lying to myself.

But I really, really liked him. I wasn't planning to break up with him from the start. It just happened.

"If you never wanted to see your ex again, you shouldn't have dated the son of our closest friends," my dad says past his arugula. "I'm sorry, Kaylee, but we're not letting a teenage breakup derail decades of family tradition."

I resist stomping my foot like a toddler, though I very much want to. I know it's horribly clichéd to say they just don't understand. Still, stereotypical or not, they *don't* understand. I *need* this vacation.

But with Dean there, California won't be a vacation. He's been . . . pretty mad since we broke up. I pleaded with him for forgiveness and friendship in tearful late-night texts, only for him to block me. Wounded, I've let him be. I've gone out of my way to avoid him at school—but there will be no avoiding him when he's sleeping down the hall from me for three weeks of family beach days and dinners. Every sunny day will feel like a storm, every barbecue a battlefield.

Mom looks up. The sympathy in her eyes is sincere now. "However," she says, "no one is going to force you to come to California. If you're uncomfortable with Dean's presence, of course we would be devastated to not have you with us, but we'd understand."

I straighten up. It's a sudden light past the rubble of the collapsed cave of my summer. I can physically feel relief racing into me, lessening the pounding of my headache.

"Really? That would honestly be great," I say. "I could stay here and spend time with Brianna before she goes to college."

The idea fits into place in my head perfectly. I don't need crystal waters. I don't need backyard barbecues. I only need weeks with the friend I *didn't* just dump. The friend who isn't furious with me. Instead of my Malibu vacation, I will have the perfect Newport *staycation*.

Wrapped up in the fantasy, I nearly miss the look my parents exchange.

And then, in unison, they laugh. Really laugh, like what I've said is just hilarious. The world-class punch line they never saw coming. I'm stuck standing here, glaring while my cheeks heat.

"No way we're leaving you on your own," my mom manages.

"But I'll be seventeen next month," I protest. "I'm plenty capable of surviving on my own for three weeks."

"It's not a discussion," my dad says, still smiling from the unexpected uproariousness of my very reasonable suggestion. "You either come with us, or you can spend the summer in Nevada with Aunt Caroline."

Staycation dreams shatter in my head. While I can't stand my narcissistic aunt, she's not the real problem. Summer in fucking Pahrump, Nevada, outside of *literal* Death Valley, is summer without volleyball. The heat makes it nearly impossible to go outside, let alone train like a professional athlete. It's not an option, and my parents know it.

"Please," I say quietly. Defiance, I realize, is getting me nowhere. "Could they just not stay at the house with us?"

"We already invited them, sweetheart," my dad replies. "They have their flights. You really want us to kick them out?"

I don't really need my dad to put the question explicitly for me to know the offer is impossible, or to feel horrible for even proposing it. Darren and Terry Freeman-Yu are practically family, and I know how much it would hurt them and divide our families if I were to pout until I get my way.

I close my eyes. The realization hits me with sudden forceful clarity—I shouldn't be behaving this way. This isn't me. I'm better than this. I call on the girl within me who doesn't make excuses. Who pushes through without letting the hardship show.

I can't keep the strain out of my expression, but I do smile. "Of course," I say to my parents. "I get it."

Without needing to hear more, I leave the room. I can do this. I can put on a brave face. No one will see me stumbling.

Malibu won't be a vacation, but no one has to know that except me.

Three

POUTING IN FRONT OF my parents is one thing.

Pouting in my room? Completely different.

I storm upstairs into my bedroom, which is one part volleyball shrine, one part yearbook. I've gridded photos of my friends, the beach, my games—everything, really—onto one wall with neat white lines separating them. It's eye-catchingly geometric. Bookshelf space, meanwhile, is reserved for my not inconsiderable collection of trophies.

Fuming, I ease myself onto my bed and close my eyes, ready to ride out the rest of this migraine.

But frustration and stress keep the pressure pounding in my head, refusing to let me doze off. On the one hand, I know I'm being spoiled about dreading a three-week vacation in California. On the other, my breakup with Dean was uniquely awful. He'd cried, which was new in my experience. Not that it's always me doing the dumping, but when it is, my exes in the past haven't shed a tear. Exactly the way I intended—

I purposefully keep relationships from ever getting serious enough for those sorts of emotions.

The truth is, I'm good at dumping people. I've practiced it unintentionally, but practice is practice, and practice makes pretty close to perfect. I've mastered making my breakups feel logistical, comprehensible, just the natural consequence of me having too much going on to commit.

But Dean was harder. Of course he was. It's why my parents warned me over and over about starting a relationship with him—how dating a friend could ruin a friendship, and dating a family friend could ruin a family.

Maybe I was vain to think we would be different, that he would be the exception to my string of short-term relationships. I've stayed friends with several of my exes, real friends, whether it's exchanging US history notes with Bryson or sending memes to Mark. Dean and I had the sturdiest foundation of friendship I could ever wish for, years of vacations and beach days and nights hanging out in his room while our parents talked for hours. I couldn't imagine our breakup shaking what we'd built.

Or, say, leveling our friendship like floodwaters. Which is what happened.

My headache is unrelenting. I roll onto my side, searching for relief. The cool of my pillow is small comfort.

I should've known. Should've known I would screw everything up. It was an open secret in our families that Dean had a huge crush on me. When we were six, he declared we'd get married, and, of course, everyone has teased us about it ever since. Deep down, I knew what it meant when we got together. I knew dating him wouldn't be casual.

I'd wanted to anyway. And why not? Despite the deluge of guilt washing over me, this little fire of indignation hasn't gone out. It's unfair—that Dean was allowed to have his crush and not have to hide it away, but when *I* began to have a crush back, *I* was the problem. I was the one told *no*. The one told to *consider the consequences*.

Dean never had to consider the consequences, safe in the idea that his crush would remain unrequited.

But I liked him, too.

I flip over onto my other side, still hoping one of these poses will help ease the pressure in my head. Unfortunately, this new position puts me right in the eyeline of one of the photos on my wall—from California, with our families in the frame. Dean is right next to me, smiling, sunscreen sticking his wavy dark hair to his forehead. Since our breakup, I've removed the photos of just us from my room, but I kept this one because everyone's in it.

I'm regretting the decision now.

I settle for closing my eyes, flat on my back. Newport is quiet on the coastline where we live. I keep hoping the peace of the night will help me doze off.

Instead, memories keep me stuck in my sleeplessness. We had a good two months together—a *really* good two months. There were playlists shared. There were bike rides on Narragansett Beach. There were photoshoots overlooking the cliffs. There were kisses in this very room while my parents, putting together "taco night" downstairs, definitely knew what was going on.

Then he told me he loved me and I said it back, and the next day, I broke up with him.

When he asked me why, I didn't have a good answer. I don't know if a good answer is even possible for heartbreak.

I can't fault him for how obviously pissed he's been on the few regrettable occasions when we've crossed paths, in class or in the halls. It hurts, but it's understandable. Inevitable. In fact—

My eyes fly open.

If there's one person who wants to go to California with our families less than I do, it might just be Dean. He hasn't said two words to me since our breakup. For all I know, he hates me, and our friendship is sunk like a shipwreck.

Dean is probably having the same conversation with his parents tonight that I had with mine, except Terry and Darren will be reasonable. *They'll* let Dean stay home. Sure, it'll still be awkward sharing a house with my ex's family, but it'll be better than Dean himself. He'll stay home, silently hating me from afar.

The thought is both comforting and painful, which I resent.

I sit up in bed, motivated by new hope, knowing what I need to do. No more hiding. No more fretting. No more dreading vacations or family events I should look forward to. I need to definitively get over this breakup.

Fortunately, getting over breakups is one thing in which

I have plenty of experience. My methodology is perfected. Tested by time, by frequency, by variety. I could probably teach community college courses on the subject if I wanted to. I can envision the flyers now—*Kaylee Jordan. Volleyball star, social media personality, breakup expert.*

Instead of moping, it's time I put my practice to work. One way of getting over someone? A rebound.

I reach for my phone. Thumbing through my contacts, I focus on the merits of this plan. It'll help me stop dwelling endlessly on why things went wrong with Dean, certainly. If I'm lucky, it'll possibly even give Dean the kick he needs to get over me. If he hasn't opted out of our vacation yet, maybe hearing I'm with someone new will make him hate me enough to bail on California. It's genius.

It's almost depressing how excited it makes me to have found this way of getting him to hate me. Instead of fixating on this thought, though, I force myself to continue through my contacts.

My fingers still on a name I programmed in as *Jeremy from Newport Fest.* I don't usually listen to the local music festival's *music,* instead just enjoying the summer weather, the wandering from stage to stage on the sand-flecked grass of the harbor mouth, and the obviously great photo ops. I remember Jeremy's band, though. They were good—they would be going-places good when they got older. This number is what I have for walking right up to him while they were leaving the stage from their set. I never texted him, though. School started and I got swept up in other things.

Time to change that.

Inspiration cuts through the painful fog of my headache. I start to type.

> At Newport Fest last year, a very tall blonde asked you for your number after your set. She was extremely charming and had lips you definitely thought about kissing while you watched her from onstage. Ring any bells?

I put my phone down, pleased with the message. I'm not expecting him to respond immediately. When he sees it, though, he'll reply.

My phone vibrates only seconds later.

> Kaylee, right? I definitely remember.

I smile as I reply, already feeling the rejuvenation of a rebound quickening my pulse.

> I know this is, like, nine months late, but do you want to hang out?

> Name a time and place.

> Nine months is nothing, btw. You were worth the wait.

Four

I WALK ONTO CAMPUS on Monday tentatively hopeful. Over the weekend, I went out with Jeremy. First to the new bakery in town, then to the nearby beach park, where we sat near the shore. He was funny. His sung Harry Styles impression was legitimately impressive. In every respect, it went great.

While he's not my boyfriend *yet*, things are tending in that direction. I posted a tasteful if leading photo of the two of us to my Stories and told Brianna to help spread the word. It'll reach Dean eventually. He'll be pissed, but it'll help us both in the long run.

Except when I head toward my locker, I see him waiting for me in what was, for two months, our spot.

Dean. He stands out to me the way he has my entire life. For the visible reasons, of course—there's no ignoring the fact that Dean is handsome, with his face full of sharp lines, his contemplative lips, his keen, dark eyes set in golden-brown skin. He wears hipsterism like he does everything, entirely without self-consciousness. On others, obscure music shirts or cuffed jeans or hair worn in a bun might be a posture, a costume. Not Dean, though. They're just what he genuinely likes. I know him well enough to be sure. His unreserved himselfness is inspiring, and magnetic.

But it's not the only thing I see when I'm with him. I've lived my entire life intertwined with Dean's, thanks to our families. He's inscribed with memories, context I share with no one else. Our every conversation, every passing glance, reminds me of our years of friendship. It's a melody of endless reprises, of new variations on the wonderfully familiar. It's like nothing else.

Until I ruined it, of course.

He's standing now where he used to wait for me in the mornings, then walk with me to my locker. Pre-dating, we didn't hang out much at school—I stuck with the jocks, Dean with the other art kids. But for the months of our relationship, this was where we brought our worlds together.

People wave to me in front of the locker hall, where the welcome morning sun reflects harshly off our campus's concrete geometry. Others call my name. I return quick smiles, hoping I don't look distracted, not wanting to be unfriendly.

As I approach Dean, I slow my steps. Surely he's not waiting for *me*. He hasn't so much as looked my way in the past few weeks.

Everything in his relaxed posture, his unreadable expression, says he's perfectly at ease. He's leaning against the stucco wall, studying his shoes. *No*, I decide. *He's not here for me.* He's just here.

When I reach him, though, he pushes himself off the wall. He lifts his gaze from his suede chukka boots, which I only know the word for because of him. For the first time, his eyes lock on mine.

I wish I didn't feel the relief rushing through me. It is definitely *not* the way the Kaylee who's over this breakup would respond. The truth is, though, I've missed Dean more than I should.

Or maybe not more than I should. Maybe it makes perfect sense. I didn't just lose my boyfriend—I lost my best friend, too.

"Can we talk?" he asks.

Just hearing his voice, spoken to me, momentarily catches me up short. I falter, waiting for my capacity for speech to return. "Of course," I finally say.

He leads me past the planters outside the school's front entrance, where there's more privacy. The memory of how we used to use this privacy sits awkwardly in our silence. My heart is pounding like it does when I walk onto the court for every game. Dean, for his part, is expressionless, offering me no hint of what's coming. *Maybe*, I wonder with wild hope, *this is where we'll begin to put our ill-advised romance behind us.*

He doesn't leave me in suspense for long. "So, what?" he snaps. "You have a new boyfriend already?"

I blink, stunned by the heat of his anger. I knew word would reach him eventually—I'd counted on it, even. I just didn't figure it would happen this quickly. "I'm not sure he's my boyfriend yet," I say, keeping my voice neutral. "But yeah, we're something."

Dean frowns. I have to ignore the wave of memories the expression summons. The Dean I know, the guy I'm hoping doesn't become the Dean I *knew*, grimaced just like this when we'd get out of movies he didn't like, or when social media platforms changed their interfaces or default fonts.

"I'm sorry if it hurts you," I say sincerely. "But I hope we *both* can start to move on." I search his expression, looking for signs he understands me. Understands I'm not moving on because I didn't care about what we had—but because I *did*, in ways I'm trying not to let destroy our friendship.

He refuses to meet my eyes now. It's not encouraging.

Nevertheless, I go on. "There are plenty of people who would love to call you their boyfriend."

Dean is bi, which didn't at all factor into our breakup. He came out to his family last year, and when he had his first kiss with a boy, I was the first person he told.

Back when we were best friends.

His expression changes, his resentment fading. "I *have* moved on," he replies. Reading my raised eyebrows, he goes on. "Don't look so skeptical. I've totally . . . moved on. I'm—moved."

I study him, the slant of his posture, the indecipherable quirk of his mouth. Despite the loud patterns he embraces on his short-sleeve button-downs, Dean is quiet, even shy, and doesn't open up to people easily. When he does, however, he's . . . every wonderful thing I've watched him become over almost seventeen years. He's funny, smart, and completely charming.

He is not, however, careless, insensitive, easygoing, or jaded, like he's pretending to be now. I let the expanding silence say I don't quite buy this bravado.

"Okay." He eventually sighs in defeat. "So I'm not over you *yet*. I'm working on it, though."

I have to smile. His confessional honesty is—well, it's Dean.

"Don't smile at me. It doesn't help. I'm trying to be mad at you. Mad at you is an essential step in falling out of love with you." He says the last sentence like he's reading from the official medical journal of heartbreak.

It's a kick in the stomach. I don't know what hurts worse—the fact he's still in love with me, or how hard he's trying not to be. "So me hanging out with a new guy is helping, then?" I ask.

"It's definitely not making me *less* mad," he says, eyes flashing. "I think I just need closure."

I sigh. "We've gone over this. I don't know what more to say, Dean. I'm sorry."

He goes on like I didn't say anything. "You told me you loved me, then twelve hours later you dumped me, and now three weeks later you have a new boyfriend—"

"Technically not my boyfriend yet—"

"Not the point." He scowls.

I stare up into the cloudless sky, wishing we weren't dissecting the end of our relationship for the hundredth time.

It's not like I don't want to explain everything to Dean in clear, painless terms. "I don't have an explanation that will make it okay for you," I say in exasperation. "I just didn't want to date you anymore."

Dean's reply is immediate. It's the one I knew was coming. "You don't just fall out of love with someone. Not that fast."

"Well, I guess I'm different." I'm going for matter-of-fact. Instead, my words lose their footing. They land sadly on resignation.

Dean looks at me, his eyes searing with hope for something I just can't give him.

There's no graceful transition, but I decide to lead the conversation where I need to. "So about California . . ." I begin.

His brow furrows, his expression shadowing with suspicion. "What about it?" he asks. "Don't tell me the not-yet-but-probably-soon boyfriend is coming."

"Ew, of course not," I reply instantly.

When Dean brightens, I chastise myself for giving him something to hold on to. Just, of course I wasn't going to bring my rebound on vacation. In fact, it's gone unspoken in the decades of our families' vacation history—no one else comes to Malibu. Not when Dean became inseparable from Trent Paul in seventh grade, bonded over some online video game. Not when I spent freshman summer dating this guy who went on to star in the *Back to the Future* reboot TV series. No one else comes. Malibu is ours.

But just because you don't go on vacation with your new rebound doesn't mean you should with your ex.

"I tried to back out of the trip altogether," I explain. "But my parents wouldn't let me. Or, they *would* let me, but only if I stay with Aunt Caroline."

Dean grimaces. "Definitely not an option," he agrees.

"Right. You get it." I keep going, hurrying my words. "I wish I could have stayed home. I'm sure this trip will be . . . rough for you. I don't know what you're thinking, but . . ." I say it leadingly, hoping he'll pick up the rest of the sentence.

His stare is blank until the moment what I'm suggesting registers with him. I see it happen, the slight widening of his eyes.

"You want *me* to stay home?" he clarifies.

I feel waves pummeling the sides of my desperate hope. "*Want* isn't exactly the word I'd use. But, Dean," I say, leveling with him. "Do you really want to spend three weeks living with me?"

He laughs, the sound humorless, like stone scraping on stone. "I *want* to spend three weeks in California."

"Be serious, though," I insist. "Really consider it." Honestly, has he not? I look into his eyes, searching for reflections of the things I've imagined. The stomach-churning quiet of family dinners, the way each other's presence is certain to make the sand feel gritty and the sunshine sticky. How could he *want* to come?

Instead, Dean crosses his arms, looking . . . victorious. "Did you think I'd just volunteer to stay home? While my whole family takes a vacation without me? Just because *you'll* be there?"

I do not like the dark delight in his questions. "It's not as unreasonable as you're making it sound," I reply defensively.

Once more, he huffs a hollow laugh. "No, it is. You really have no idea how spoiled you're being. Look, I can't force you to love me again. I can't force you to explain why you stopped. But *you* can't force *me* to give up my summer vacation. I'm not thrilled with the circumstances either, but it's the way it is."

I'm proud of my capacity for patience. I've practiced it, honed it. Right now, however, my patience has just run out. I put a hand on my hip, not caring how childishly indignant I look. Fuck looking perfect when Dean is driving his foot into our summer.

"Fine," I say. "Well, I hope you do find a way to move on before the trip. Because I have."

Dean winces, and I wilt. My rebelliousness flies out of me instantly. I regret how mean that was. It's just, I'm not looking forward to my vacation becoming a sun-soaked living reminder of how I couldn't make it work with someone as great as Dean.

"Sorry, that was harsh," I say.

He rolls his eyes, but there's no anger in it. "Don't bother. I hope I move on, too."

I smile weakly. "Right. Well, am I at least making you mad?"

Dean considers. "A little," he concedes, sounding encouraged. "Maybe you could storm off?"

"Oh, good thinking. I'll do that," I reply, swallowing my smile with pursed lips. Spinning around, I take several decisive, angry steps away.

I hear Dean's voice over my shoulder. "So should I include you in our surfing lesson reservation?"

It's a pointed question and not Dean's first playful reminder of my memorable face-plant. I kind of don't mind the pleased flush it brings to my cheeks. I keep walking, smiling where he can't see.

Five

I LOVE DRIVING. I got my license as soon as I could, sick of my volleyball-famous mother dropping me off at my clinics and practices. I'm proud of my mom, but having her at every first introduction instantly set the bar imposingly high.

After class, I drive to the café near Jeremy's school where I said I'd pick him up. Dean's refusal to refigure the vacation situation stuck with me for the rest of the school day, leaving me hopelessly distracted, including embarrassingly spacing out in Spanish when Ms. Huerta called on me.

However, I remind myself I'm doing exactly what I need to. I'm getting over the breakup. I'm rebounding. I'm following my methodology. Hitting my marks. Doing what I've practiced. It's how I become the person I need to be.

If dating Jeremy doesn't work, I'll move on to one of my other heartbreak survival guide routines, like hobbies, maybe. In the wake of my freshman-year split with Isaiah Hunter, who's now varsity quarterback, I watched like thirty seasons of *Survivor* in three weeks. I even filmed my own audition video.

I'll be okay, I reassure myself. I'll get over this. Unwinding for the few minutes I spend passing by the old-time storefronts on Newport's picturesque streets, I lower the window for the wind to play with my hair, which is back to its highlighted, sunny look.

When I pull up in front of the cute facade of Daylight Coffee, where I've accompanied Brianna in her pursuit of elegantly decorated lattes, Jeremy's waiting for me. I smile. This boy is rebound energy personified. Tall, limber, with long guitarist's fingers, brown waves of hair, one or two perfect freckles on sandy skin. He stands up from the wire-frame table—holding, I notice, two coffees. One for me.

The gesture is sweet. But the coffee will need to be, too, if I'm going to get the drink down.

Opening my passenger door, he gracefully folds his legs into the seat, which doesn't require much effort because my usual passenger is the six-foot Bri. Holding the coffees, he leans over the console to give me a kiss that's longer than a peck, if not a full-on make-out. We haven't graduated to pecking yet, the casual comfort of kissing hello.

Dean and I reached pecking pretty early. It wasn't unexpected, given how much romantic history it felt like we had because of how much *history* history we actually had. But despite the naturalness of our relationship, we would sometimes surprise each other, too, drawing the other in for long, heart-fluttering, knee-liquefying kisses. He—

No. I halt the train of thought. This is not about Dean. I'm here with Jeremy. Rebound Jeremy. Nice Jeremy, with the extra coffee I don't want.

I give him a bright smile. On our first date, he pointed out I'd seen *him* play, but he's never seen *me* play. The wordplay made me smirk, and I told him for our next date, he could come to a pickup game, which is where we're heading now. Brianna and two of our friends who now play for Brown are waiting down at Narragansett. It's probably my favorite place to play in my home state, though to be honest, the competition isn't crowded. Rhode Island isn't exactly a beach volleyball state, which is one reason I look forward to our California trip every year. I'm grateful for the friends I've made here, training my hardest on the East Coast's sand, but if my mom hadn't retired, I would still be spending winters in California like I did when I was little, before Mom stopped training year-round.

"Good day?" Jeremy asks as I'm pulling out of the parking lot.

"Better now," I reply.

"I got this for you." He puts the coffee for me into the center drink holder, like I hadn't noticed the cup's conspicuous presence.

When we pull up to the first red light, I sip hesitantly from the smile-shaped opening in the plastic lid. Honestly, I don't know what I'm drinking. It could be vanilla, or espresso, or pumpkin spice. To me, it all tastes like battery acid.

"Yum," I say.

Jeremy reaches for the cord to plug his phone in. I'm hit with more whiplash, remembering how Dean would play new songs he'd discovered for me on our drives to each other's houses. He was never pretentious, never preachy, never out to impress or intimidate me like music guys are. He just wanted to show his best friend what excited him.

I'm wondering if Jeremy's going to do the same when, once more, I stop myself. With the road winding through the New England trees toward the beach, I decide to be present with Jeremy, who says all the right things, who got me coffee, who just put on the same Harry Styles song he sang for me on our previous date. I'm not here to think about where things stand with Dean. The whole point of breaking up with Dean was to stop thinking about where things stand with Dean.

"So do you, like, want to play in the Olympics?"

His question pulls me out of my refocusing efforts. Glancing over, I find earnestness in his eyes. He's not prying like volleyball guys do, out of skepticism and competitiveness. He's really interested. He wants to get to know me.

I soften. "I'm going to try. Qualifiers are still a few years out, and I want to find the right partner first," I explain. "Most players go to college or play pro before trying. I'm not going to put too much pressure on myself."

Jeremy nods. "Your mom didn't play in college, though, right? I mean, I saw she has the record for volleyball gold medals. She went straight to the Olympics. I was just wondering if you wanted to do the same thing."

I fight to hide my grimace. My fingers involuntarily clench the steering wheel.

So Jeremy googled my mom. It doesn't mean he'll be weird about it. I need to work on not reading comparisons coded into every facet of my life. In fact, it's normal to have questions like this, I remind myself. Most people find it interesting when they learn I'm related to an Olympian. It's a nice, engaged, boyfriendly thing to discuss.

I repeat my reassurances in my head. *He's interested. He wants to get to know me.*

Instead of observations, they sound more like prayers. It's not helping. I dash them from my head, focusing on the road, which is curving toward the parking lot, revealing the sparkling ocean. "That's the plan," I say. "I'm not as good as my mom, though. I'm good, don't get me wrong. Really good. One day I *will* go to the Olympics. But I'm not going to break my mom's records, and I'm not trying to. I just love this sport."

I like the charge of conviction I feel in my words. They're the truth. I do love volleyball. The idea of being the best in my family is one I never let go of, because I never held it in the first place.

Still, not competing with my mom doesn't relieve the pressure her legacy places on my life. I want to do her name proud.

Jeremy looks impressed. "You're really mature about this," he says. His voice is gentle, not doubtful or wheedling. "I don't know if I could handle living in someone's shadow."

I hit the gas a little hard at the next green light. While I'm not looking to outdo my mom, Jeremy's phrasing grates on me. It's not the nicest comment, but besides, it's not how I see things. I don't live in my mom's shadow. Shadows hide you in the dark, making it so you have to shine even brighter to be seen. Instead, I live in my mom's *spotlight*. Everyone is watching me. From professionals to jerks on Instagram.

In this world I'm committed to, I have a reputation before anyone has seen me play. It's a privilege, I know, even if the spotlight is sometimes searing.

Which is where Jeremy comes in. I need flings like these, free of consequences. I need flirty texting. I need front-seat make-outs. I need . . . freedom.

It's why, in some guilty yet desperately necessary way, Jeremy is good for me. With him, I can make mistakes and walk away. Escape expectations without having to play the Instagram-friendly, volleyball-famous role of Kaylee Jordan. I can unwind, then wipe the slate clean with someone new.

Not like with Dean. He was a mistake I won't make again.

I pull onto the sandy pavement of the beach parking lot. "It's not easy," I go on. "Which is why I need *someone* to help me have fun."

Jeremy grins. "That I can do."

When I park the car, he kisses me again. This time, I keep my mind on his smell, his thumb gentle on my jawline, the way our mouths move together. Him.

Six

I STAND ON THE court with Bri, facing down Leah, our former indoor volleyball teammate from Newport High. She's now a freshman at Brown, and she's brought one of her teammates to be her partner.

The sun shines low in the sky, sticking my sweat to my skin. Feet planted in the sand, I bend my knees, preparing to spring in whatever direction Leah serves. On the sidelines, Jeremy sits on the sand with Patrick, Leah's hallmate at Brown, and his long-distance girlfriend Siena, who's in town for the weekend. My chest flutters whenever I notice how intently Jeremy is watching, not scrolling on his phone or chatting with them.

Leah tightens her blond ponytail, then puts on sunscreen for the third time. Honestly, I'm shocked her pale complexion hasn't burned yet. When she tosses up her serve, she powers the ball over the net to where I can easily reach. I bump the ball to Brianna. We've played together long enough for me to know her rhythms, so when the ball is just leaving her fingers,

I'm already approaching the net. I quickly spot the court and spike with medium force between my two opponents.

Leah drops to one knee for the dig, but the ball hits her forearm wrong. It flies slanted off the court too fast for her partner to save.

I hold my hands out to Bri for quick high-fives, our ritual after every point scored, while Jeremy cheers and Patrick calls out reassurances to Leah. I blow Jeremy a kiss, enjoying the feeling.

Walking up to the net, I let the smell of the ocean wash over me, indulge in the summertime prickle of the sun on my shoulders. I wait for Brianna to serve, feeling perfectly myself. When my friend puts the next point into motion, I spring to life. While this game is just for fun, I play hard, diving for digs, blocking with high jumps that make my legs scream.

I love the sport, but I also love the competition. I can't give this up for the summer, even if it means escaping the family vacation. Not just because it would set me back on my training, either. But because it's pure joy.

I'm going to California. And so is Dean. We'll . . . figure it out.

When we score the final point, we shake hands with Leah and her partner, Claire, under the net, one more ritual repeated into routine. I walk off the court and collapse into the sand near Jeremy, who hands me my water. I gulp it down immediately, not minding how the sand sticks to the sweaty skin of my thighs.

A couple feet away from me, Siena holds up her phone for

what is not her first selfie with Patrick in front of the ocean today. I smile—it's sweet. In fairness to their photography, the water is stunning right now. While the sun is moving lower in the sky, it's not yet sending orange onto the perfect blue of the horizon line.

"That was incredible," Jeremy says, his hazel eyes lit with genuine enthusiasm. He's loosely holding his knees to his chest, the cuffs of his black jeans speckled with sand.

I grin, leaning back on my elbows. "It's no concert, but it's definitely not boring," I concede.

Siena's laugh floats over to us. I look over, noticing that while Siena has her phone camera raised, Patrick's surprised her by smushing a kiss to her cheek.

While Jeremy gazes out over the glittering strands of sun-light on the water, I exchange a glance with Leah. Patrick's long-distance relationship is semi-famous in our friend group. When Leah moved in at Brown in September, she offhand-edly commented that her new hallmate's LDR wouldn't last the month. Ever since, we've watched like we would someone rock climbing without a harness as each day passed and Siena and Patrick *didn't* break up.

"You should visit more often, you know," Patrick says with gentle longing hiding under the playfulness in his voice.

Siena's face softens beneath her sunglasses. "It's not my fault you chose to go to school on the opposite coast."

"I know . . ." Patrick replies. His drawn-out syllables say they've had this conversation before. "I hope I make the vis-its worthwhile, though."

Instead of the mushy confirmation I'm expecting, Siena cocks her head sarcastically, pretending to consider. Patrick laughs—then, with deft strength, scoops Siena off her feet. Patrick is sneakily well-built, like he works out for the sake of it instead of to look jacked, which complements the boyish charm of his openhearted features and swirl of brown hair. While Siena squeals with delighted surprise, Patrick carries her back over to our group, where he deposits her right onto the sand close to me.

Finding everyone—minus Jeremy—watching her, Siena just grins, no shadow of embarrassment crossing her features. Honestly, I'm envious of her in moments like this. She's the kind of laid-back, effortless cool I could never be, not when I conscientiously tailor every visible facet of myself. Siena is comfortable in her own skin, unafraid to try new things in a way I respect, if not relate to. She shakes sand out of her iconic bangs. Like a Californian, she's worn her checkerboard Vans right onto the sand.

"Yeah, yeah, go ahead and make fun," Patrick says dryly to our stares.

"You've been married how long again?" Bri deadpans.

He lowers his sunglasses to shoot her a look. "Don't joke about that. The random dude Kaylee brought to the beach will think you're serious."

"He's not random," I protest quickly, not wanting Jeremy to be offended by Patrick's dry sarcasm. "He's my date."

"It's okay. I am somewhat random," Jeremy chimes in. I give him a smile.

"The *point is,*" Leah says, "you and Siena act like an old married couple."

Siena settles back onto the sand. She crosses her outstretched legs, looking off into the distance like she's enjoying sounding full of wisdom. "You know, there was a time I would have been insecure about that, but not anymore. Patrick knows I don't want to get married until I'm at least thirty."

Claire scoffs. "God, why wait that long? You two can't keep your hands off each other."

"Come on, can you blame me?" Patrick replies. "We're only together for a couple days every few months. But hey—" He turns to Siena. "Thirty? Earlier this year it was thirty-five. I like this new timeline. Not that I wouldn't wait however long you wanted," he goes on. "We have the rest of our lives, after all."

His sentimentality makes Siena roll her eyes, but there's no hiding the pleased blush under her smile. She slips her hand into his.

The sureness in Patrick's voice hits a sore spot in me. I can't imagine having their conviction. *The rest of our lives?* I couldn't even make it last with Dean. *Dean.* Despite years of foundation, the winds of uncertainty knocked over whatever hopes I'd built for our relationship in two months.

I study Siena, how content she looks. The echo of her easy, flirty, tender conversation with Patrick fills my head. How is she not crushed under the pressure of that level of commitment? Just imagining myself in her position, some small version of the stuck feeling I get in relationships steals into me, like noticing storm clouds moving in toward clear skies. How is Siena so sure she won't get bored? Or lose herself? Or get heartbroken? Relationships sometimes seem like sandcastles to me. No matter how tall or intricate they get, they're so, so easy to swipe into nothing.

With Dean, it was better to end it first. I know it was.

"Besides," Patrick says to the group, "you act like we've been together forever. This time last year, we were broken up." Over his sunglasses, he levels me a look.

I squirm. "What are you implying?"

He shrugs pointedly. "Oh, nothing," he replies. "I just happen to know that people who break up do, on occasion, get back together."

"So?" I fire back. Even in the summer weather, I feel my cheeks heating. While I'm conscious of Jeremy next to me, he's not the reason I'm on edge. This line of conversation is veering close to those streaks of insecurity I try to keep out of my view. They're neither pleasant nor productive.

Leah tosses her hair. "Dean's going to California with you, isn't he?"

I round on her slowly. Ganging up on me with Patrick now! I don't reply, because she already knows the answer. I shared the Malibu situation in the groupchat I have with her and Bri when I needed to vent, but now her prying is starting to irritate me. I know Leah was opposed to my breakup with Dean. I mean, everyone was opposed to the breakup, but Leah—the self-elected straight talker of the group—was the only one to inform me of this to my face. I had wondered if she knew how much her words matched the judgment I was piling on myself, then concluded she probably didn't.

Clearly picking up on my demeanor, Jeremy shifts in the sand next to me. "I'm getting the vibe Dean is an ex?"

"We didn't date that long," I quickly clarify.

Brianna snorts unhelpfully.

Jeremy looks between us, his expression clouding while he pieces the conversation together. "And you're going to California with him?" he asks.

I permit myself one split second to narrow my eyes at Leah. Then I use familiar muscles to smooth out my expression as I face Jeremy, making myself look calm. Neutral, reassuring. "Yeah, but it's a family thing," I explain. "It'll be my parents, his parents, his sisters, and him. It's one big family vacation. Nothing to worry about."

I nearly have myself convinced by the end of my description, although of course my worries are very different from Jeremy's. *One big family vacation.* Reminding myself of this reality might just be how I'll make this summer easier. I'll focus on how I'm not *only* going with Dean. I'm going to hunt for seashells on the beach with Jessie, to enjoy Darren's unbelievable chicken skewers.

Feeling renewed, I shoot Bri raised eyebrows, silently asking her to back me up.

"Of course," she says, understanding. "Besides, I'm sure Dean is totally over you by now."

She grins cheekily, swiping sand from her knees. I return her smile through clenched teeth. She's messing with me. Honestly, it would be funny if it weren't at my expense. Bri has left me only one possible response—one I'm not sure I can sincerely give, remembering the guarded fire in Dean's voice this morning.

"Totally," I repeat. "Totally over me."

I reach for Jeremy's hand, squeezing gently when our fingers interlock. He squeezes back. But like the sun starting to sink toward the horizon, some of the brightness in his eyes has gone out.

Seven

THE FINAL WEEKS OF school fly by. Every day feels like I'm on the court—each moment is structured, calculated, deliberate, yet when I get to the end, I don't know where the minutes went. It's one rushing blur of finals, paid promotion for my account, training, dates with Jeremy, and a photoshoot with my mom for a *Sports Illustrated* story.

One semi-bright spot is Dean. He's no longer completely shutting me out, though things haven't progressed past distant between us. He'll look in my direction, sometimes even wave. But we're not talking. Even so, I can tell he's trying, which makes me feel like maybe, just maybe, we'll be okay.

If, that is, Malibu doesn't put us in such close contact that he decides he hates me again.

I'm in my room packing the day before our flight when my mom walks in holding her iPad.

"*Sports Illustrated* published the story," she says. She doesn't hide the excitement in her voice. She sounds the way she did during the whole interview—like she's been waiting for this for years.

I'm not unsympathetic. I've wondered on plenty of occasions how she must've felt, how she emotionally managed the seismic shift of ending her professional career. What her life was like in those first months, even years, of waking up without new qualifiers to train for or new opponents to size up.

Other things filled her days, I know. She's told me she retired because she worried she was missing too much of my childhood. She built her clinic from the ground up, too.

Still, pulling herself out of the world she'd called home for most of her life surely wasn't easy. The hunger to celebrate her onetime place there—well, I get it.

I dump every swimsuit I own into my suitcase while Mom walks over to show me her iPad screen. The photo they chose is one of me in midair, spiking a ball my mom has set for me over the net.

I was prepared to hate the photo. There's one unlikely truth I've discovered in posting so often on social media—while I expected it would lessen my self-consciousness of how I look, it hasn't. It's made it worse. The flaws I see in myself feel like insults I've heard hundreds of times instead of only once.

Surprisingly, I don't dislike this photo. I look powerful. My mom remains in focus, slightly behind me. The metaphor of the whole thing is obvious, but effective. It's engaging even to me, one of its subjects. I like the girl who is part of the story this snapshot tells.

Next to the photo is a graphic of my mom's and my stats.

I scan the numbers, their meaning sweeping coldly over me. The chart is comparative. Charitably, it's meant to indicate I'm on my mother's path, positioned to be the next big thing in women's volleyball. It includes not just our records on the court, but the impersonally presented details of our bodies. It notes I'm one inch shorter, but wonders if I have enough puberty left to gain that inch.

I scan the article. While it's positive, I can read the unwritten suggestion in its premise. I have ground to make up if I'm going to match my mother. The photo becomes a question. *Will* I score the point my mom has set up for me?

I pull my eyes from the screen, finding the intensity stretched over my expression in the picture unbearable. It looks like desperation. I start to hate the photo. But I hide my reaction, forcing my lips into a brave smile. *This is a privilege*, I remind myself. It's incredible exposure. It's *Sports* freaking *Illustrated*. Coaches and potential partners will see this, not to mention new fans who will find my social media. The privilege can't be separated from comparisons to my mother, so I just can't let it get to me.

"Great, right?" my mom says.

Her enthusiasm makes my smile more sincere. "Really great," I say. "I love the photo."

Clicking off the tablet, she changes her focus to my open suitcase on the bed. "You almost done packing?"

I don't get the chance to reply. My phone, lying on the cloudlike folds of my white comforter, lights up. Glancing down, I see a text from Jeremy. When my phone recognizes my face, it unlocks. Jeremy's full message displays, long enough to fill the screen.

My heart sinks. I don't need to read what he's written to know. Something this long from the boy I've been dating for one month could only be one thing.

I'm being dumped.

"Everything okay?" Mom asks.

"No," I reply, her question sparking frustration out of my hurt. I hold up my phone for her to read. "I just got dumped because Jeremy's uncomfortable with me going to California for three weeks with my ex. Which, by the way, is completely reasonable . . ." I flatten my eyebrows at her accusingly.

Mom is unmoved. "Was Jeremy even really your boyfriend?"

I exhale out my nose. "Not technically, but we were getting there. Hence him feeling the need to write me a whole novel to break things off."

Her eyes move from the phone to me. "Your tone tells me you think this is my fault."

"Because it is."

"*Or* . . ." Her eyes wide, Mom fixes me with one of her focused stares, like she would when I'd complain about homework after practice. It fuels the fire in my cheeks. "*You* shouldn't have gotten together with Dean in the first place for this exact reason, among others. Kaylee, you treated a dear friend like a shiny toy, and I'm sorry you're facing consequences for throwing him away, but this is not my fault."

I drop my phone on the bed, my gaze following it. "Wow, Mom, you make me sound like a terrible person," I say dryly, hoping the sarcasm I load onto my reply hides the hurt of her depiction. "I'm a teen girl. I'm allowed to have breakups."

Her ocean-blue eyes linger on me. "You are," she acknowledges. "By all means, date and dump a hundred Jeremys. But Dean deserved more caution."

I slump down onto the bed, chin propped in my hand. "In the Kaylee-and-Dean breakup, my own mother is Team Dean. Super."

"I'm on your side in life, sweetheart." Mom's voice softens sympathetically. "But Dean's the heartbroken one. If he had broken your heart, then I'd be sitting courtside on Team Kaylee."

"Right, well, we all know *that* could never have happened," I reply.

"Exactly," my mom says.

I falter, having meant what I said sarcastically. *Exactly?* My mother's response is *exactly*? *Exactly, Kaylee, we know you couldn't possibly be heartbroken over the end of your friendship with the closest person in your life, because girls like you just don't hurt the way other people do?* Her casual comfort is, ironically, what summons the sting of tears, which I quickly blink from my eyes.

My mom doesn't pick up on what I'm feeling. "I'm sorry about Jeremy," she says sincerely, rubbing my shoulder with a comforting hand. "Maybe when you get back from California, you can work things out with him."

I find I don't have much enthusiasm for the idea. "Yeah, maybe," I say weakly.

When my mom walks out of the room, I shove my suit-case aside, not wanting to think about California right now. I hate this. While my mom was in the room, I was distracted from the real hurt of Jeremy dumping me, but now it's there. First the miserable circumstances of our trip, now this? I'm not without fault for how things ended with Dean, but I don't think I deserve for it to swallow up every shining light in my summer.

Even though I know I shouldn't, I open the *Sports Illustrated* story on my phone. I scroll recklessly to the end of the piece to read the comments, pretty certain of what I'll find. Sure enough, the first one leaves my cheeks stinging. Oh look, strangers on the internet think I'm "no Judy Jordan."

I click the phone screen off, feeling even shittier. Which has me reaching for my laptop.

When I need to refocus, I watch old Olympic volleyball matches on YouTube. I've seen every US match, but lately I'm studying China's players. Reducing every game into individual plays pulls me out of what's bothering me. While I know rigorously scrutinizing the skills I need to polish is perhaps not the healthiest coping mechanism, it works for me.

Of course, even while watching international players, I sometimes see my mom playing as the opposition. Though I'm not looking for her, I can't help noticing her.

My mom is incredible. She does everything not just *right*, but with intuition, premonition, even style.

Like usual, she inspires me. I grab my notebook from my desk and start writing down the skills I still need to perfect.

Eight

OUTSIDE THE OVAL WINDOW of my seat on the plane, the exhilaratingly blue water glimmers in the sun. The California coastline.

It waits in the distance past the tan reach of the city under us. When our plane touches down, the perfect warmth of the summer day welcoming me like a hug, I can't fight my excitement. I know I'll have to deal with Dean, with the pressure cooker of me, my ex, and our families living in one house for three weeks—but in this moment, what takes over is the pure joy of my favorite place in the world.

The feeling stays with me while my parents pick up the rental car, putting down the fee so underage drivers—me—can use the white Jeep. We head out onto the freeway until we reach the Pacific Coast Highway, the wide road along the coast with the ocean glittering endlessly on one side. On the other, the high cliffs of the canyons shoot into the cloudless sky.

I resist the impulse to post a video to my Stories of the idyllic drive, holding myself to the social media hiatus that's become my tradition for this trip. I enjoy social media, I honestly do. But it's somewhere I have to be perfect, to consider optimization, metrics, timing, post order, not to mention how I look in every photo. I try to reduce the amount I train during our California weeks, too, treating this time like my recovery period. I sort of have three jobs—school, volleyball, social media—each of which, for these weeks, I put to rest. Vacation is for recharging.

Or trying to, while my ex is right down the hall.

Eventually we reach the winding highway into Malibu itself, then to the house my parents have on Escondido Beach. They rent the place out on Airbnb during the year, but for the next three weeks, it'll be home.

It isn't just natural beauty I'm basking in. It's some of the best memories of my life. Growing up with my mom often traveling for tournaments, I could always count on this being the time my family was together. It was made more complete by the Freeman-Yus, who I've always considered my second family.

Long before Mom and Dad owned a house here, this trip was a tradition they and Dean's parents started shortly after college. Everyone except Mom went to undergrad in California, and when postgrad life pulled them to new cities, they decided to reunite every year on the beautiful coast of the city where they met. They would stay in the cheapest rentals they could find, which often come up in their slightly drunk dinner table reminiscences every year.

Our families' history is inscribed into me, proudly unforgettable. Terry Freeman and my mom were beach volleyball partners in high school. Then my mom went pro, intending to go to college later, which she never did because her career took off. Terry played for UCLA but gave the sport up halfway through to focus on engineering.

It was at UCLA that Terry met Darren Yu and his roommate John, my dad, who she introduced to my mom. On their first Malibu trip, my parents officially got together—which I'm pretty sure means they hooked up on the same beach where I now play volleyball with Dean's sister, Lucy. I try not to think about it. Terry and Darren were married here, and when our parents had kids the same year, it was only natural the California trip expand to the new generation.

Driving down PCH, I find myself starting to struggle to hold on to my usual excitement. I wish I could look forward to this trip the way I have every year, when the sun dazzling down on the Palisades made me feel like stress was melting off me.

Instead, I'm starting to dread what I'll find when we reach the house.

How will spending time with Dean's family even look now? I haven't exactly gone over for Freeman-Yu game night recently. They'll be polite, obviously, but they're Team Dean, too. How could they not be? While I've always considered them family, there's nothing like present circumstances to remind me they're really, really not.

Honestly, it's why I've avoided them over the past weeks, working out late in the school gym the night my parents had them over for dinner, even dropping off Dean's *Twin Peaks* DVDs—which he owns due to his "respect for physical media"—in the mailbox instead of bringing them to the door. I haven't wanted confirmation that the love I shared with Dean's family was broken, too, when I broke Dean's heart.

Before I'm ready, we pull up to the house. Despite the fact that we only visit for these yearly vacations, I remember every detail. It's two stories, the whitewashed wood reflecting the California sun, with white trim under the gently slanted roof. The house sits on stilts over the wet sand of the beach, where the water rises during high tide. Hibiscus flowers spring from the hedges out front. Palm trees rise high over the roof, their upright trunks and heavy foliage wrapping the whole place in seclusion.

I'm here. I'm really, really here, and I need to unwind. I wait desperately for eager relief to flood over me.

It doesn't. Instead, memories do. Games of tag played on the sand. Spraying each other with sunscreen on the porch before running down to the beach. Growing up under the high palms.

This house has seen the ways we've changed, played host to different versions of ourselves. It remembers the me who pretended she wasn't self-conscious in her first bikini. The way Dean tried not to stare. It remembers how happy we were just last year, the indulgent smile he'd give me, hiding how flattered he was when I'd try to drag him into the water from the sand where he was often rereading his favorite Pauline Kael collection of film criticism.

Not just me and Dean, either. It saw the version of my mom who sat on the beach every night the year my grandpa died, sometimes with Terry, sometimes by herself. The Jessie who had a powerful *Unicorn Kingdom* phase—not, in fact, very distant in memory—and who insisted we watch the pastel-colored cartoons over and over. Memories hold this place up just like the walls.

I wonder if this year's memories will be a wrecking ball instead.

My parents hurry to pull the luggage out of the trunk and head inside. I drag my feet, needing the extra minutes to reassure myself that however the Freeman-Yus react to me, I'll be fine.

I haven't quite convinced myself by the time I set foot inside, the rosewood floorboards creaking welcomingly under me. Instantly, Jessie and Lucy, Dean's sisters, dash into my parents' arms. Jessie, six years old, is boundless enthusiasm, her straight black hair in two messy braids. Lucy, thirteen, is shyer and still getting used to her growth spurt, not to mention her mouthful of braces.

I stand awkwardly in the entryway, not wanting to draw attention to myself.

Terry walks in from the dining room. I feel myself stiffen, hating the automatic defensive reaction, the product of my storm-clouded thoughts in the car. Disappointing or upsetting people is hard for me even when they're *not* practically my second mother. I haven't fully relaxed when Terry walks right up to me and wraps me in a hug.

"I'm so glad you're here," she says. "I need my rom-com movie night alliance."

I could cry with relief. "We need to strategize. Stay strong in the face of the Lord of the Rings fellowship."

Terry laughs. Letting me go, she looks at me, really taking me in. I do the same, sheepish and grateful. Terry is the parallel-universe version of my mother, tall and elegantly built like her, but paler, with stylish round glasses perched on her nose.

"It's good to see you." Her voice drops gently. "You know, you didn't need to be a stranger."

I smile, a little ashamed that I actually thought this woman who watched me grow up would ever reject me.

With Terry's gaze on me, I feel the first flicker of something I haven't since our plane touched down. Hope. If Dean's family has forgiven me, maybe Dean himself isn't far behind. *It's not like he burst into tears or* totally *simmered with rage whenever he saw me at school*, I remind myself. Maybe we won't make each other hate this trip. Maybe I can spend these weeks not with my ex, but with my friend.

When I look around for him, though, I don't find him.

My dad asks the question in my head. "Where's Dean? I need to discuss with him whether we should include the Hobbit movies in our programming."

While I wasn't wondering about the Hobbit thing, I face Terry quickly, intensely curious.

"Please, no," Terry replies. "Enough Lord of the Rings. Let us have peace."

Everyone laughs.

"Dean's in his room. He . . . didn't want to come down," she goes on.

It's like jumping into one of the ice baths my mom sometimes prepares for workout recovery. The cold punch of disappointment drowns my relief. This is the opposite of progress with Dean, basically the death sentence for the weeks of relaxation with my friend I now feel incredibly foolish for imagining.

Not helping things, my dad shoots me a look like this is my responsibility. *Figure it out, Kaylee. Fix this.*

I ignore him, not needing the reminder of what I rehearse in my own head in countless versions every day—*Figure it out, Kaylee. Be everything, Kaylee. Get it right, Kaylee.* Indignantly, I hold on to my frustration that they're putting Dean's emotional well-being on me. I'd rather feel that than the hurt. Grabbing my suitcase, I march upstairs.

The bedrooms branch off the upstairs hallway, into which one square window spills sunlight. Dean's room is across the hall from mine. When I pass his door, it's shut. I pause, considering knocking. Guilt works powerfully in me. I live my life by the word *should*—I should smooth this over, reassure, comfort. Perfect doesn't look like letting someone keep his door shut because he's too pissed to even say hello.

With effort, I stop myself, releasing the fist I lifted to knock.

He's *not* my responsibility, I remind myself. No one forced Dean to come on this trip. Making sure he enjoys it is not my job.

I head into my own bedroom, closing the door behind me.

Nine

MY FEET POUND THE soft sand, my legs throbbing.

I couldn't stay cooped up in the house wondering if Dean would ever emerge from his room. Instead, I changed into a one-piece and quick-drying shorts and walked down to the waterline. With the sun on my shoulders, I set off running down the coast.

Honestly, I hate running. But the transition from indoor volleyball, which I play at school, to beach volleyball is brutal. Just covering the court on the sand is exhausting, even if the dives have softer landings. I have to run on the sand to build enough endurance to even last twenty-one points. Here, fortunately, it's so beautiful out that I'm not completely miserable. Here, each breath lacerating my lungs is scented with Malibu's gorgeous ocean.

After I've run what I guess is three miles, I dive into the water to cool off. It's dreamlike, impossibly refreshing on my sunscreened skin. With the tide swaying me gently, I pause, squinting, surveying the perfect turquoise stretching out be-hind me.

When I walk back to the house, I find the parents grilling teriyaki skewers on the deck suspended on the house's stilts over the sand. Terry, holding the tongs, is loading up plates while Darren and my mom sit with Jessie and Lucy under the patio table's umbrella.

My steps falter on the stairs up past the wooden stilts when I spot Dean. He's standing with my dad by the outdoor bar, looking like himself—black T-shirt, well-fitting bur-gundy shorts, hair in his usual bun. He's smiling.

It's gutting. The feeling is clichéd, but like never before, on this beach—*our* beach—he looks like someone I used to know.

It makes me want to grab the plate Terry prepared for me and head inside with the excuse of needing a shower. But I stop myself. If Dean wants to hide from me, that's his business. I'm going to be an adult about this. I'll face him, un-bothered, and we'll get through it.

I walk up to the grill, where the heat washes over me. The smell is heavenly. Plate in hand, I continue over to where my dad is talking to Dean.

Their conversation dries up the moment I get there. I swivel suspicious looks between the two of them, intuiting their topic of discussion. "Should I go elsewhere so you can continue talking about me?" I ask.

My dad laughs, grinning sheepishly. While Dean's cheeks heat a little, he meets my eyes, which is more than I've got-ten from him since we arrived.

"Not everything is about you," he says.

I exercise familiar muscles of swallowing disappointment. Not the greatest start. "Oh yeah? Fill me in, then," I reply dryly. "What were you talking about?"

The guys exchange a look. *Busted.*

Dean covers quickly, putting on confidence as he bites into his skewer. "How's Jeremy?" he asks casually.

I blink, thrown. I didn't expect him to bring up Jeremy, to rub salt in his own wound. I didn't even know he knew Jeremy's name. Recovering my composure, I shrug, hoping it doesn't look robotic. "We broke up," I inform Dean.

Dean scoffs with entirely too much satisfaction.

I narrow my eyes. "What's that supposed to mean?"

My dad frowns, studying his chicken skewer.

"Just, you know"—Dean watches me, waiting to see where his words will land—"another one bites the dust."

Anger flares in me. He's struck one of my sore spots. Worse, he knows it. I hate that he sees me this way, hate how weak a defense of myself I have. Sure, if you lay out my romantic history on one long time line, it doesn't look great. But there are *two* people in every relationship, even my relationship with Dean—the one I continue to catch the most heat for.

When I open my mouth to retort, my dad preempts me. "Play nice, you two," he says, the humor in his voice not fully hiding the warning.

Dean and I shoot my dad identical annoyed looks. I regret it instantly. Not for my dad's sake, of course—but because I don't like having stepped inadvertently into a rare moment of unity with Dean. It hurts to be reminded of every other shared reaction like this, every eye roll, every smothered smile in response to our parents over the years.

Ignoring my dad, I wrench my focus back to Dean. "Actually, Jeremy was the one to dump me," I inform him coolly. "And you don't see me hiding in my room moping about it."

I watch my words find their mark, feeling like I do when I slam an unreachable spike over the net. Dean's eyes flatten. He mechanically sets his plate down on the bar top next to him.

Without saying a word, he walks inside, shutting the sliding door behind him.

I'm only a little remorseful. I'd feel worse if he hadn't been rude to me first, making fun of my relationship history. Not even I have such unwavering instincts for forgiveness.

The way my dad is eyeing me, he evidently wishes I did.

"He started it," I say weakly, conscious I'm relying on the judicial philosophy of a six-year-old.

When he doesn't reply, I figure silence is my easiest out. I'll just walk away, see if I can rope Jessie into playing tag on the sand or explaining every intricate detail of whatever show she's currently obsessing over. Clutching my plate, I turn to leave.

I find the other three parents watching me, frowning. It's clear they heard my parting remark to Dean.

"Oh, Kaylee," my mom says, rubbing her temple.

I hate how wearily embarrassed she looks. "What?" I shoot back, my voice pitching up. "Didn't you hear what he said to me?" I look to my dad to corroborate, but he only shakes his head, disappointment settling over his features.

Darren shifts in his seat. He's wearing trunks and a Hawaiian shirt, and the bronze of his skin, deeper than Dean's and the girls', is darkened from spending the day playing with Jessie in the sun. "Maybe this wasn't such a good idea," he says.

Terry's mouth flattens into a thin line. Hearing her dad's words, Jessie's eyes fill with tears.

"I don't want to go home," she says, her voice wavering.

"You don't have to go home, bug," my mom says to her. She wraps an arm around Jessie, consoling her like she's her own daughter.

While I just stand, helpless and hurt, my dad walks ahead of me. He nods in the direction of the beach for me to follow. Knowing I have no choice, I do.

The sun is setting, the clouds orange with deep purple streaks. The water shimmers with the rippled reflection of the vanishing light. It's exactly the first evening in Malibu I wish I could enjoy.

Instead, while I walk, indignation burns up the back of my neck. Just because I can't take Dean's belittling comments without getting emotional, it means I don't deserve any sympathy? He's somehow wound up with a monopoly on misery, leaving me looking like the villain.

I don't understand this—like, existentially. I'm just *different*? I'm the family-splitting, vacation-wrecking diva here by default? I'm not entitled to my own parents seeing me struggle with something and having compassion?

Why not?

The wounded whisper of the question follows me out onto the sand, where my dad is walking with slow strides. It's a power move, one I've seen him do with Mom, and a clever, ultimately harmless one. It says, *Your long volleyball legs give you no advantage here. You keep* my *pace.*

Dutifully, I fall into his measured step. He waits until we're out of earshot to stop on the sand.

"Look, I know you're in a bad spot," he says, and I straighten up, not having expected even the small allowance of understanding. "But you have to be more compassionate. Dean is heartbroken. Everyone knows it. You're smart, so I know you know it, too."

My shoulders return to their slump. I feel foolish for having had hope. Usually, I would let it go, school myself into compliance. But this is one slight too many. Under this dazzling sunset, I let my disappointment sour. "So?" I snap.

His eyes widen, genuinely. I know when my dad is performing. Right now, I've really surprised him. It only makes me more stubborn.

"I *could* be the heartbroken one," I go on. "I've just taught myself not to be. I don't get to be heartbroken."

Honestly, I don't even know why I'm explaining this to him. It's incredibly obvious. Being heartbroken isn't compatible with being likable. With being a champion. No one wants to feel sorry for the girl who has it all. The truth of it clings to me everywhere, like little spikes on the imaginary crown I wear to every volleyball practice or school dance—not often biting enough to draw blood, but never forgiving enough to forget.

And why should people feel sorry for me? I can handle my feelings so they don't burden others. But that doesn't mean I don't *have* feelings.

"I know it feels that way," Dad says gently. "But no one is telling you not to be upset. The thing is, you're just the greatest person in the entire word. No wonder Dean is distraught to be without you."

This makes me laugh a little, grudgingly. My dad, recognizing he's scored a point, smiles.

"That said," he continues, "I'm not telling you this for Dean's benefit."

"Really?" I ask. "Because it feels pretty obvious that everyone here is on his side." I hear the slouch in my voice, how I'm no longer managing to keep my sharpness light. I just sound sad.

Dad shakes his head, his mouth flattening with sincerity. The measured softness of his voice doesn't ease the intensity of the stare he fixes on me. "No way. I'm on your side, always," he says. "Which, right now, means reminding you Dean was your best friend. He was your best friend for longer than he was your boyfriend and longer than he's been your ex. And you're in danger of losing that friendship forever if you keep on like this."

It hurts to hear—this time, not because I think he's being unfair or because I just want to enjoy my vacation. It's because he's right. Dean *is* important to me. I don't want to lose that relationship in my life. I just don't know why repairing it has to fall entirely on me.

I guess it does, though.

My dad puts a hand on my shoulder, then walks back to the house, leaving me cold in the warm California night.

Ten

I EYE THE COFFEE maker hesitantly while the morning light glares in through the wall of windows looking out onto the shore. The time change pulled me out of bed early—it's barely six. When I got downstairs, I found Terry and Jessie eating breakfast, and, fuzzy with sleep, I trudged over to the kitchen counter.

In front of the small Keurig, I stand, torn. I *wish* I liked coffee. I like the *idea* of liking coffee. It would be conducive to my life in so many ways, from the productivity kick of caffeine to the obvious social media appeal of pretty drinks. Instead, whenever I venture into coffee, I find myself feeling like I'm swallowing down hot dirt.

Still, I keep thinking if I continue to try it, I'll develop a taste for lattes, cappuccinos, and all the variations with indiscernible differences.

"How about I make you eggs?" Terry offers behind me.

"I can make them," I reply. But Terry is already up, reaching for the pan. It's the way we've always been. Terry is like a second mother to me. I used to dress up in her clothes when Dean and I were kids. Whenever my parents couldn't pick me up from school, I'd find Terry's Volkswagen at the front of the line of parents' cars.

Knowing there's no point in resisting, I settle into the kitchen booth next to Jessie, who's playing an iPad game while eating Eggos. I offer overenthusiastic encouragement despite having no understanding whatsoever of the game's objective, which makes her giggle and shove me away.

While I'm an only child, on these trips, I don't feel like one. I can't imagine having sisters who feel more sisterly to me than Jessie and Lucy.

Obviously, the comparison doesn't extend to Dean. He's the farthest thing from brother territory.

Terry brings my eggs over to me. They're prepared just the way I like, salt and generous pepper with no ketchup. Holding her mug of coffee, she sits down across from me. Once more, I endeavor to find the steam's pungent smell enticing. Once more, I do not succeed.

"How's Brianna doing? Are you and she playing any tournaments this summer?" Terry asks, staring past the rim of her mug, which is starting to fog up her glasses.

I dig into my eggs. "Oh, no, we're not partners anymore," I say. "She's going to Stanford in the fall, where she's going to play indoor."

Terry's eyes crinkle with concern. "I'm sorry. You two made a great team."

I reach for my napkin, hesitating to reply. We're stepping onto slightly sensitive ground. I know Brianna's and my split mirrors the choices my mom and Terry made when they were eighteen, my mom opting to forgo college and go pro while Terry played for UCLA. "Yeah," I say eventually. "I'll miss her, but we'll stay close." The unspoken part of my confidence is obvious. *We'll stay close just like you and my mom did.*

Terry smiles, hearing what I'm not saying. "And you're still not planning to play for a college team? You know that's the first step for the majority of players going pro." While her voice is light, it reminds me how riptides sometimes hide under the even, glassy surface of the ocean.

"I know," I say. "But no, I'm not planning to. Not right away."

Terry looks like she wants to say more. She sips her coffee instead.

I stay silent, enjoying the perfect sprinkling of pepper on my eggs a little less.

"Kaylee," Jessie says next to me. "Will you take me to the beach today to play mermaids?"

The request lifts my spirits immediately. Not just because it distracts from the pinched stillness over the conversation, either. "Um, *why* do you think I got up so early? I've been waiting for you to ask."

Jessie grins hugely. "I was going to ask Dean, too," she informs me. "But he was crying in his room until late last night. I heard him because I was too excited to sleep."

I wince, dodging Terry's gaze. *Crying?* I expected Dean's

snark last night. I handled him hiding in his room when we got here. *Crying in his room* feels like something new. I'm shaken, like I've just realized I'm going skydiving with a life preserver instead of a parachute. I put my fork down, no longer hungry.

"Jessie, it's not nice to gossip about your brother," Terry says. She places a hand on my forearm, and I venture to meet her eyes. "He'll be okay. It's not your fault," she reassures me softly.

Her words comfort me a little, but I still feel awful. It is *partly* my fault. It's partly Dean's. But fault doesn't even matter. Dean was my best friend, and now he's heartbroken.

What my dad said returns to me like it was carried in on the morning breeze rustling the palms outside. He was right. I have to do something—I have to help him. Not because I owe him, not because I was wrong to dump him or because my parents are forcing me. But because we used to be friends.

Because I still care about him as a friend.

Terry slides out of her seat to refill her coffee, and my gaze wanders to the stairs leading up to Dean's bedroom. I start to remember how *little* I've thought of Jeremy since we got here, how quickly and seamlessly I got over *my* last relationship. More of my conversation with my dad returns to me.

I could be the heartbroken one. I've just taught myself not to be.

I stare. The idea settles over me gently, like the new day brightening outside. Who recognized dating Jeremy would make the past few weeks bearable, even if it ended poorly?

Who knew to watch thirty seasons of *Survivor* to reset her romantic outlook? I'm not just a friend who wants to ease Dean's heartache, I realize.

I'm the perfect person for the job.

I'm going to help Dean get over me.

Eleven

DEAN, THE HIPSTER, GENUINELY does enjoy coffee. Or at least he's much better at faking enthusiasm for the drink than I am.

My face scrunching up, I brew a steaming cup into his favorite mug, the Hermosa Beach Pier one we've had for decades. While the rest of the house is waking up, I walk up the stairs, working hard not to slosh acid bean juice on me. Reaching Dean's room, I knock quietly, just loud enough for him to hear over the pained vocals of the desperately sad electronic R&B floating through his door.

"Come in," I hear from inside.

I crack the door open, knowing he probably wouldn't have given the invitation so freely if he'd known who was knocking.

"It's me," I say.

Dean is lying fully clothed on his bed. Like he got up,

got dressed, and then couldn't leave his room. The sight is another reminder of how much work I have ahead of me. Despite the fact that my cup of coffee is starting to feel like a very small candle in a very heavy rainstorm, I don't let my resolve waver. I *never* let my resolve waver.

Dean sits up, looking horrified. He hastily cuts the volume on the portable Bluetooth speaker he brings everywhere.

"Can *I* come in?" I ask cautiously.

He eyes me warily. I can practically see the emotional calculus running in his head, displayed in the details of his familiar features. Is it worth it to kick me out, extending the messy scene we're making in front of the families? Is the effort of shutting down my every interaction with him a little too exhausting for seven in the morning on vacation? Finally, he slowly nods.

Shutting the door behind me, I walk in.

"Feel free to mock me, because yes, I'm still moping," he says humorlessly.

I bite my lip. He's right to rub my nose in what I said last night. If I'd handled myself perfectly, I wouldn't have made fun of his feelings.

I hold the coffee out to him. "No mocking. I swear," I say.

Skeptically, he takes the mug from me. He might soften slightly when he notices the coral reef design. I can't quite tell. He doesn't drink, though.

"I'm sorry about what I said last night." I keep my eyes on him, wanting him to know I'm not hiding from my remorse.

Dean looks at the floor, where his closed blinds draw

slashes of sunlight. He pauses before replying. "Yeah, well, me too," he says finally.

I grasp on to this hopeful sign. Before I lose my nerve, I sit down on the window seat, which houses a laser printer and a couple plants. "I was thinking we could try something," I start, chasing confidence I don't feel just yet. "You're going through a bad breakup, and clearly you could use a friend to talk to about it."

"I *have* friends," he protests.

"I know—I know you have friends," I hastily clarify. "I just mean, what if you *pretend* I'm not your ex? What if I'm just your friend? You know, your friend who you combined allowances with to buy that pirate book from the elementary school book fair. Your friend who helped you ask Taylor to homecoming freshman year. Your friend who you can talk about your breakup with."

Dean's eyes narrow. But he sips his coffee, and almost immediately color seeps back into his cheeks.

"I'm not sure I can do that," he replies.

"Just try. In exchange for the coffee you're already drinking," I press him.

He places the mug down, looking somewhat amused, which I consider another victory. Excitement starts to speed my pulse. I straighten up when Dean clasps his hands, fixing his gaze on me with what looks like indulgence.

"This isn't going to work, but okay," he says. "Two months ago the girl of my dreams dumped me. She's totally moved on, but I don't know how to get over someone like her."

My mouth opens, then closes. I—didn't expect such stinging honesty right out of the gate.

"Please, friend. Make me feel better." He sits back, looking smug.

I shake off my surprise. *Game time.* "Well, firstly," I venture, going for playfully prescriptive, "your ex must not be very bright, because who would break up with you?"

He rolls his eyes. Everything in his demeanor now impossibly casual, he reaches for his coffee. "She's actually very bright. And beautiful, and brave, and everything I admire."

His compliments hit me in soft places, which I cover. He's trying to make this hard for me, hoping I slip on the sweetness of his words. I won't let him. "Okay, *that's* your problem," I say matter-of-factly, in the voice my mom would use to help me with my serve. "We need to bad-mouth this girl. Let's pick apart her flaws."

Dean shakes his head, incredulous. "No. No way."

It's the first non-calculated reaction I've gotten from him in this line of conversation, which makes me double down. "Come on. You have her on a pedestal. She's not *that* great. She . . ." Grasping for insults I can use on myself, I find one quickly. "She *sounds* pretty emotionally unavailable. And, I mean, clearly she didn't appreciate you."

Dean stays silent. I can't read his expression.

"Also, I have a hunch she snores. You can't get serious with someone who snores," I say.

His lips twitch. "I don't mind wearing earplugs."

"She has small eyes," I point out. Once more, I'm not surprised how swiftly I'm able to hunt down more self-criticism.

While I do not enjoy focusing on my flaws, I'm effortlessly conscious of what they are.

"No, she doesn't," Dean replies.

"She talks at an annoyingly high volume."

He opens his mouth, then closes it. "Okay, yes, that's true."

"Hey!" I say, laughing. Dean laughs, too, and we're really laughing, like we used to. My chest feels somehow full and light simultaneously. Dean, I'm gratified to find, looks close to happy for the first time on this trip. "See?" I say gently. "I can help you. It's not easy getting over people. I'm only good at it because I've had a lot of practice. A *lot* of practice."

His expression starting to sober, Dean listens. I charge on, knowing it's now or never for my pitch.

"I have sort of my own heartbreak survival guide, which I can share with you. I can—I *want* to help you get over me," I say.

Dean's eyes slip from me. He gazes out the window, where the morning marine layer is starting to burn off, leaving the ocean unclouded. "I'm not sure I want to get over you." There's no mistaking the honesty in his words.

"Dean . . ."

He meets my eyes again, and a searching look passes between us.

"We can tiptoe around each other for three weeks until we go home," I say, hoping he hears the imploring undercurrent in my voice. "Or we can try to move past this."

"There's a third option."

I blink, unsure what he means until the sparkle in his eye clues me in. "We're not getting back together," I say flatly. I decide not to share my reasoning. It's not like I can no longer imagine wanting to, objectively—even having pretty much literally just rolled out of bed, he's unfairly good-looking, with his intense eyes, his rakish hair. But I'm not interested in going backward.

He shrugs. "I had to try."

"Look, I'm not going to force you to do anything, obviously," I say. "I'll let you think about it. Whatever you want, just know I'm here to help." I stand up and head for the door, pausing near his speakers. "Should I resume your incredibly depressing playlist?"

"Yes, please," he says.

I'm reaching for the play button when I hear him sigh, defeated.

"Wait." He speaks slowly, his words carefully considered. "What would that look like, exactly? You helping me?"

I face him, not daring to hope.

His expression remains cautiously curious. I work doubly hard to keep my voice gentle, *at a normal speaking volume*, not wanting to scare him off with my enthusiasm. "Well, I'll walk you through the steps I take. I'll distract you with hobbies, days out, fun. I'll remind you how wonderful you are. How you don't need anyone to be happy."

I'm not fighting to soften my voice by the end of my proposal. I don't need to, not when I'm speaking from the deepest part of me.

Dean quirks an eyebrow. "Sounds like we'd be spending a lot of time together," he ventures, new interest in his voice.

I search his eyes for where he's going with this. "I mean . . . yeah, we *are* on vacation together. You sleep ten feet away from me."

This confirmation transforms Dean's expression. He looks rejuvenated. "Right. Days at the beach, dinners, long walks. Sounds like dating," he says. Delight flickers in his dark eyes. He stands up. "I'm in."

I'm honestly unable to believe what I just walked into. When I repeat his description in my head, it . . . Okay, while I understand where he's coming from, I don't think I share his characterization. Can't two old friends walk on the beach without it being romantic? "Dean, the point is to help you get over me," I say warningly.

"And you're sincerely welcome to give it your best shot. Really," he replies without hesitating.

I narrow my eyes. "Okay, I'm . . . not following."

"I'll do what you advise, but don't be surprised if spending time with me reminds you how good our relationship was," he explains evenly, leaning on the dresser. "How fun. How soul-stirring. How perfect."

My expression flattens. "That won't happen," I say sternly. "I didn't break up with you just because."

He cocks his head. "Hey, why *did* you break up with me?"

I have to smile, just a little. "You're impossible."

Dean receives my deferral with good grace and a knowing grin of his own. Straightening up from the dresser, he puts out his hand. "Should we shake on it, then?"

Without thinking, just thrilled he's embracing my plan, I

take his hand. The skin-to-skin contact is like lightning, surprising me with a sudden force of feeling.

I press it back instantly, not letting the memory of holding his hand on the way home from our first date flash through my mind.

"Get ready for the beach," I say. "We start now."

Twelve

I GIVE US TEN minutes to change into swimsuits.

I'm waiting for Dean at the bottom of the stairs when he bounds down, buoyed by obvious enthusiasm for his own agenda. It doesn't bother me. I know what I'm doing. What matters is that Dean doesn't hate me right now. As long as he's willing to spend time with me, I'm relieved. I'm confident that with a couple weeks I can get him well on the way to getting over me, and then we'll just be friends. The way we were.

He's dressed characteristically cool, even for the beach, pairing his plain white tee with floral-print trunks in nicely contrasting greens and pinks. His hair bun is loose, with carefree strands falling out. When he sees me, his eyes light up.

"Okay," he says. "What's first?"

I smile. Regardless of its reason, his eagerness is contagious. In my head, I flip open my heartbreak survival guide. "The first thing I do after a breakup is say yes to every invitation, even when I don't feel like it," I explain. "It's important to get out into the world. To be around friends. To stop *moping*."

The glance I give him on my final word doesn't perturb him in the least. He nods, looking game for whatever I have in mind.

I start walking through the house, leading him to the back doors out to the deck. Past the railing, the ocean waits invitingly.

"And today's invitation is brought to you by—" I pause dramatically while we step outside.

In the hammock on the patio is Jessie, ready in her swimsuit, sunscreen smudges everywhere on her round little face. She whips her head up, pigtails swinging with the widest smile.

"My little sister," Dean finishes, the enthusiasm in his voice starting to deflate.

I match Jessie's grin. "She asked us to play mermaids with her."

"*Finally!*" Jessie leaps up, the hammock wobbling in her wake. "Kaylee, what's your tail look like? Mine is silver, and I have purple hair, and I can make giant bubbles for all my human friends and also for Toaster to come visit me at the bottom of the ocean. What are your powers?"

"Toaster doesn't like to swim," Dean points out unhelpfully.

I glare. *Party pooper.* Toaster is the Freeman-Yus' twelve-year-old, very ill-tempered cat. Who, yes, would definitely hate visiting Mer-Jessie's undersea queendom.

"That's why he'd be in a bubble," Jessie replies witheringly. "Duh."

I laugh. "She has you there."

"Kaylee," Dean implores me under his breath. "You can't be serious."

I raise my eyebrows, unflinching. "We had a deal, did we not?"

In defeat, Dean exhales exasperatedly. Grumbling something incomprehensible, he starts walking with us in the direction of the water.

"Dean, do you feel better today after crying?" Jessie asks.

I tense, not wanting the reminder to dampen Dean's spirits, not when he's out here, grudgingly participating.

Dean, however, looks unshaken. "Yes, I do. Crying is nothing to be ashamed of."

Softening, I hide my chagrin at having misjudged his reaction. When he's comfortable, the Dean I know is quick in conversation and naturally unselfconscious. I don't fight my smile as he dives into describing his mermaid characteristics to Jessie. He picks a black tail and the power to listen to music underwater—of course. I go with a pink tail, bright-blue hair, and the power to swim super fast.

When we reach the shore, it's empty of people since it's still early. Tourists will flock in from Los Angeles later, but right now, the sunlight bathing over the tranquil water feels secret, even stolen. No footsteps pockmark the surface of the sand, no shouts of kids on the breeze. We're catching the shore fresh-faced.

I don't have words for the vividness of everything. The serene sounds of the gentle waves, the exhilarating scent of the sea, the gorgeous blues where the water meets the sky, even the welcome ordinariness of the sand receding up to the row of houses lining the coast on stilts like ours. I feel this way whenever I'm here. Like I've stepped into someone else's photograph.

Holding my flip-flops in one hand, I let the soft sand shift under my feet, enjoying the sensation instead of focusing on whether I have the perfect stance to jump or sprint. In the moment, with Dean working with me on my plan, I feel a little of what I'd hoped I would find in Malibu. I feel *good*. We have plenty of progress to make, but this perfect morning really does feel perfect.

It's something.

In front of us, Jessie runs into the water, immediately plunging her head under the surface to blow bubbles—for Toaster, presumably. Grinning, I drop our towels, kick off my shorts, then begin walking toward the ocean before I realize Dean isn't with me.

I turn, finding him watching me, still standing with the towels though he's taken his shirt off. I can't quite read the funny pinched expression on his face, but I do recognize the way his eyes have glazed over a little.

He shakes his head, like he's trying to pull himself out of it.

"You're really bad at this getting-me-over-you thing if you think me seeing you in a bikini is helping," he says.

The boldness of his comment changes the shade of my smile. Swallowing it, I walk back up to him. There's no use hiding, not when we're going to spend every seaside day together for the next three weeks. Besides, I don't want to. I quite like how I look in this yellow bikini, which is not something I'll sacrifice even to my very promising effort to ferry Dean past our breakup.

"I'm able to be around you shirtless without it being a problem," I point out.

There's humor in the frown Dean gives me. "You do realize that was actually an insult."

My cheeks redden for the first time since I took off my shorts. "*Actually*, it was a compliment. I didn't wake up between dating you and breaking up with you and suddenly find you physically unattractive."

Dean stares, taking my remark in like it's momentous when it's obviously not. I made it clear while we were dating exactly how attractive I found him. I walk into the water, not bothering to wait for him to work through this. It's refreshingly cold, like gulping down hydration in between points on the court. I glide my feet easily under the glassy surface. I've sunk down to my neck when Dean joins me. We float near Jessie, who keeps diving to the bottom to search the soft sand for "treasure."

After lazing in the water for a few minutes, Dean suddenly holds up a hand like he's figured something out.

"Wait, so physical attractiveness *didn't* factor into our breakup? That's what you're saying?" he asks.

Staring up into the flawless sky, I inhale, inflating my lungs like life preservers. "Okay, lesson number two, and I know this one will be hard for you," I say. "But to get over an ex, you have to stop wondering *why* you broke up. It *doesn't matter*. Knowing why changes nothing. You'll be broken up either way. Like, look at me. Jeremy dumped me because he found out I was going to California with my ex." While keeping my voice light on the subject isn't easy, I call on practiced muscles for controlling my demeanor. "I have a definitive answer as to why," I continue, "and it doesn't matter. I'm still going to California with my ex, and he's still someone who would dump me over that. It doesn't make me feel better to know he didn't trust me enough to stay with me."

"But you didn't love Jeremy," Dean counters. I think I hear the prickle of defensiveness in his voice. The hidden question.

I exhale, letting myself bob in the water. "So? It still hurts that someone I cared about saw me that way."

"Sure," Dean says impatiently. "But when you're in love, part of you needs to know why it ended. I guess you wouldn't understand, since you clearly didn't love me back."

He doesn't let me reply, choosing now to push off from the ground and swim suddenly after Jessie, pretending he's a shark. She squeals and splashes away.

I watch them, Dean's parting words stinging. I really thought I meant it when I told Dean I loved him, but . . . maybe he's right. Maybe I didn't. How could I have, when I fell *out* of love with him so quickly, over nothing? It's unnerving to second-guess something so fundamental. It feels like sudden undercurrents have pulled me off my feet, far from the peaceful shore.

I hate that I can't tell Dean how wrong he is about me. But I can't. I wouldn't believe myself if I did.

Thirteen

I PROD MY CEVICHE in silence.

The families have driven to our favorite local restaurant, where we're seated outdoors. Returning here is something I look forward to the whole year—sitting under the white sloped roof, reviewing the newspaper-sized laminated menu even though we know what we want, countering the evening heat with water from the huge plastic cups. Restaurants in Malibu come in two varieties, ridiculously fancy—hundred-dollar sushi or cloth-napkin finery—or incredibly casual, like this place, with picnic tables on the flagstone patio where the seafood, served on plasticware or in paper-lined blue baskets, is the freshest I've ever had.

Hence, the ceviche. I focus on the perfect citrus-seafood-onion combination in my first bite, trying to enjoy myself.

I'm not loving how much *trying to enjoy myself* I'm doing on this trip, but right now I'm stuck on Dean's comment from this morning. I haven't pressed him on our getting-over-me plans since then, wanting to give him space and not over-whelm him with tasks. Or that's what I've told myself. I'm probably just being cowardly after what he called me on at the beach.

I've only just taken my second bite when my phone starts blowing up on the table.

I grab for it, heart jumping into my throat, pounding so painfully I can barely swallow. Glancing over the messages, I figure out what's going on. Brianna's texted me that the national ranking of high school volleyball players has been posted, followed by a string of exclamation points. A second later, my phone is flooded with friends congratulating me.

For what, I won't know until I find the list online.

I type in my login info to get behind the paywall, my eyes trained on my phone while the rest of the table talks about the new pancake house we drove by on the way here. Then I wait. The meaning fades out of the parents' words. My knee starts bouncing under the table, hard enough for Dean to notice.

He eyes me curiously. I ignore him. I just need to know what—

The page loads.

My name is . . . second. Second in all the players in the United States, juniors *and* seniors. Second. I understand why everyone is congratulating me—objectively, it's a huge achieve-ment. The next junior on the list is number twelve.

I put my phone down, searching for pride. It's there, deep in me, a warm glow I try to nestle into. I can't quite do it, though, for one reason. The voice in the back of my head, the familiar, inescapable itch, the faint presence of everything I wish I could ignore—the whisper reminding me my mom ranked first as a junior.

If I didn't have the reference point of my mother, I'd be all-caps yelling in my texts to my friends, sharing in the celebration. Instead, I know this will just be one more stat trotted out in articles about us. In any other family, this would be a conversation stopper, an instant cause for celebration. In mine, it will feel like an empty imitation of greater achievements.

I glance up. The parents continue their conversation happily unaware, sharing their enthusiasm for new pancake options. The list ranking, the confetti grenade I'm clutching, waits expectantly for me to pull the pin.

I can't do it. I can't bring myself to share the news with the people around me. It's not that they wouldn't be thrilled for me. It's just that, even if they think they mean it—can they really? *How*, with my mom sitting right here?

I flip my phone facedown on the table, knowing I'll have to process these feelings later. And I will. I just need more time with them on my own before I bring the ranking to my family. If I can cut out my own disappointment, bring out my inner pride, then when my mom says she's proud of me, I'll be able to hear her words for real instead of having them ring hollow.

Looking up, I find Dean's eyes haven't left me. He searches my expression, questioning. For a second, I'm not sure which version of him is curious—the friend I shared everything with, or my ex, goading or guarded depending on the conversation.

I ignore him, not wanting to let vulnerability in right now. Instead, I turn to Lucy next to me. She's going into eighth grade, and every time I see her, she's gotten taller. I'm 6'1" and I'm confident Lucy will surpass me. "What'd you do today?" I ask. "We missed you at the beach."

"I slept," Lucy replies. "I've been so drained from practice, and while I was on the plane, I had to submit a makeup final I missed for a tournament, so I was coming off an all-nighter."

I grimace in sympathy. Lucy plays club volleyball, and I know well the struggle of cramming schoolwork and practice into days with not enough hours. "Ouch," I say. "Well, we're dragging you out with us next time."

Lucy smiles, all braces.

"Us?" my dad interjects from the other side of the round table. "Do my ears deceive me? Surely you and Dean weren't at the same beach this morning."

I keep my expression unmoved. "We were. With Jessie."

Now we have the whole table's attention. "Oh, thank god," Darren says. "That's a relief."

"I know," my mom chimes in. "We were worried you'd end up drawing a literal line in the sand to keep away from each other."

Dean frowns. "We were fine."

My dad gives him an indulgent look. "All we're saying is we're glad you're tolerating each other. Now we can put the whole Kaylee-and-Dean saga behind us."

"Amen," Terry says.

I whip my head toward her. Terry sounds *too* relieved,

fervent, like my dad's just said something she's thought be-fore, maybe even said before herself.

My mom chuckles. "It wasn't that bad."

Terry huffs not quite a laugh. "I'm just glad it was brief. You two got it out of your systems."

I'm stunned by her words. They rip new ragged edges into the patches I've neatly put over Dean's and my relationship. It's not that I want to be with Dean and need Terry's ap-proval, but it hurts to hear that his mom, who's like family to me, didn't want me dating her son. Why? She knows me—the real me—and still I'm not good enough for Dean?

It stings worse than the rankings.

Dad shrugs, reaching for his beer. "It would've been nice if it had worked out, though. We already feel like one family anyway."

Terry doesn't look heartened. "They're teenagers, John. Don't put that pressure on them. It's better this way," she says. "For everyone."

I feel my chest crumple. It's literally difficult to breathe from the gut punch of her judgment. I have the urge to pick my phone back up, to escape into the stressful world of high school athletics.

"It's not pressure. It's a thought," my dad replies evenly, impossible to intimidate. "Of course I didn't think it was a good idea when they got together because we knew where it would lead. I'm just saying, under *other* circumstances—"

"There are no other circumstances," Dean cuts him off harshly. "Kaylee and I dated. We broke up. Now we're . . ." He looks to me, hesitancy clouding over his expression. "Friends, or something. It's none of your business," he says to the table.

My dad looks surprised, possibly even proud of how deliberately Dean silenced him. In the pause, Mom holds up her drink. "Well said, Dean. I for one am excited not to have to talk about this anymore."

I blink. Was that an offhand comment, or did the parents have other discussions about us? I can feel hidden layers moving in this conversation, like the rock shelves under the sea. Silent, until they churn up tsunamis. The way everyone is tense, the bitter edges to their tones, is uncharacteristic, the ominous hint of a rift I've never seen before.

Part of me wants to press into it, figure out where it's coming from—fix it. I hear the siren song of my fiercest instincts, to strive, to polish, to perfect. I *need* to know what problem with me, what flaw, is causing such a strange division in our families. *Fix it, Kaylee. Figure it out. Make it work.* The words pound with the rhythm of my heartbeat.

Still, I stop myself. I want to know why me being part of the Freeman-Yu family would be such a bad thing, but I'm not sure I can handle the answer. Not right now.

"Yes," I hear myself say. "It's done, so let's all just move on."

Everyone nods, eager to change the subject from this unexpected source of tension. But while the table returns to the eternal Movie Night Debate, I don't know if I'm imagining it or if some of the strain remains in the way Terry looks at my parents.

It feels like we really haven't moved on at all.

Fourteen

I LIE IN BED, unable to sleep. The roaring of the waves, welcoming in daylight, now sounds insistent. I stare up into the ceiling of my dark room, knowing deep down that sleep isn't coming for me yet.

On the way home from the restaurant, I could feel a migraine coming on, but I managed to prevent the worst of it by catching it with aspirin at the right time. Still, my head feels tender, like I just battled through one of the devastating headaches. Sleep is the best treatment, but my mind is fighting itself too much.

I'm stuck on the rankings, hating that I even compare myself to my mom. Hating how the habit sharpens points of pride into shortcomings, making me feel like I need to be constantly striving even when I should be celebrating. It's not rational or fair—I shouldn't compare myself to one of the best volleyball players ever.

But I do.

I don't know where the cycle started, whether I'm just made to constantly stretch myself until I'm close to snapping, or whether living my entire life reaching for her greatness has left me unable to stop. If she weren't my mom, I wouldn't spend every single minute comparing myself to the legendary Judy Jordan.

It's my instinct to call Brianna, to hear her say I don't need to waste time in the demoralizing cycle of comparing myself to my mom. She knows how those insecurities prey on me even if it's not something I allow myself to share often. What stops me now is knowing I ranked higher than her on the list—how selfishly needy would I be to want reassurance over a rank like mine?

I will myself to be satisfied with what I've done on my own. But for some slippery, infuriating reason, I can't.

Annoyed with myself, I swing my legs out of bed. There's no use sitting with my thoughts right now. I decide I'll go downstairs, where Darren is probably watching something random on TV. Heading into the hall, I walk gingerly to keep the floorboards from creaking, knowing it's past Jessie's bedtime and remembering poor Lucy's sleep debt. Sure enough, when I start tiptoeing down the stairs, I hear televised voices floating up.

But when I reach the living room, it's not Darren on the couch, legs kicked up onto the sectional. It's Dean. With him is Lucy, whose sleep schedule I guess *is* incredibly messed up right now. They're wrapped in blankets it's honestly too warm for and quietly watching a movie.

I only need to see a couple seconds to determine it's one of Dean's indie films. He was always trying to get me to watch them while we were dating. I'd agree, then quickly get bored and decide to make out with him instead. He didn't complain, although he did confess to rewatching the movies on his own later.

I put those memories from my mind. Right now, one of Dean's movies is exactly what I need to put me to sleep.

"Mind if I join?" I ask from behind the couch.

Dean glances at me over his shoulder. "You'll hate it," he says with no contempt in his voice, only a strange loaded something, like a resisted inside joke. He scoots over, making space between him and Lucy, who seems to be mostly texting friends rather than watching the movie.

I settle in, hit immediately with the familiar scent of Dean. Two months ago, I would have tucked myself into his side. I don't now.

His voice comes suddenly from next to me, low and soft. "Can't sleep?"

I cut him a glance out of the corner of my eye. He's watching me, not rapt, but not careless, either. "No. This will do the trick, though," I say playfully, winking.

He doesn't smile. It's a few seconds before he speaks. When he does, his eyes shift back to the screen, like he's figured out what he was looking for. "You're irritated about the ranking."

I straighten up. "How did you . . . ?"

The light from the TV casts over Dean's features in rippling waves of luminous gray. "I subscribed to the newsletter when—" His expression flickers faintly with displeasure, the look of someone who's just stepped in a puddle. He carpets the reaction over instantly, continuing without emotion. "When we were together."

I don't know how hearing this makes me feel. "Oh," I settle for replying.

Dean says nothing. Silence returns—or, silence except for the dialogue of the characters in this very talky movie. I face forward. Suddenly, the idea of focusing on whatever nuanced dramedy Dean's chosen for us doesn't sound so bad, not when the other option is continuing to delve into my deepest insecurities, this time with my ex.

I've nearly managed to figure out the plot when Dean speaks up, his voice unimaginably gentle.

"Second is really incredible, you know," he says.

I don't move. Hearing him say so is—I don't know. It's exactly what I need, yet somehow impossible to believe.

"And as a junior," he goes on. "You should be really proud. There's no one in our grade who even comes close to you."

I pick the fringe of the nearest pillow, then pull it into my lap. I hate how much I want to deny his compliments. How hungrily part of me fights for its right to feel small, insufficient, unworthy. How badly it wants to remind him—to *prove*—I should be judging myself instead of celebrating myself.

I refuse to give in to the instinct, but I can't quite manage to defy it, either. So I redirect. "Hey, so your mom seemed really opposed to us. Do you know why?"

Dean's gaze leaves me and fixes on the screen.

My curiosity piqued, I stop fussing with the pillow. "Dean. Why?"

Dean sighs. Then, like he's realizing something, he faces me, slowly smiling. "I'll tell you if you tell me why you broke up with me."

I slouch back into the couch, stymied. I should've seen *that* coming. Note to self—asking Dean any questions at all, about anything, this entire summer, is futile. When the couch cushions shift next to me, though, I realize my insistent ex isn't the only one with interrogatory tricks up their sleeve. I round on Lucy. "Do *you* know?" I ask her, going for gossipy with an edge of *I'm the older girl you totally look up to so you better start talking.*

Lucy squirms. She looks up from her phone, her gaze skirting between me and Dean.

"For the record, I thought you were a cute couple, but I'm going to bed now and not getting involved," she says, rushing the final words, then immediately getting up.

She texts the whole way up the stairs. It occurs to me she's probably not really going to bed.

I huff. *Whatever.* It's fine—I don't really want to unwrap this question so late at night anyway. I return my focus to the movie, which has not improved. I have no idea how far into it we are and don't want to ask. Instead, I settle for sitting quietly, watching with sleepless eyes.

Finally, I figure out that the movie Dean's chosen is about . . . a breakup. *Of course* it is.

I roll my eyes. Dean needs to stop wallowing. I'm not, like, categorically anti-wallowing—it's an important first step. We're two months post-breakup, though. Dean needs to move on to step two.

"Tomorrow we're going to talk rebounds," I announce.

"What? No. No way." Dean's head whips to face me. He doesn't hide the live-wire agitation in his voice. "Firstly, how could you possibly help with that? Secondly, I'm not ready." He crosses his arms defensively, like he's physically walling himself off from the prospect of romantic intervention.

The force of his reaction sort of makes me smile. "I'm not going to force you, of course," I reassure him. "Baby steps. Training, if you will. You don't have to do anything except consider it. Then before you know it, you'll be ready."

Dean grumbles inaudibly, no doubt something about regretting shaking on this agreement.

We fall back into silence, watching the movie. But no matter how much I try, I can't get invested in the plot. While the pretty people on-screen emote their way through their lovelorn story, my turbulent thoughts pull me deeper into my head.

"Did she think our personalities were incompatible?" I know my question comes out of nowhere, but I don't care. I can't pretend I'm not still curious. "Because I know we had a bit of that grumpy-sunshine thing going on."

Dean laughs. "You think *you're* sunshine, I take it?"

I look over, mildly incredulous. "I mean . . . I am? I

talk to strangers on the internet pretty much every day. Besides, you're all . . ." I wave my fingers at him. "Broody and artistic."

Mr. Broody—who, perfectly supporting my case, is still wearing what he wore to dinner, his nicely cut olive-green shorts and a black tee with some words in French on it—just stares, supremely skeptical.

"I'm *so* sunshine," I insist. "You think *you're* sunshine? You're not sunshine. I'm sunshine."

"You really can't handle the possibility that someone has found a flaw in you," he says.

The playfulness drops from my expression immediately.

"A *real* flaw," he goes on. "Not just joking about whether you snore or whatever. That's why you're so hung up on my mom's opinion of us when you don't even want to date me anymore."

I have to physically restrain myself from pouting. "That's not it. I get plenty of online comments telling me all about my flaws. I can handle my flaws."

"Sure, but those people don't matter," Dean replies easily, like he knew what I was going to say. "You work so hard to keep your life looking picture-perfect, even to the people closest to you—*especially* to the people closest to you. The thought that someone on the inside can see the cracks is driving you wild."

His assessment leaves me a little stunned. Not because I'm convinced he's entirely right—I'm not sure he is, or maybe I just don't want him to be. I *do* know I have nothing I can say to rebut. I want to. I really do. Yet nothing comes. It's unsettling in its own way.

My head still feels tender, the faintly foreboding pre-throbbing of the migraine I thought I'd left behind. I ignore him and curl onto my side to face the screen.

I watch the film until I fall asleep.

Fifteen

I WAKE UP THE next morning on the couch, under the blanket Dean was wrapped in last night.

He tucked me in when I nodded off. Knowing I maybe shouldn't, I let myself indulge in the thought, in whatever it means. It's certainly something good friends, ones who've forgiven each other for romantic impasses, would do. The image of him gently draping the blanket over curled-up me is sweeter than the ocean scent drifting into the room, more heartening than the soft sunlight filtering in the living room windows.

I tap my phone to wake up the screen, which reads 6:12. It's incredibly peaceful this early in the morning. The house is silent, my headache is gone, and Dean doesn't totally hate me. I feel unusually good.

I head quietly up the stairs to my room. Truthfully, though I don't love the weariness of mornings when I'm not helped out by the time change, I enjoy being up early. The freedom to plan my routines and collect myself without interruptions or evaluating eyes on me is very, very welcome. Right now, for instance, I respond to emails with precious, methodical calm. Then I even get in some yoga and meditation.

I'm feeling so renewed and recharged that I have new perspective on last night. I don't know why Terry didn't want me to date Dean. We're not together, though, so it doesn't matter. I can't believe I forgot to follow my own advice, the very same I gave Dean—knowing why someone doesn't want you doesn't change anything. Finding out can only hurt you worse.

Hours later, I'm drinking guava juice in the kitchen, planning out Rebound Training Day in my head, when Dean walks in. He's dressed in trunks and a tank top, his hair up.

I grin. "Perfect," I say.

His steps slow. He eyes me suspiciously. "What's perfect?"

"You're already ready for the beach."

Dean relaxes. He walks over to the box of pastries Darren picked up around seven before heading to Surfrider Beach to surf with my dad.

I preempt his biting into the glazed cherry Danish he picked out. "You can eat in the car, right?" I ask over my shoulder on my way to the key rack near the front door, where I find the keys to my parents' rental car. I negotiated the use of the Jeep with my dad earlier this morning.

"Um, I don't plan on it," Dean replies.

Keys in hand, hip cocked, I stand in the entryway. "Well, you can always just eat something in Venice, I guess."

He sets his Danish down, frowning. "Venice? Kaylee, why? The beach outside our literal door is better. The boardwalk will just be crowded with tourists."

I smile. "Exactly."

It requires more convincing, but finally I get Dean—with his Danish—into the car and on our way to Venice Beach.

The road follows the contour of the coastline, the iridescent shine of the ocean literally right outside our window on one side while the sandy cliffs rise on the other. The landscape is majestic to the point of being intimidating. Our winding, two-lane stripe of pavement feels hard-fought, won from the rugged heights of the California coastline, unlike the endless easy reach of the rest of the city. It's just like everything else in Malibu for me, inspiring sheer wonder undimmed by the number of times I've been here before.

Until we hit the Pacific Palisades. When the narrow coastal road opens up into the flatter streets crossing PCH, we find ourselves in traffic. While we wait for other cars to inch past the light, I content myself with gazing out the windows, enjoying the sunlit view of the landscape where sand meets sea. What's a California vacation without traffic?

Dean, however, squints doubtfully out the windshield. *Does he seriously not see that he's the "grumpy" in our dynamic?* "We'll turn back if we can't find parking, right?"

"We'll find parking," I say.

Dean watches us slowly stop behind the car in front of us,

clearly unsatisfied with my response. "You said you wouldn't force me to rebound," he reminds me, changing tack.

"And I won't!"

He slides farther down in his seat, sulking. "Okay, then what exactly is the plan today?"

The light changes. We don't move. Even I start getting somewhat impatient with the unchanging details of the sun-soaked highway. I mean, I *hope* we'll find parking. "If I tell you," I say, "you'll just force me to turn the car around, and I'll panic because the road is crowded, and we'll get in a huge accident, and you'll ruin my volleyball career. Is that what you want, Dean?"

He groans. "This is a terrible idea. You're just going to get jealous if I start dating someone else."

I dart him a glance, my eyes leaving the congestion of cars in front of us for a second. "No, I won't."

Dean scoffs.

"I won't!" I insist. "You're my friend, and I want you to be happy."

"I want you to be happy, too," he says. "But there's a difference between wanting you to be happy and having a front-row seat to the happiness you find with someone else."

I soften. "I'll be fine," I say. I'm not promising idly, either. If Dean needs persuading, I'll remind him it's the whole point of my deeply internalized guide to getting over someone. *Being fine* is life itself. When every day is one nearly unrelenting deluge of sports stats and social media notifications and comparisons, being fine is essential. "Plus, I thought you weren't interested in a rebound," I go on, keeping my voice light. "Or *are* you ready to move on now?" I raise an eyebrow.

When he doesn't reply for a second, I wonder if I've upset him. I genuinely wasn't trying to, and I'm on the verge of attempting to smooth this over when he speaks up.

"Let's say we get to Venice and I have a meet-cute with someone," he says, pronouncing the term like it's foreign. "I invite them to tag along on our beach day. While you sit on the sand, I take them into the water, where I wrap an arm around their waist and pull them close. You remember how that felt, right?"

I fix my eyes on the road, my cheeks heating. *Yes, Dean, I remember.* I know what he's doing, too. It's clever, I'll give him that, but it won't work.

"When I kiss them," he continues deliberately, "I set the pace slow at first. We're on a public beach, after all. But I deepen the kiss just enough to hint at more soon."

I control my breathing, feeling his eyes on me. I remember how Dean kissed, too. I remember in searing detail how every press of his lips came with swooping flips in my stomach. He's a good kisser, but skill didn't really come into it. I'd kissed more skillful kissers before, but no one *wanted* like Dean.

Which is what I try to forget when I plaster on my smile. "Yup, that's how it would go," I say with silverware-in-an-electric-socket cheer. "I'd be okay."

Dean frowns. He turns to face away, out the passenger window. Even though I know he was trying to provoke me, I still feel bad for not reacting the way he wanted. But I'm trying to help him get *over* me. What does he expect me to say? I can't open the door to him just to remind him he can't walk through it.

"I don't believe you," he says stonily.

"Well, you know what you'd have to do to prove me wrong," I point out, effortfully upbeat.

Dean doesn't reply. I decide not to press the conversation, for once out of energy for cheering up and fixing things. Sometimes it feels like an endless job, like I'm the guy we learned about from Greek mythology who pushes the rock up the hill forever.

After a couple minutes of driving, Dean suddenly points to a small, dusty stretch on the shoulder of the road, right where the verdant incline of the hills hits the highway. It's meant for car trouble, not for parking. "Pull over for a second," he orders me urgently.

"Dean, I don't think we can park there—"

"I'm going to Venice to do god knows what. The least you can do is pull over for five minutes."

Reluctantly, I flip on my turn signal, not really feeling like fighting him on this. Maybe it'll improve his mood heading into Rebound Training Day. I merge onto the shoulder, slowing while Dean reaches under the glove compartment. When I stop, he unzips his camera from his bag.

Unhesitating, he hops out of the car. While I watch, puzzled, out the windshield, Dean proceeds to climb *on top of* the rubber-plastic cylindrical trash can positioned on our stretch of shoulder.

Despite myself, I find I'm starting to smile. Not out of enjoyment of his precarious position—in fact, I kind of wish his perch would stop wobbling—but because of how Dean it is. How fearless, how untouchably fixated on pursuing his passion.

He raises his camera, then begins capturing the landscape. The perfect cut of California highway firing down the coast, the mountains, the view, even the white footnote of our car in the midst of the huge scene. It doesn't take him long to get everything, then lower himself deftly to the dusty ground.

He hustles in the passenger door, looking like the opposite of the Dean who doubtfully observed the traffic we'd hit. He looks like 110 percent of himself. "Okay, *now* we can go," he declares.

I crank the key in the ignition and pull forward, the Jeep's tires crunching on the dirt. While I merge onto the road, I wait for Dean to explain himself. "What was that for?" I ask when he doesn't.

He pages through the photos on the LCD screen of his camera, which beeps with each scroll. The rapid-fire sound fills the car, the camera chirping dozens of times in Dean's fast perusal. Knowing how many snaps I often need to get each Instagram post right, I won't say I'm surprised.

"There's this thing I want to do," he replies distractedly.

"Get our car towed?"

This earns me the swiftest of sarcastic glances. "No," he replies. "I want to take the perfect photo."

I smile a little, appreciating his earnest ambition. I'm

surprised how plainly he put it. "What will you do with the perfect photo when you have it?"

Dean's brow furrows, like he's somehow surprised by the question. "Nothing. I'll just have it," he says with the slow clarity of someone who finds the response obvious.

We suddenly enter one of the tunnels winding through the mountains. Past the initial *whoosh* of the entrance, the car is plunged into silence shaded only by the constant growling undercurrent of our tires on the road. I say nothing. Personally, I can't understand Dean's reply. There's no way for me to separate my goals, my entire life, from how public everything I do is. From how much of myself I put up for celebration or consumption—sometimes not knowing where one ends and the other begins.

But I don't press him to explain. It's kind of beautiful to imagine Dean taking the perfect photo, then quietly storing it away on his computer. It makes me almost sad, though, knowing he won't show it to me.

Sadder than when he described kissing someone else.

Sixteen

"**WE COULD HAVE SAT** on the beach in Malibu," Dean complains.

We've parked the car, miraculously wedging the Jeep into the only tiny parallel-parking space we could find, and settled on the crowded sand. Dean is rubbing sunscreen on his shoulders, his eyes concealed by very consciously cool sunglasses—circular, polished black lenses with dark wire frames.

He fit right in with the neighborhood we walked through to get here. Venice is like hipster Disneyland. On Abbot Kinney Boulevard, boutiques in clapboard-walled bungalows hold collections of crystal jewelry next to the ultramodern facades of the city's finest restaurants. Girls in Converse walk French bulldogs while cinephile-looking guys lean on the bike racks waiting for their reservations. Even Dean, I noted with pleasure, no longer looked completely dissatisfied by the change in scenery.

We continued the short walk down the boulevard out to the Venice Boardwalk. This beach is the most touristy, manufactured part of the city, packed with families, walk-street vendors, international travelers, and young vacationers. Given the boardwalk's landmark status, it's no surprise this beach is ten times more congested than Malibu, but the seascape is no less gorgeous—powdery sand ceding to iridescent water.

I pull off my shirt, which leaves me in my bikini and favorite pair of worn jean shorts. Dean's gaze drops to my bare stomach for a second, or I think it does under his shades, before he faces the shore.

"We're not here for the beach," I answer him. "We're going to practice checking people out."

Dean turns back to me, dipping his chin to eye me warily over the tops of his sunglasses. "That sounds ridiculous," he pronounces.

I lean back on my elbows on the beach towel I laid out for myself, enjoying the hot prickle of the sun on my chest. "I assure you it's not," I say. "It's proven methodology."

Dean frowns, looking not unamused. "Right. Kaylee Jordan relationship recovery science. Nobel Prize–winning stuff."

Swallowing a smile myself, I elaborate patiently like I didn't hear him. "Sometimes after a relationship, I get lonely, but I don't have a new crush or interest in anyone in particular, so I just . . . people-watch and pretend." I let my eyes sweep the other beachgoers, like I'm warming up.

"Pretend what?" he asks, his voice low.

"Pretend I'm interested in who I see," I say. "Sometimes it

requires real effort. You have to persevere. Remember when I dated Logan last year? I had to practice checking people out for six days straight after I dumped him. Until then, I didn't even *start* to feel genuine physical interest in other guys because I couldn't get the image of Logan's abs out of my head. Like, *ho-ly shit*. You would know what I mean if you'd seen them. Six-pack of the *gods*. I've seen Olympians who were less cut—"

"Kaylee, could we focus," Dean says calmly.

I clear my throat. "Yes, I mean, when I—practice, I . . . make up stories of how we meet, how we get together. It sort of flips a switch in my mind, reminding me of who's still out there. Telling me it's okay to want someone new, even if I'm still bruised."

When Dean's frown deepens, self-consciousness washes over me like cold water. I want to take the words back, not liking the vulnerability they exposed. I suddenly realize it's one unexpected consequence of sharing my breakup survival guide with someone else—instead of doing my very best to uphold my smiling persona, I'll be showing someone the work it takes. The hurt I wade through to re-create myself whenever I need to.

This isn't someone, *though*, I remind myself weakly. *This is Dean. If there's one person who maybe gets to peek behind this curtain . . .*

I plunge onward, projecting unflappability. "It's practice."

Dean drapes his towel on the sand, then lies down on his stomach so our heads are close together with our legs pointing in opposite directions. He raises his camera, which hangs from his neck from its strap, and starts photographing the shoreline, the birds landing on the sand.

"I think I'll need a demonstration," he says.

I grin, pleased he's not finding a hundred ways to object. Scouting the beach, I stop when I notice a guy about our age sitting what I could only describe as moodily under an umbrella. He's reading. I note his short curly hair, his scowl, the pencil tucked behind his ear, and the drably designed cover of his paperback. Something cerebral, no doubt.

"Him," I say with conviction.

Dean follows my gaze. "Him?" he repeats. "Seriously? I know you're attracted to the brooding artist type, present company included, but he's pushing it, don't you think?"

I ignore him, developing the story in my head, enjoying myself. "All day, I notice he keeps getting distracted by me while he reads. Maybe I make a point to walk in front of him when I get lunch. Then finally," I elaborate triumphantly, "he puts his book down to watch me get in the water. I throw him a wink over my shoulder."

Dean coughs. "Your imaginary guy sounds like a creep."

"Shush. I'm safe in my imagination." I look over, eyebrows raised, chin high. I won't let him find fault with the perfect little Venice Beach rom-com I'm directing on the fly. I continue my fabrication. "He's a poet, and when I get back to my beach bag, I find he's ripped out a page of his book to write a poem for me, which he's signed with his phone number."

His shoulders slouched, Dean looks comically imploring. "Come on. That wouldn't actually work on you, would it?"

I shrug. "His name is Timothy, and he cries after we make love for the first time. Your turn!" I say brightly.

Dean snaps more photos, twisting to get the shot he wants. "God, no. Pass."

I flick him on the arm, earning no reaction. "Fine," I say, undeterred. "I'll do it for you." Resolutely, I look around the beach, the patchwork of towels, the sun scattering silver over the turquoise ocean. My eyes finally land on a blonde in a strappy red one-piece running into the water with two other girls. "Her," I confirm.

"Who?" Looking up from his camera, he swivels his head like he can't immediately pick out who I mean.

"The knockout in red," I say, like *Duh?*

His expression flattens. "Be serious, Kaylee."

"I am." I sit up, defensive. "Why not her? She's stunning."

He gestures with one emphatic hand. "She's obviously social and athletic and, like, popular." He pronounces the final word suspiciously, like he finds the whole concept sinister.

I cock my head, unamused. "So? *I'm* those things."

"Yeah, well, we didn't work out, did we?"

I shake off the glare he sends me. At this point, I'm immune to Dean's glares. I study the girl, searching for sparks of inspiration. "You stand in line in front of her at the public showers. She tells you you have great hair and—asks to borrow your shampoo."

"I don't bring shampoo to the beach," he interrupts unhelpfully.

"Not relevant." I wave my hand. "But then she accidentally

finishes your bottle and feels really bad about it, so she makes you walk with her to CVS to buy you a new one."

I shift my gaze to Dean, waiting.

"Okay, fine," he grumbles. "That's cute. Not helpful or realistic, but cute."

"Or him!" Feeling charged by my half victory, I quickly fix on my next subject, the guy with broad dark shoulders who's sleeping on the sand.

Dean follows my gaze—with more interest this time. He dares to glance quickly over his sunglasses. "Maybe if he weren't obviously twenty-five."

I don't concede out loud that this point is valid. "Okay, how about anyone in that group playing paddleball?"

Dean looks over his shoulder. "Paddleball? Can you see me playing paddleball on a crowded beach?" His scorn for our game, I notice, is starting to sound forced. "They almost just stepped on that child. Kaylee, I couldn't possibly date someone who plays *paddleball*," he says seriously.

I pout, playfully this time. "Well, if I'm doing such a bad job of picking people for you, then—"

His eyes fix on something behind me.

"Her," he says, his voice coming out low.

My heart seizes. Surely with excitement, I decide. Yes, I'm pleased with the sudden success of my plans, despite Dean's determined resistance. This is good. This is my heart *leaping*, not squeezing. This is what hope feels like.

I nonchalantly look over my shoulder, following his eyeline. I find a teen girl with bright red hair sitting on a towel with a boy her age. At first I think they're together. Then I notice they share the same narrow nose, the same spattering of freckles. His hair is more blond than red, but the similarity is undeniable. They're siblings.

"While shooting the beach, I take an incredible photo of her," Dean says, his voice expressionless. His eyes don't lie, though. Past his glasses, I see sparks of intrigue. "It's so good I have to walk up to her to show her. When I do, I ask if she wants me to email it to her."

"Dean!" I shake his shoulder. "That's so smooth! Wow, honestly, that could be your move."

As his eyes fall back to his camera, his cheeks redden. Not, I know, with embarrassment.

Seizing on the opportunity of his interest, I chase the idea starting to come to life in my head. "Can I borrow that?" I ask, nodding at his camera.

His expression hardens with suspicion. "You said we were only practicing," he reminds me.

"We are," I promise him.

Dean watches me warily for several long seconds, gripping his camera like Gollum with the Ring. *Ugh, my dad would be delighted I even thought that reference.*

Meeting Dean's stare, I hold my hand out expectantly.

Our sun-drenched standoff continues for moments longer before, finally, Dean deposits the heavy camera into my open palm. I smile my most winning smile.

Then I get up and turn on my heel, heading directly for the girl Dean pointed out. Dean hisses my name behind me. I ignore him. I reach the siblings' towel, where they're eating ice cream from the boulevard's creamery.

"Hi, sorry," I say eagerly. "Could you take a photo of me and my friend?"

The girl smiles. I notice she has a cute gap between her front teeth. "Oh, of course. My hands are sticky, though. RJ?" She looks to the boy, who stands up.

I wave Dean over, ignoring the daggers he's staring at me. Looking very much like he doesn't want to come, he hauls himself to his feet and shuffles over.

Moving to stand next to him, I fling my arm around his shoulders. It's the ultimate nonromantic picture pose, of course, the cheerfully empty cousin of the unquestionably couple-y diagonal-down-the-back waist clutch. Dean stands stiffly while RJ lines up the shot. When he's snapped a few, he hands the camera over.

"Make sure you like them first," RJ says. His voice is soft, earnestly friendly.

Dean receives the camera like it's a human child. While I wait, he taps through the photos, the camera resuming its chorus of beeping. His expression doesn't hide his reactions— his eyebrows lift, his mouth slackening, first with interest, then with respect. "These are really good. Are you a photographer?" he asks RJ.

"Not really," RJ says, sweeping a self-conscious hand over his rose-gold hair.

The girl gets up, paper cup of sorbet in hand. "He's lying," she informs us with no small measure of delight, or maybe it's pride.

RJ shoots her a look. "I'm a— Well, I *want* to be a filmmaker."

"That's so cool," I say. "Are you from here?" I direct the question to the girl, wanting to get her talking.

"No, we're here for the week. Our older sister is getting married on Saturday," she explains. "We're actually looking for stuff to do while our family is caught up in endless wedding prep. Are you two locals?"

I don't register the question for a second, focused on Dean, who I half hopefully notice manages to make eye contact with her. He doesn't reply, though. Patiently and a little peeved, I step in. "No, but we come here every summer."

Her eyes brighten. "Really? Oh my god, I've been so overwhelmed with all the beach options. Where should we visit? The wedding is in Malibu, which is gorgeous, but the beaches seem so secretive. I'm Emma, by the way," she says. "This is my brother, RJ."

"I'm Kaylee, and this is Dean." I nudge him forward, silently communicating, *Stop staring at your camera screen.*

"Nice to meet you." Emma smiles.

Despite my urging, it nearly startles me when Dean suddenly speaks. "Escondido Beach," he says. I hear signs of strain in his voice, like he's worked up his nerve. "That's where we're staying and it's more secluded. Way less crowded than Zuma. You should, um, totally come visit."

Emma and RJ exchange a look. "Escondido," Emma repeats. "Thanks. We will."

We wave our goodbyes. Returning to our towels, I'm brimming with pride. Dean did it. He's doing it. He didn't have to invite Emma to come visit. He *chose* to. It's so much more than I expected of him today, even in my wildest hopes for Rebound Training Day. I sit back down on my towel, crossing my legs. "You did great," I say with earnest excitement. "I wonder if we'll see them. It could be fun to hang out, right?"

Dean holds up his camera to take more photos. "Yeah, whatever." He surveys the sand through the small viewfinder. "It's not a big deal."

But it is. I know it is. For the first time, he was really trying, instead of just indulging my project. It's the beginning of the beginning of something, but the beginning of the beginning *is* something.

I lie back on my towel, grinning to the sound of Dean's camera shutter.

Seventeen

I DON'T FORCE DEAN to talk on the drive home. He sticks with silence while he thumbs through the photos he took today, slower this time, deleting the ones without potential. He probably wouldn't care if I turned on music. I don't, though, privately enjoying the soundtrack of his careful concentration.

I drive the same route home, the curving path of PCH along the cliffs into Malibu. My ankles are sandy, my shoulders still warm from the sun, my hair streaked with salt water. It's one of my favorite feelings in the world. Everything disappears. I can stay perfectly in the moment, free from rankings or likes or legacies.

It's nearly six when we reach home. Sunset hasn't started, but the sky is pale, the light lavender of late afternoon. While the house is empty, it's not quiet. Returning the keys to the hook next to the front door, I hear the shouts and pauses, the strikes and thuds of the rhythm I know best in the world.

Out on the sand, I find our parents have rigged up the volleyball net and the couples are facing off. I smile, having seen many versions of this match before. I know what my mom and Terry would prefer is to partner like they used to, but the dads aren't good enough to make it a fun game.

Dean's sisters watch from the patio hammock, even energetic Jessie hushed for the time being by the spectacle of her mom's skill. I follow Dean over to them. We sit down on the deck, dangling our legs over the edge from behind the railing.

My mom is going easy on them, playing for fun rather than to win. But Terry, I observe, can hold her own despite not having played seriously in decades. I take in every second of their game play, not even wanting to blink. While this is nowhere near the Olympic matches I watch on my laptop, I still love the chance to see my mom play.

As a kid, I didn't understand my mom was one of the best players in the world. She was just my mom, who sometimes went to the Olympics. Which was cool, but also meant I had to miss summer with my friends. It was a job, just like any of my friends' parents' jobs.

Only when I got older did I really appreciate what my mom could do. How good she really was. My mom became my role model and my hero.

I wish it was still the only thing I felt when I watched her play.

On the court, my dad sets the ball to my mom in the middle of the net. Darren moves to block while my mom moves forward. I hate the twisting in my stomach—the shallow stabbing pressure of jealousy—when she suddenly unleashes her full skill, spiking the ball through Darren's block like a missile, her motion one part dance and one part domination.

Darren and Terry laugh and applaud my mom, who bows her head gracefully.

I don't want to be jealous of her. I know I shouldn't be. It's ugly, unseemly, the idea of being envious of the person who's given me everything, including life itself.

And I'm not. Not really. I'm just aware of the gulf separating us, and I just want to be . . . enough. I work desperately hard to be *enough*.

Dean nudges me with his shoulder. I turn to find him watching me, his eyes concerned. "What's wrong?" he asks, the undercurrent of his voice nearly inaudible.

I flush, furious. Furious at being caught, at being accidentally vulnerable. It's how Dean is, though, uncommonly perceptive in everything. Of course he'd notice the slightest shift in me.

I flip my hair, desperate to cover my feelings. Hiding from my unguarded moment. *No one likes the princess who doesn't make it look easy.* It's like my mind is ever-ready with its warning recitations, slipping them in whenever I flicker. "Nothing," I say, giving Dean my shiniest Instagram smile. "I'm fine."

When he only narrows his eyes in scrutiny, I realize I need to change my strategy.

I stand up and hold my hand out to Lucy. "Want to take them on with me?" When Lucy only bites her lip, her gaze skirting to the side, I wave her on enthusiastically. "Come on, Luce, I need you."

The praise gets Lucy to smile bashfully. She hops up out

of the hammock, making me grin for real this time. We head down the stairs onto the sand, Lucy following me. When my dad misses a point, I pick up the ball and face my mom and Terry, who've come together on opposite sides of the net. "How about you ladies pick on someone your own size?" I say to them.

My mom looks delighted at the prospect of playing on Terry's team. She ducks under the net, jogging to Terry's side, where they high-five.

I hand the ball to Lucy. "You serve," I say. She takes it, looking nervous. I notice the stiffness in her stance, the uneasiness in her eyes. I know the feeling. "It's just for fun," I reassure her. "We're going to lose. But one day, we'll beat them. I guarantee it."

When Lucy serves, the ball soars strong and steady right to the middle of the court. My mom gets the dig, and Terry sets her perfectly. I'm in place, ready to block as my mom rises up to spike.

She still makes the hit—but Lucy saves it, popping the ball up perfectly for me.

Dean, Jessie, and the dads cheer loudly on the sidelines. It fuels me as I run to where the ball is sinking from the lavender sky. I go for the spike, but my mom is there, with her imposing six-foot-two block. In the moment, I suddenly see nothing except the one-inch difference on the *Sports Illustrated* chart.

The hard thump of the ball hitting her hands echoes over the court. We lose the point, of course, but my mom slaps my hand under the net. "Nice one," she says. It's not her mom voice. It's her professional-volleyball-player voice, detachedly friendly and a little winded.

I swell with pride. Losing the point doesn't even bother me.

I throw myself into the rest of the match, valiantly fighting my mom, who, though retired, is still a world-class champion. I'm proud of every point I score—each one while Dean cheers.

Lucy, for her part, is incredible. She scores a kill that my mom misses for real. I can see my mom is genuinely impressed.

While everyone congratulates Lucy, I fend off envy, forcing it into the corners of my heart where I pile up feelings that are better ignored. I remember how the kind of enthusiasm Lucy's receiving would've thrilled me when I was thirteen, talented but unsure of myself in every way.

But seventeen-year-old me needs it too, from time to time. When you have to be perfect every day, perfect becomes ordinary. Expected. But there's no way to be *better* than perfect, either—which means there's no room to be better than ordinary. No room to be exciting. No room to be impressive.

You just keep on *being*. Ordinarily perfect, and perfectly ordinary. Starving in the spotlight.

I get the feeling under control and plunge it under the demands of each serve, each block, the quick, focused sequences of the game. Like usual, it works.

We lose, but it's fun. I love this sport—even if I'm not the best Jordan to play.

Eighteen

THAT NIGHT, I'M WALKING back to my room after showering when I notice the light still on under Dean's door.

My first instinct is to veer over and knock. Which is—huge. For weeks, I've considered spending time with Dean to be something either to be prevented or something to be patiently tried in dutiful hopes of restoring our friendship. Since our breakup, it's never felt natural, the way it did before we dated.

Going to the beach today, having honest-to-god fun together, maybe didn't just help Dean. Maybe it helped me a little, too.

Even so, I hesitate. The dark, empty square of the window at the end of the hallway reveals nothing of the night. Maybe I'm pushing it if I venture into Dean's room. Or maybe he's decided Rebound Training Day was no fun and he's back to hating me now. I have plenty of reasons not to knock.

Still . . . if I don't, I'm stuck having to wrestle those feelings I didn't want to deal with on the court. I'd really, *really* rather not.

I muster up my resolve.

Without letting myself lose my nerve, I knock softly on Dean's door, two quick knuckle taps.

"Come in," I hear.

I wonder if he knows it's me.

Entering, I find the light is coming from the lamp on his nightstand, not the overhead. It casts illumination in a soft sphere of which Dean is the center. I shut the door behind me, not wanting to wake up the parents. It's intimate, I recognize, being in my ex's bedroom late at night, but I charge on, refusing to pause for long enough to let implication set in.

Dean is working on his laptop, seated on his bed. He looks up in slight surprise. "You can't possibly have a task for me this late at night," he says. His face falls in horror I'm not sure is pretend. "Don't tell me the next step of your program is to post a thirst trap or something."

I laugh. "Wait," I say half-seriously. "Would you? It's not a bad idea, honestly."

Lifting one eyebrow in contemplation, Dean slaps his hands on his legs. "I don't think the internet is ready for these thighs."

This time I have to swallow a laugh I know would wake the house. While my shoulders shake, something satisfied, wistful, and somewhat stung crosses Dean's features. I wonder if he's thinking this—this conversation—feels momentarily just like old times. Like the us of every past California trip.

Or maybe it's only me.

The feeling flees quickly out of Dean's expression, which goes neutral. "What did you come in here for?" he asks, looking back down at his computer and clicking intently like whatever he's working on is under deadline.

I perch on the edge of his desk. "Let's do a checkup," I suggest, knowing I need a reason to prolong this conversation. Which I *do* want to prolong, I realize.

His eyes flit to mine, a little amused. "A checkup on what?"

"To see if my regimen is working yet."

Dean removes his hand from his computer's trackpad, skepticism entwining with the humor in his eyes. "All right . . ." he says slowly.

Ignoring the fact I'm wearing my lilac pj's, I adopt a very professional demeanor. "Okay, first," I start, "how sad have you been today, on a scale of one to ten? There's no wrong answer here. I just need honesty so I know how to plan."

I fix my stare on him, enjoying the performance. The question itself isn't performance, however. It's one I ask myself when figuring out what I need after a breakup.

Dean considers my question.

"One," he says.

Real incredulity cuts into my doctor act. "One?" I repeat. "With one being not sad? Or one being sad?"

"Not sad," he confirms. His voice is casual, sure. "I had a lot of fun today."

I grin. "Excellent. That's great. Huge progress." In fact, I don't point out, it's better progress than I expected. If four hours in Venice gets him down to one on the Kaylee Jordan Sad Scale, my job this summer will be very easy. "Next question," I go on. "When you think about your ex, what emotion do you feel the most?"

Dean laughs. "The most? Right now . . ." He purses his lips, picking his words. "Light annoyance."

"Wow, fantastic!" I clap my hands together.

"You're happy to hear you're currently annoying me?" he asks, not really sounding annoyed.

"I'm delighted," I confirm enthusiastically. "How do you feel compared to the beginning of the day about the possibility of moving on?"

His eyes slip from mine.

"Closer to wanting to move on, I guess," he says.

I don't know how to read the new subtleties in his expression. Nor do I expect the feeling that washes over me, the one I get when I defeat an opponent who really wanted the win, who played with the same desperation I did. It's a surge of pride, stained with something sour.

This is what I wanted, I remind myself. It was the point of today. I don't want to date Dean, which means accepting that he'll move on. I push the stab of selfish sadness away. "Great. You're doing . . . great," I say. "Your progress in just a couple days is impressive."

"Yes, I'm very impressive generally," Dean comments.

While I can't help smiling, I otherwise ignore him. "So going forward, I want to focus on hobbies. I think getting that perfect photo is a great post-breakup task. It'll remind you of how much there is outside of your relationships, how much worth *you* have."

Dean starts to smirk, like he's laughing at a joke I'm not in on. "How convenient. I happen to be working on that hobby right now." He raises his eyebrows innocently. "Want to see?"

Slightly suspicious, I unseat myself from the desk and walk over to him and his computer.

"It's not perfect," he says, "but it's pretty damn close."

I'm expecting to find the photo he leapt out of the car on the side of the road to take. Instead, on the screen is—me. It's from the pickup game earlier today, when my mom blocked my spike. The photo, though, is of the moment before I lost the point. I'm still rising up, reaching my mom's level. It's clear in the image my mom already has me beat, but it doesn't matter. I look fierce. Strong. I look like a champion.

It's not something I would post even if I wasn't on my social media hiatus. The composition is perfect, of course. The golden-hour light wraps me and my mom perfectly, heightening the drama. It's just—I have enough people in the comments comparing me, usually unfavorably, to my mother. I don't need to encourage them with this image of her ready to decimate me.

Which saddens me, because seeing the shot for myself, in Dean's bedroom—just Kaylee, not @Kaylee_Jordan—it's exactly the sort of photo I'd want to post if I didn't have my profile, my name, my following. So this photograph is just for me.

"Good, right?" he asks. "I also got this." He tabs to another photo. It's from the beach—I'm sitting with my legs crossed, my back to him while I stare out at the water.

Dean tabs again.

Me, laughing as I point to one of the people I picked out for him. I look happy, gorgeous. It hurts in a good-tender way, knowing this is how he sees me, even now.

Tab. Me, driving, eyes fixed in wonder on the deep turqoise sea. *Tab.* Me, sitting in the car while he's on the side of the road. *Tab.* Me, high-fiving Lucy, my cheeks flushed from exertion, the hugest encouraging smile on my face.

There's more. Dozens and dozens.

Of me, looking every way I want to be seen.

"So this probably means I failed your checklist, right?" he asks, unabashed, his eyes sparkling with amusement.

I step back. "Yes." I sigh.

"Don't worry," Dean replies congenially. "I'm sure you'll come up with something to help."

I roll my eyes, knowing it's the response he's expecting. "Good night, Dean," I say dryly.

He holds up a hand in farewell. "Night," he replies cheerfully.

I walk out, closing the door on him, leaving him to his photos. His photos of me. It's not ideal for the getting-over-me effort, honestly. I'm used to excelling, not to obvious setbacks like Dean working in devoted detail on my photos in the middle of the night. I know I should be discouraged.

But I'm not. Not completely.

Nineteen

THIS VIEW IS SPECTACULAR. It's one of my favorite sights in the entire world.

The morning mist rises up Topanga Canyon, the unexpected rough glade of rocky wilderness just ten minutes from LA. From the cliffs, views of the ocean reach out in one direction, the city in the other. Below us is nothing but steep slopes of trees. In the warm fog, I'm breathing hard, but I'm exhilarated. This view is so, so worth the three hours of hiking it takes to get here.

My mom pants next to me, wearing a matching smile.

It's just us on this morning hike. In past years, we were able to get the rest of the families to come, until they wised up. I guess climbing a canyon didn't make for everyone's ideal morning. My mom still valiantly encourages everyone that *it's really not that bad*, which never works, not when Dean inevitably points out, *You're literally a professional athlete*.

I don't mind. The hike is now mother-daughter time.

Honestly, there's something sort of hilariously perfect about *our* mother-daughter time involving half the day spent in grueling physical exertion.

I look forward to it every trip. No matter what's going on in our lives, we have six hours of talking on this trail every summer. Three years ago, I remember returning to the Jeep right as my mom got a call from the volleyball coach at Newport High saying I'd made varsity as a freshman. We drove straight to Sidecar for celebratory doughnuts still in our dusty hiking boots. Starting the hike down from the spectacular vista, I hold the memory close.

We're walking single-file, my mom behind me. I hear her voice over my shoulder. "So next year, you think you'll still have time for this?" she asks hopefully, and with no hint of judgment.

"Of course," I say. I look back, incredulous. "I'll make time, even if I'm competing professionally. Like you did."

When she smiles, I catch something somber in it. "Just, you know," she says delicately, "there are some excellent university volleyball programs out there. You'd have much more flexibility."

I stiffen, so hard I nearly trip while bouldering down a nearly vertical part of the trail. Suddenly, the mist is no longer refreshingly outdoorsy—just stifling, plastering my hair to my forehead's sheen of sweat. The height is no longer exciting—just precarious. "I don't need more *flexibility*," I say lightly, hoping I sound normal. The conversation feels like she's pushing something, leading up to a point.

I owe her the benefit of the doubt, I remind myself. She's probably just trying to figure out my priorities. To let me know she supports my choices.

Still, I can't read the vague indication in her voice when she finishes the short section of bouldering, coming down next to me on the widening path. "Flexibility isn't the worst thing," she says.

I'm starting to get impatient with the hidden nuances of this conversation. "Do you regret not going to college?" I ask. "Is that what this is about?"

The question sounds more defensive than I like. More defensive than has to do with my mom's college regrets. Honestly, I'm not sure I could've hidden the sharpness in my voice, because in the space of my last few steps, I've figured out what's happening here. While we may be chatting about flexibility, what we're really discussing is—*am I good enough?* I'm desperate to steer the conversation as far from the subject as possible, scared to hear my ugliest fears confirmed.

My mom, for her part, doesn't sound offended. "Sometimes I wish I'd had those college experiences, but not to the level of regret," she says measuredly. "I'm happy with the choices I made. They were *my* choices."

We trudge side by side down the dirt of the trail. "This *is* my choice," I reply.

My mom studies me, and I feel intensely uncomfortable. The mother-daughter hike ahead of us transforms into something weighed down by the sense that my mom—my idol—doesn't have confidence in me. It's suffocating like no elevation or leg-searing descent could be. I don't want to be discussing this. I just want my mom to be proud of me, happy I'm following in her footsteps.

When I look at her, though, I find her expression has shifted. She's smiling.

"Good," she says. "You'll be amazing. I have no doubt."

Her praise works into me, loosening my muscles. While I search with hungry instinct for signs that she's forcing her compliments, feigning her praise, I find none. She only sounds sincerely, genuinely proud.

Still, I can't quiet the voice in my head. *My mom has to say that. She's my mom.* I don't know why it won't shut up. I don't know why some self-destructive part of me always wants to convince me I'm not good enough. With the same care I'm placing on every step down this mountain, I remind myself I need to concentrate on what my mom has actually said and done. Which is support me.

We keep hiking, heading down the rocky path. It's patient going, the kind of measured movement where I start to forget the passing minutes, the strain in my legs, even the whispers of doubt in my head. I honestly don't know how much time has gone by when my mom suddenly speaks up, new vigor in her voice.

"I have something exciting I wanted to share," she says. "I'm planning to start playing again."

I look up from the ground. "You do play."

"No, like compete," she clarifies. "I've been thinking of coming out of retirement."

I open my mouth. Nothing comes out. The simple announcement catches me off guard, scattering my thoughts. I nearly slip on the dry soil, and while I manage to find my footing, the feeling doesn't stop. Like reality is suddenly sliding out of my grip.

My mom goes on, filling my stunned silence. "You know, I stopped so young. I was afraid of people watching me decline, of falling short of expectations, and I wanted to be around more for you. But, well . . ." She hesitates. "You're grown up now, and I wonder if I cut my career short out of fear."

My feet move mechanically now, navigating the terrain on their own. I start silently, urgently checking the realism of what she's suggesting. My mom is forty, which, while on the older side for a professional athlete, is not unheard of in volleyball. And my mom is still good. Really good. Better than me.

Suddenly, I have names for the writhing feelings in my gut—resentment, fear. Even jealousy.

If she comes out of retirement, we could be in direct competition. She could really, literally win the matches and earn the opportunities I'm fighting for. Tournament titles, Olympic spots. Real professional hopes she could pull out of my reach. What's more—our stats would be directly comparable every day of our overlapping careers. They wouldn't be the hypothetical stuff of human interest stories, or confined to the question of whether I can carry on her legacy. Every day we play in the same world, I could fall short in cold, hard math.

When she glances up, I force myself to give her a quick, considering glance, contorting my lips in what could generously be called a supportive smile.

Inside, I'm collapsing. I feel horribly, horribly selfish. "Oh," I get out, then can't manage to say more.

I feel like something is being stolen from me. Which sounds so childish, so spoiled when I think it. But I can't stop. I can't. My worst instincts rise up in me, furious—this was supposed to be *my* time. My moment. Of course I was already competing with my mother's legacy. Now, with the world-record holder coming out of retirement, there won't even be a competition.

I hate myself for wanting the spotlight fully on me. I just can't imagine the future I'm left with, either, of vanishing into the cold of a very long shadow.

My mom, I notice, has no idea what storm is swirling in me over this surprise of hers. She navigates the rocky path carefully, nothing but quiet pride on her features. She likely hasn't even considered what this will mean for me. Maybe it's not fair of me to consider it, either. My mom shouldn't give up on her dreams forever just because she's a mother. I have to be okay with this.

I *will* be. When have I ever not been okay?

Slowly, I get a grip. One very simple, harsh reality stabilizes me. *I'm not entitled to being the best at the thing I love.*

I just can't find the words yet. I can't *say* I'm okay. In the growing silence, only the rustling of the forest surrounds us. I push myself harder, knowing that handling this right is the one thing I can reach for. Whenever I'm struggling, my one consolation—my final refuge, my fragile handhold—is not letting it show. Right now I feel even the handhold crumbling with my hopes for my career.

So I grasp on to what I do have. Which . . . is my mom, who will still be my inspiration. No matter what. And volleyball, which is still mine, even if we share it.

When I smile, it's stronger this time. "Hey, doughnuts after this?" I say. It's not the perfect response I should give, not excited exclamations or eager questions. Not yet. But this offer is close to celebration. If she isn't looking closely, it'll pass.

"I was hoping you'd suggest that," my mom replies, her voice bright.

I grin despite not really wanting the doughnuts—despite knowing this will darken my perfect memory from three years ago.

Twenty

WHEN WE GET HOME, I promptly look for Dean.

Doughnuts were nice, but empty. I mean, not literally. The powdered, cinnamon-dusted globs of cake sit like stones in my stomach. The chitchat with Mom, though, doesn't exist in my memory. She could've told me we were moving to Milwaukee—I would have heard nothing past the heavy curtains of comparison shrouding my thoughts.

My mom heads upstairs. The house is quiet except for the beach breeze swaying the windchimes. I check the kitchen, wondering if Dean's making more of his noxious coffee, and then the living room, but he's not there. Undeterred, I head up the stairs. I push my mind with familiar muscles in happier directions, productive directions—I don't want to think about my mom or volleyball right now. Helping Dean get over me is the perfect distraction.

Checking his room, I come up empty once more. In defeat, I head across the hall. I pick up my phone off my desk, where I left it behind like I do every year. The hike is supposed to be just time with my mom.

When my screen comes to life, my heart leaps a little.

In my notifications is an email from Dean. It's a Dropbox link. The message is simple. *You're free to use these if you credit me.*

I open the link despite knowing what I'll find. Wishing I felt excited or flattered instead of resigned. Sure enough, Dean's sent the photos he took yesterday—me on the beach, playing volleyball. Facing off with my mom. With the editing he was doing last night, they look like life in the best possible light.

But they're still me, playing volleyball, facing my mom.

I scroll until I find the first one he showed me last night. The one where I'm leaping up to spike into my mom's inevitable block.

With the photo's gorgeous, kinetic composition filling my screen, I force myself to look, despite the stressful reminders the details flare in me. My limbs straining with exertion. My mom's perfect form. The contrast in our expressions, how the intensity on my face looks like this shot means everything to me, while the calm in my mom's says this is one more victory in thousands for her.

I look and look, until after a minute, the sick stress in my gut relents. I start to see *myself* in the best possible light. How powerful I look. How undaunted. The photo takes on new meaning. Even if I don't *win*, even if I'm not remembered—immortalized—for winning, there's extraordinary grace in the trying.

I can do this. It might take time, but I can get comfortable with the idea of my mom occupying the place I once thought I could claim for myself.

I hear footsteps approaching down the hall, and I turn, hoping to find Dean in my doorway. But it's Lucy.

Her eyes focus right on my screen. "Wow, cool photo," she says with unhidden enthusiasm, even a little aspiration.

"Thanks," I say. "Hey, do you know where your brother is?"

"He went down to the beach with some people I've never seen before," she replies, still studying the photograph. "He told me to tell you when you got home."

I put my phone down, checking the one place I hadn't yet looked—out my window. On days like this, the white window-sill looks like the thin frame of the most gorgeous painting I've ever seen, strips of color making up the beach, from sand to sapphire-blue water to pale sky. Sure enough, in the waves I see three figures. When I squint, I can make out Dean, Emma, and RJ.

"I'm going to join them. Want to come?" I ask.

Lucy shakes her head without hesitating. "Your mom said she was going to set up a target and give me some spiking tips." Her posture straightens several inches, her voice luminous with pride.

I soften, remembering when I would've felt the same way. Then I chastise myself—I will not get jaded. I *would* be excited the way Lucy is. I *will* be. It's what loving this sport means. "Have fun," I say earnestly.

Leaving my doorway, Lucy continues on to her room. I

reopen my phone, where Dean's file of stunning photos waits open on my screen. Decisively, I hit download, filling my camera roll with them. After my hiatus, I'll choose one to post. Not the one of my mom blocking my spike, of course—probably one of the ones where I'm sitting on the beach.

It takes me ten minutes to change into my swimsuit and walk down the stairs to the shoreline, where I find the three of them in the water. RJ floats on his back, perfectly peaceful. Dean, with his waterproof camera, is snapping photos of Emma, who's modeling for him with no hint of shyness.

I watch them—watch Dean composing his shots while he circles Emma. I'm not jealous. I'm proud.

"Hey, you two made it," I say, perhaps a little too loud.

Not seeming to mind my volume, Emma brightens when she notices me. She throws her hands wide, like she's trying to hug the daylight. "This beach is incredible. Thanks for the recommendation."

"How was your hike?" Dean asks me without looking up from his camera.

"Fine," I say, not quite pulling off nonchalance. I hear the weird, pinched cheer in my voice, the squinting-in-the-sunlight strain of normalcy. I know Dean notices, because he glances up from his camera.

Before he can ask me any follow-up questions, I turn the conversation back to Emma and RJ, inquiring about everything they've been up to. As I learn, they're from Seattle, where Emma just graduated high school and RJ is going into his junior year. They've made themselves scarce today because their sister, the one whose wedding they're here for, is having last-minute vendor problems.

"How long are you here for?" Dean asks.

"The wedding is tomorrow, and we fly out two days after that," RJ replies, now standing, submerged up to his shoulders in the water. "We're planning to surf before we leave. If you're interested . . ." His eyes flit to Dean.

"I don't know how," Dean says. "I've always wanted to learn, but *someone*"—he looks to me pointedly—"refused to take lessons with me."

"We can teach you," RJ offers. He says everything softly, with nuances in his voice I can never quite catch. He seems sort of the opposite of his heart-on-her-sleeve sister, which makes them a delightful pair.

Dean hesitates. Him I have no problem reading—confidence starts to swirl in his eyes, like he's psyching himself up. It's nice to see. "Sure," he says, cradling his camera. "Yeah, that could be fun."

"For *you*," I can't resist interjecting.

Dean splashes me in reply. "Come on," he says wryly, needing no confidence boost when he's teasing me. "So you face-planted when you were eight. You're much more coordinated now."

I glare, realizing I should've known he would dredge back up my public humiliation. Truthfully, I work hard to look effortlessly perfect. Eating it in the ocean in front of hundreds of people is not exactly the image I want. "I'll watch," I say.

Swiping the water with his hand more gently now, he

studies me with soft interest. "It's okay to be bad at stuff, you know." While he makes the remark lightly, I hear the undercurrent of something sincere. It's comfort put playfully, something I think I might not notice if it weren't coming from him.

"Not in my experience," I say. When his forehead lines with curiosity, I hurry the conversation on. "I'll have more fun watching you fall a dozen times anyway."

Dean rushes over, scooping me up and dropping me suddenly so my head submerges. I come up laughing, my now-wet hair slick down my neck. I don't hesitate before diving for his knees to take him out in retaliation.

When we come up, spitting seawater with huge grins on our faces, Emma laughs. "You two are adorable," she says.

I straighten up stiffly. Right on cue, the lightest summer breeze drifts over the ocean, cooling the water on my skin. "Oh, we're not a couple," I clarify hastily.

"We used to be, though," Dean chimes in.

I shoot Dean a very pointed glare, while the siblings' eyebrows rise in unison.

It's Emma who inquires in understandable confusion. "And you're on vacation together?"

"It's fine," I say, eager to move past this part of the conversation. "We're friends."

"Friends," Dean echoes. There's humor hiding in his easy, immediate reassurance. I send him the fakest of smiles. I should've figured no matter how much progress he was making in getting over me, he would never pass up the opportunity to tease me. It's exactly what—well, what friends would do.

"Wow," Emma says. "Damn. I mean, it was miraculous getting both our parents out here for our *sister's wedding*, and they were married for fifteen years."

"Yeah, that's impressive," RJ comments. "I don't know many people who've managed to stay friends with their ex. I guess it was an amicable breakup?"

"Oh no, not at all," Dean replies cheerfully.

I palm my forehead, incredulous at Dean.

"*No*," Emma whines, smiling. "Kaylee, why?"

Everyone's laughing—which is good, because *everyone* includes Dean. If he can joke about it, then he's getting over me. I have to smile, now enjoying this conversation just a little.

"*Excellent* question, Emma," Dean says with professorial flair. It wipes the smile from my face. The sparkle in his eye clues me in to exactly what's coming. Sure enough, Dean faces me inquisitively. "What was the reason again?"

The glance I give him is dry enough it could soak up this entire ocean, leaving only shells and suffocating sea life. "Let me answer your question with one of my own," I say, imitating his posturing demeanor. "Aren't you glad we broke up early enough in our relationship that we could go back to being friends?"

"If that was the reason, why didn't you consider it before we got together?" Dean asks.

I dunk my head underwater in response. For the next few seconds, I enjoy the submergence, the perfect peace of my billowing hair surrounding me in the glittering sea. It calms the headache I feel building.

When I come up, I'll need to force my way out of this conversation for real. This, Dean doesn't realize—or maybe he does—is why I didn't explain myself when we broke up. Because he doesn't *want* an explanation. He wants to convince me to regret my decision.

Which I don't. I *did* have the right to date him. I *did* have the right to dump him when I knew staying together would only end in heartache.

I surface, and Dean is watching me, clearly still expecting a reply. I decide on an honest one. "I did. I just couldn't resist."

Pleased surprise flits over Dean's features. He hears the unsaid last word. *I couldn't resist you.*

"I am glad we can be friends," he says.

The smile he gives me is real, honest. Our guests probably don't even notice the quick moment we share, but I hold on to it, like one of the fragile sand dollars I've occasionally found on the shore. It leaves me with no doubt about what he's just said.

He returns to taking more photos, and I watch, the sun somehow seeming warmer on my shoulders.

"Can I see your camera?" RJ asks Dean.

Dean looks up at him, then wades over, casting rolling ripples over the surface of the water. While Dean dives into Nikon specs, I tip back to float on the shimmering liquid glass of the Pacific. I know Dean can really get going on this subject, and it sounds like RJ is genuinely interested in sharing opinions on lenses and shutters.

With my ears submerged, the world goes quiet under the soft sounds of the current. I welcome the precious relaxation coming over me. The questions preoccupying me when I got here have drifted off into the horizon. I start visualizing the next few days with Dean—new steps in my regimen, undoubtedly, but ones I think will start to feel like vacationing with my oldest friend.

Somehow, when I lift my head up several relaxing minutes later, he and RJ are *still* going. Emma shares a kindred glance with me.

"These are great, man," RJ says enthusiastically, now looking at the photos on Dean's camera. "Do you have an account or website or something where you share them?"

"No," I say over the water, "but he *should*. He could honestly be a professional."

Dean rolls his eyes, flattery putting pink into his cheeks.

"Wait." Emma speaks up, her expression suddenly unreadable. "Do you do weddings?"

"Like, photograph them?" Dean asks. "No, I'm not actually a professional. Kaylee is just being Kaylee."

"I mean, I am. Being Kaylee means being right about things," I point out.

Dean can't quite manage a scowl in reply.

"The vendor who dropped out of our sister's wedding is the photographer," RJ explains. "He broke his ankle. He's sending his assistant, but Phoebe is still freaking out."

Dean looks from RJ to Emma, doubtful. The sun reflects off the curve of his hair bun, sleek with water. "I'm sure the assistant is still better than I am," he says. "I've never done anything like that. I don't know if I'd even be up to it."

"She'd pay you," Emma says. "Her fiancé is loaded. This morning she was calling every photographer in LA. She wants a backup in case this new guy is no good or, like, also breaks his ankle or something. I don't know. But the wedding is tomorrow, and, as you can guess, everyone's booked."

"Dean," I say encouragingly. "You'd do an amazing job. It sounds pretty low pressure, with the assistant there as backup and everything."

Dean pauses, visibly conflicted. He looks down, studying his camera like it's a Magic 8 Ball he can shake for the answer.

"Maybe. I'll consider it," he says.

He sounds drawn to the idea, but like something is holding him back. I don't know what. Once when we got detention together freshman year, he walked out of the hourlong session showing me his elegant thirty-shot series "Faces of Detention," snapped when the teacher went to the restroom for five minutes. Dean loves photography, no matter what or when.

"It'd be a huge help," RJ says. "Let me give you my number in case you change your mind."

Dean blinks, then nods. I watch the two of them walk out of the water up to the shore, where Dean grabs his phone from his beach bag.

The more I envision it, the more I love this idea Emma and RJ have dropped into our plans. A photography gig is perfect, I'm realizing. I was just saying how we should focus on Dean's hobbies, and I've told him hundreds of times he could really make a living with his photography. Maybe he just needs to be shown it's possible.

Still, for some reason not even his oldest friend could figure out, Dean didn't love this idea. I saw him hesitate.

I just need to figure out why.

Twenty-One

THE SUN IS SETTING when Emma and RJ leave to return to their hotel. Before they say their goodbyes, they entreat Dean once more to really consider the wedding.

He and I walk back to the house in comfortable silence, with the sky over us showing off in incredible stretches of orange, pink, and blue. I decide not to press him on whatever his issue with photographing the wedding is. I think he'll eventually warm up to the idea. For now, I just want dinner.

But when we walk into the kitchen, we find all four parents looking abashed and tense. They immediately fall silent, the conversation ending with sharp haste.

"What's up with you guys?" Dean asks, his voice heavy with suspicion.

I dart glances around the group, not needing Dean's question answered. It's obvious they were talking about us. This is the quiet of walking past cafeteria tables right after a messy breakup or a memorable loss on the court.

With well-honed responses from those situations, I put on unbothered bravado. "No need to be worried," I say. "We're not back together. We were just hanging out at the beach with some people we met in Venice."

Terry doesn't look relieved the way I expected she would. She looks skeptical. When she speaks up, her tone suggests she's speaking for the group. "We're thrilled you two are getting along again, but . . . are you sure it's such a good idea to be spending so much time together?"

She shifts her focus to Dean, whose features go rigid. He's furious. Understandably—where was this concern before our families decided to vacation together? Where was this concern while we grew up together? "I'm seventeen," Dean grinds out. "You don't need to regulate who I spend time with."

The room goes quiet once more. There's only the gentle sound of waves under the insistent hum of the kitchen's overhead lights.

Terry looks pained, her mouth pulled taut, like she wants one of the other parents to step in and support her. No one does.

"I just know how important Kaylee is to you, honey," she says to Dean.

The moment is mortifying. Dean shifts on his feet, a bright flush rising in his cheeks. Of course, it's horribly embarrassing for me, too. She's speaking about me like I'm not even in the room. But Dean is the one whose feelings are being openly discussed in front of an audience. He looks on the verge of storming out of the kitchen and slamming every door on the way to his bedroom.

My dad clears his throat. "I think what your mom is trying to say is, we just want everyone to be mature about this . . . situation."

It does nothing to repair the moment. Dean is done. He slams his sunglasses down on the counter, and everyone winces.

Without one more second's pause, he spins and leaves the room.

I linger rigidly in the kitchen, impulses wrestling in me. This conversation is beyond infantilizing. I hate the blush heating my own cheeks, the hot prickle of scrutiny on my neck—the unfair sting in every detail of this situation. The heavy rhythm of Dean's footsteps pounding up the stairs tempts me, beckoning me to follow.

But I don't stomp out of rooms. I can't. I wouldn't even recognize the Kaylee who did.

Instead, I decide I'm going to handle the parents as gracefully as I can, even if they really, *really* don't deserve it. "I can control myself, you know," I say coolly. "No matter how much time Dean and I spend together, I'm not going to mess with his feelings." I clench everything in my core, holding my demeanor together. *Get through this. Shake the winner's hand and walk off the court. Don't get mad until you're alone.*

Terry's eyes fix on me, and I'm relieved to see embarrassment written in her features. At least we're all in this humiliating hellscape together. It's not much comfort, but I'm glad I'm not suffering alone.

"I know you can," Terry says soberly. "But you also have no idea how much Dean will always care about you. You have an enormous amount of power over him. He'd do anything for you, and you have to be responsible with that."

I grit my teeth. My first reaction is rage. Rage that no one seems to care about *my* feelings, not to mention how they're vastly underestimating Dean. But I temper myself.

Deeper down, though, I'm torn. It's one of the ugly off-shoots of perfectionism—the incessant second-guessing. I can't not self-examine, turn facets into flaws in everything I do. Right now this sinister microscope is forcing me to wonder if there *is* something to what they're saying. If I have been selfish, trying to hold on to Dean in a way I have no right to anymore.

I make sure to iron the unsteady emotion out of my voice before I speak. "The last thing I want is to hurt Dean again," I say to the parents, my inquisitors.

The entire room seems to narrow down to the sad smile Terry gives me.

"I'm not sure that's possible," she says. "Just being near you is going to hurt him. It may not be today, or even on this trip. But it will."

I'm humiliated to find tears stinging my eyes. When I cry, it's preferably in my bedroom by myself, in the dark. It's never in front of my parents, certainly never in front of Dean's. It's insult on top of injury, though I'm not sure which is which.

What is Terry saying? I can't even be friends with Dean

again? I'm still struggling to comprehend this shift from her treating me like one of her own daughters to the suspicious intruder in her son's life. Why is she so ready to cut me out? *What did I do wrong?*

My efforts to control my composure don't fool my dad. He fixes his gaze on me, and I know he's able to discern how I'm holding in my tears. He's always had the preternatural ability to know when I'm on the verge of crying. Ever since I was little, even when my mom wouldn't, he would know.

"That's not fair, Terry," he interjects, his voice soft but firm. "Dean's feelings are not Kaylee's responsibility. She's a kid, too."

Him coming to my defense only makes holding my tears in harder, though I'm grateful. I swallow down the painful lump in my throat.

Terry, for her part, looks chastened by the reprimand. "You're right," she concedes. "Which is why we doubted whether we should even take this trip this year. We're the parents here, and we need to look out for our son. Just like you look out for your daughter."

She directs this final comment toward my parents. I notice something strange in the charge of her voice, like the peculiar humidity of storm clouds starting to form on the horizon. It's—skepticism, or something close. On the rare occasions I've seen her squabble with Darren or punish Dean, the competitive edge of the former college volleyball player comes out in Terry. I see hints of it now.

Without even waiting for my parents to reply, she walks out. Darren, with a regretful look, follows.

I round on my parents, who appear understandably thrown. "What the hell was that about?" I ask.

I have to give my mom credit for the genuine reassurance in her smile. "Don't worry about it," she says gently. "Like Terry said, we're the parents here. This isn't about you."

"How is it *not* about me?" My eyes widen. "The four of you were literally in here discussing my sex life."

Dad winces. "Kaylee, please."

"I understand why you're upset, I do," my mom continues evenly, impressively unfazed by her seventeen-year-old daughter shouting *sex life* in the kitchen. "But trust me, this really isn't about you. We have decades of history with Terry and Darren. We're family, and sometimes old stuff surfaces in unexpected ways. We'll be fine," she promises. "Everyone will be fine."

I frown. While the performance my mom is putting on shows no cracks, it's not exactly casual, either. It calls to mind a flight attendant telling passengers to *remain calm* and *put your tray tables up* while the plane spirals downward.

Mom smiles wider. "Please go shower now, sweetheart," she says. "We're going to make hot dogs in twenty minutes."

Is she serious? Of course she is. If I thought the barbecue on our first night was inhospitable, though, somehow things seem to have worsened. I can hardly imagine reconvening in *twenty minutes* for some sizzling dinner under the crimson sky.

Still, I know it's the end of the conversation, even if my mom's reassurances have raised more questions than they answered. There's something more beneath the surface here. I want to know—but also part of me really doesn't. I've worked *hard* to make this vacation normal for everyone. I don't want to unpack hidden resentments or find out why Terry has turned on me.

With quiet footsteps, I head upstairs to my room, hoping the problems don't become too big to ignore.

Twenty-Two

DURING DINNER, EVERYONE UNEXPECTEDLY returns to normal. Or close—Dean remains somewhat sullen and gruff, but not so much it's out of character for him.

Still, I go out of my way to put distance between us. I sit far from him at the dining table and make conversation with Lucy, our seats facing the window where the room looks out onto the ocean softly illuminated by moonlight. I don't want what Terry said to join with the chorus of critical voices in my head, warping how I see myself. But I can't totally discount her words, either. I *don't* want to hurt Dean, and, furthermore, I don't want to turn the heat up on whatever drama is simmering between the parents. The point of getting Dean over me was to avoid tension like this.

When the parents start negotiating the high-stakes question of the night's movie choice, I watch them, searching for signs of the cracks they've covered up. I don't find any.

In fact, the discussion is reassuringly ordinary. Lucy makes her customary Hail Mary play for *Mamma Mia!*, receiving no support. When my mom introduces Sandra Bullock and Keanu Reeves's *The Lake House*, I don't join her with my usual enthusiasm—even though I really do want to see it—but Terry does. Ultimately, the only way to persuade my dad to stand down from *The Hobbit: The Battle of the Five Armies* is to compromise on our tenth Malibu viewing of *The Lord of the Rings: The Two Towers*.

After clearing the table, while everyone settles onto the couch for three hours of battles with talking trees, I head outside. I love the beach at night. It's empty, with the moonlight reflected on the quiet water. The lights from the houses behind me give the night a faint glow. The tide has risen close to the stilts of the homes, shrinking the beach itself to a small sliver. I dig my feet into the sand, nestling into the warmth remaining from the heat of the day.

Watching the water, I search for the solace I usually find here. It doesn't come. Instead, I feel cornered. Helpless. Exhaustedly confronting how everything I've hoped for this summer—everything I planned to fix—is going the exact opposite way. I'm working *so hard* to do the right thing. To help Dean, to repair our friendship. I thought it's what everyone wanted.

But maybe it's not.

I sit down on the sand, drawing my knees to my chest. Maybe I can't make everyone happy. The thought threatens to rip me in half—it feels like defeat. I'm not someone who lets herself be defeated, not when I'm frustrated, not when

I'm confused, not when I'm intimidated. Surely, I can do this. Surely, *I* can do this.

While I'm pondering how, I hear soft footsteps behind me, then Dean's legs in familiar gray sweatpants appear at my side. I look up, and he drops into the sand next to me.

"You've been avoiding me," he says.

There's no malice in the statement, no judgment. But it's not exactly generous or selfless, either. It walks right in the middle, with uncomplicated sincerity.

I stare out at the ocean, not sure how to reply. There are too many pressures to navigate. Too many conflicting wants. They wind my stomach into knots, constrict my chest, leave me motionless. Sometimes I feel like I'm drowning on land, my lungs full of expectations, my mind locked only on survival in the form of not failing everyone.

"Kaylee," Dean says.

His voice is featherlight. Despite myself, I can't help looking to meet his gaze, biting my lip.

His eyes catch the moonlight. "Don't listen to what my mom said. I want to be your friend."

I smile weakly. I want so desperately to believe him, to trust that of everyone in this house, he's the one who's right. But I don't know how to trust him when I barely trust myself. Still, I turn from him, facing the stretch of sand. "Would you tell me, though?" I ask quietly. "If it hurt to be around me?"

"It hurts all the time."

I look back to him, stunned by the honesty of his words.

Terry was right. I haven't been helping anyone but myself. "Dean—" I begin.

"No." He cuts me off, his voice firm, his jaw tense. "Listen to me. I *want* to be your friend. It wouldn't just hurt to lose that. It would be crushing."

I nod, half understanding him. It's just hard to be convinced when right now I feel like every possibility has problems. The wind rustles the palm trees with one unexpected gust, as if it's either supporting Dean's confident reassurance or matching my turbulent thoughts. Like everything right now, I'm not sure which.

"Besides," Dean goes on, pulling me out of my head for the moment. "You're going to get me over you, right? How can you do that if you listen to my mom and avoid me?"

He's grinning playfully now. The sight lifts my spirits in ways I honestly cannot fully comprehend, like seeing stars in the daytime. I guess—Dean's certainty helps me deal with the perfectionist's paradox of being unable to make everyone happy. It leads me out of my hall of diamond mirrors. No matter what anyone says, I *know* walking inside now would hurt him. So I don't.

"Right," I say, finally feeling decisive.

"Good," Dean replies. Satisfied, he shifts his gaze to the ocean.

I let mine follow. Internally, I kick myself into gear, remembering my mission. I'm helping him, which means—hobbies. "Why don't you want to photograph the wedding?" I ask.

Dean takes a deep breath, like he knew we would have

this conversation. "It's not that I don't want to," he starts measuredly. "It could be fun, and I want to help them out. Genuinely, I do. It's just . . . it's sort of a step toward turning photography into a job."

I frown, sincerely not understanding. "Yeah, I don't see the problem there. You'd get paid to do something you love."

"Photography is my passion," he explains patiently, like he's had this discussion with himself plenty of times and doesn't resent having it with me. "I don't want my passion to become a career or the thing my livelihood depends on. It would turn into something I do because I *have* to, not because I *want* to. Photography means too much to me for that."

I feel my brow furrow. Though I'm trying, I'm really not following. I want nothing *but* for volleyball to be my career. To have the privilege of waking up knowing I get to do my favorite thing in the whole world every day. I've never wanted to live my life otherwise. Sure, the stakes get higher when your favorite thing becomes your job, but that doesn't change everything you enjoy about it. And if you're good enough, why wouldn't you at least want to try?

"You know, you can still . . . want to do things you *have* to do," I say, finding it difficult to explain something I feel with unchanging conviction. "That's sort of the whole point of loving your job. Why wouldn't you want to spend every day doing what you love best?"

I expect more contemplation from Dean, more deliberate debate. Instead, he grins widely. Not like I've said something funny—more like I've said something wonderful. "I know you don't get it. I think it's great that you love volleyball and that you want to pursue it professionally," he says. "I'm just different."

"You're really good, though," I insist. "You could do it if you wanted."

"It's not about whether I'm good. I *know* I'm good," he replies, flashing me a smile. Then fog rolls in over his expression. "Do you ever wonder what would happen if one day you . . . fell out of love with volleyball? If you woke up in the morning, and the idea of playing one more game filled you with dread?"

I reply immediately. "It's not possible."

I hear what he's really saying, of course, same as I can hear waves in my head while staring out over the calm ocean in front of us. *You fell out of love with me overnight. Why couldn't volleyball be the same?*

It's just different, in ways I'm not sure how to explain. Love is less complicated when it comes to my sport. I've considered walking away from it. I have. But the thought of giving up volleyball is much, much worse than any comparisons to my mother.

Dean doesn't press the point. He doesn't ask the question I know must be consuming him. *Then why was I different?*

I'm grateful, because I don't know.

Instead, he faces the ocean, staring like he's looking for something he's not sure he'll recognize when he sees it. "I want photography to be just for me," he says softly, his eyes remaining fixed on the hidden horizon of night. "I . . . can't imagine the heartbreak of the thing I love most in the world not loving me back."

I want to say so much. I want to say photography will always love him back. I want to say *I'll* always love him back in some way. He's Dean. He understands me, he makes me laugh, he makes me think. His presence in my life is just like the mountains or the sky, no less profound for the fact that it never really changes.

When my eyes wander to him in the darkness, the thought flashes into me—I could kiss him. I might even want to kiss him.

I yank my gaze back to the sand. *No. No way. Definitely not.*

Kissing Dean wouldn't be fair. Not when I would inevitably retreat the way I did the first time. Which I probably would—because maybe I do feel a little about Dean the way he feels about photography. Maybe I am scared how deeply, how messily it would hurt to fall for him and lose him.

His voice cuts through the night, barely louder than a whisper. "That said, I know this wedding is just *one* gig, and, well, there might be another reason to do it."

I work my hardest to chase off my thoughts of love and heartache. Mustering up what cheerful charm I can, I raise an eyebrow. "Emma?" I ask.

Dean's cheeks darken in the moonlight. "RJ, actually."

I hurriedly hide my surprise, thinking back on today. *Of course.* I remember how RJ gave Dean his number, how they stood close together while discussing every camera model ever invented.

Dean watches me, gauging my reaction.

"RJ seems really cool," I say honestly. "He's an excellent reason to do the wedding."

"Is he? You're not jealous?" he asks with urgency I can't quite decipher. Is he disappointed I'm *not* jealous, or sympathetic if I am?

I know I have only seconds to reply or else the pause will seem like its own strangled sort of answer. I keep my eyes on his. "I'm not," I tell him, not 100 percent honestly. I am a little jealous. Of course I am. Isn't everyone jealous when their ex moves on? Just a normal, ordinary amount of jealous.

But it's only because Dean and RJ have shared interests. They have a foundation. *That's* what I'm wrestling with—not the idea of Dean moving on to just anybody. Their connection isn't just sparks and heat. It could be the roaring fire you only get when you lay the wood carefully, constructed just right. RJ could be something more for Dean, not only a rebound.

Determined not to give in to how those possibilities make me feel, I focus on what I find next to the jealousy in my jumbled-up heart. There's relief there, too. If Dean moves on, then we're really done. Whatever we were will be consigned to the past, and this fragile thing between us will be safe in our friendship.

I'll be safe.

Twenty-Three

I'M OFFICIALLY GOING TO be a photographer's assistant.

Last night, when we headed in from the beach, Dean texted RJ a link to some of his photos. Not ten minutes later, Emma and RJ's older sister called Dean, pleading to hire him. She asked for his quote, which Dean made up on the spot, and said he—and an assistant—would have their meals covered.

Dean doesn't really need an assistant. Of course, I volunteered anyway. I've been around a photoshoot once or twice, and I figured my presence couldn't *hurt*. Plus, I'm determined to make this fun for Dean, on the off chance he does decide to consider a career in photography.

This morning, the morning of the wedding, we're heading to Santa Monica to go to the mall, having surprisingly enough not packed wedding-ready clothing for our family vacation. Not wanting commentary from the parents, we hustle out the door. I decide not to dwell on the inevitable tense conversation they'll have about Dean's and my excursion, releasing the thoughts from my mind like a fistful of dande-lions in the Malibu breeze.

The drive through the canyons feels nearly normal, like the layers of new context to Dean's and my relationship—from friends, to a couple, to exes—have nearly melted completely off. He voluntarily explains to me the interconnected storylines of the nine-hundred-page winner-of-some-prize-or-other novel he's reading. I return the favor, breaking down some of the in-teresting trends I've noticed in my social media metrics.

When we get to the Third Street Promenade, Santa Monica's half-old-timey, half-mega-commercial stretch of mall, I march us into the first department store I see, despite Dean's pre-dictable insistence on finding something cooler. The point of this is to find semiformal clothes that won't pull focus, not to find unique pieces for our wardrobes.

The store is on the end of the Promenade, where the topiary-decorated wide walk-street gives way to the glittering shine of the multistory complex constructed more recently. With me practically dragging Dean, we pass the usual sus-pects of other stores—smoothie chains, Urban Outfitters, watch places with Hemsworths in the window. Our destina-tion of choice is one of those huge, three-story department stores that carry nearly every brand imaginable. Low shelves surround the escalators running up and down in the middle, and soft generic pop welcomes us in.

After fifteen minutes of browsing, I've settled on a light maxi dress with birds of paradise print, fitting for the beach wedding Emma described. Dean has done nothing except grumble about how none of these shirts have enough "billow" to them.

With my choice draped over my forearm, I watch Dean hold up a perfectly serviceable white Hawaiian shirt, examine it for one whole minute—and return it to the rack.

"Dean."

He half looks up, glum.

"Pick something," I say sternly. "It's okay if you're not the coolest person at this wedding where you don't know anyone." When he shoots me an exaggerated scowl, I meet his gaze, letting him know I'm not entertaining his little sartorial rebellion. "If you haven't picked something by the time I've tried this on, I'm choosing for you," I inform him.

"Fine . . ." he replies.

As I walk past him, I stop to pull out an orange shirt and shove it into his arms. Without giving him the opportunity to protest, I continue into the empty dressing room.

In the wooden stall, with the harsh lights of the fluorescents glaring down on me, I pull on the dress. I straighten its straps in front of the mirror, where I inspect my reflection for my verdict. The dress is perfect for the wedding, elegant and unassuming, the pattern party ready. It has halter spaghetti straps that put my muscular shoulders on display.

I chew my lip, wondering if it works on me. I look like I could knock down the walls of this dressing room with one well-placed shove. While I'm proud of my strength and love the way I look in a volleyball uniform, delicate dresses like this one always make me a little self-conscious.

From conversations I've had with other volleyball players, I know I'm not alone in my sometimes-complicated relationship with my body. When I started pursuing my sport more seriously, I learned how beach volleyball is one of the few women's sports more popular than the men's. While I want to believe it's because of the female players' skill, it's hard to ignore the way they're on display in the bikinis they compete in.

Since I'm in high school, I still compete in a tank top and spandex shorts. When I go pro, though, I'll be expected to jump to the customary bikini uniform, which . . . is honestly something I'm not sure how I feel about. I definitely don't like the implications of putting players in bikinis when they're no longer underage. It's controlling and sexualizing.

The thing is, personally, I *like* how I look in a bikini. If it were truly only my choice, maybe I would choose to compete in one.

But it's not my choice. It's decided by people I've never met. Even at my level, I already feel the pressure of too many expectations put on my body. On the beach. On Instagram. Not to mention just, like, in the world. It feels like scavengers pulling off little pieces for themselves, small voices claiming ownership with their exhaustingly contradictory comments. I have to be athletic and muscular enough to win, but curvy enough to look good in a bikini—sportswoman and model wound up into one.

When it catches me on my worst days, it feels like the rest of my life. My body, like me, needs to be everything to everyone.

In a delicate, flowy dress, I'm aware of those expectations and of the ways I fall short. They cling to me like the freeing, lightweight fabric of this dress doesn't. Sometimes I feel like I should've gotten used to shaking them off without letting myself care, but I'm not sure it's even possible.

Still—I like this dress. I want to wear it, even if people's first thoughts will be about my shoulders.

Hearing someone enter the dressing room area, I glance under my door and recognize Dean's shoes. "I hope you picked *real* options," I call out. "We have an hour before we have to be there."

When I push open my door, I find he's managed to— *oh, thank god*—pick out three shirts and a pair of pants. He's on his way into the dressing room next to mine. Seeing me, though, he stops sharp.

"How do you do that?" he asks.

His eyes roam over every inch of me, including my shoulders, with—well, it doesn't make me feel scrutinized or judged or insufficient. Even so, like I can't fend off the whirlwind of persistent expectations, I can't quite wrap my head around what his eyes are saying. "What?" I reply.

"Walk into a random department store, find a dress in ten minutes, and look that incredible," he says. "Maybe I *should* let you pick for me."

The heat rising in my cheeks comes quickly. I can't help it. His praise is exactly what I needed to hear. I feel the danger of this moment, though—as if on our perilous climb up to ordinary, harmless friendship, we've just glanced down into the dizzying depths of what we once were to each other.

I rush to speak before his words work deeper into me. "Let's see what you've got first," I say.

I push him into the stall. While I watch his feet under the door, his shorts drop to the floor. I'm very conscious of how Dean is basically getting naked two feet away from me with only a thin door with slats that *really* don't block everything out between us. I turn around. Dean doesn't come out, and I figure it's because he's trying and already discarding what he brought in.

Finally, he opens the door. I face him, fearing I'll find the Dean I dragged into the store in his familiar black shorts and white tee with rolled sleeves.

Instead, my mouth drops half-open.

I'd vaguely guessed the choices he walked in with would look good together. I'd noticed bold colors, nicely contrasting fabrics, pleats. Guys can't go wrong with pleats.

Nevertheless, I did *not* imagine just how good even Dean's reluctant eye would be. He's standing in socked feet wearing high-waisted dark pants and an orange-and-yellow short-sleeve button-down. With the shirt tucked in, it tapers attractively at his waist. Beneath his shirt, I can make out the white tank top he's wearing.

It's . . . extremely hot.

He obviously can read it all over my face. "I knew it," he says smugly.

I meet his eyes, conscious of how I absolutely hadn't been looking at his face. How many different kinds of fire can possibly ignite in my cheeks in one afternoon? "Knew what?" I ask with apprehension.

Leaning on the dressing room's doorframe, he smirks. "You're not over me," he explains. "I just hope you don't wait until it's too late and you've missed your chance to get back together."

I say nothing. I'm speechless. My mouth is dry, like sand— desert sand, Death Valley sand.

Dean is smoldering with pride and self-satisfaction. "Shall we buy these, then?"

Twenty-Four

WE WEAR OUR PURCHASES out of the store, turning in the middle of the mall so we can tear out each other's tags. Dean drives us to the venue while I do my hair and makeup in the car.

The Malibu Beach Estate is one of those expansive beach clubs built right on the edge of where the rocky hills meet the coast. Palm trees crisscross high over the sloping wooden roofs of the bungalow-style buildings. Golf carts sprint past decorative fountains.

When we park, though, we hardly have the chance to take in the lush details of the majestic entrance before being swept up to the bridal suites. We have several hours before the ceremony itself, hours in which we'll capture the getting-ready process in the club's impressive complex of cream-colored halls.

It turns out Dean *does* need an assistant. I keep track of his camera equipment, rearrange furniture, and corral groomsmen while Dean and the other photographer get shots of the groom. After, we move over to the bride and repeat the process. I'm swept up in the hustle, consumed by the endless chaotic logistics of the day.

Until the couple's first look. Only when the groom sees the bride on the sweeping staircase do I stop running around long enough for feeling to steal over me, sudden and profound. The intimacy of the moment, of the glimpse we're getting into the lives of a pair of strangers, hits my heart in unexpected places.

We start to head for the beach, where the ceremony will take place. While we walk with the group down the flagstone paths around the pool, I hand Dean one of the waters I grabbed in the room where the bride got dressed. "Hydrate," I instruct him.

"Thanks." Dean takes the water bottle gratefully. "This is nonstop."

"It's kind of cool to be a part of, though," I say.

We're in the midst of the whole group of wedding party and family, now continuing on to the sand. Finishing a long swig of water, he hands me back the bottle so he can capture photos of the flower girls running to catch up to the bride.

"Surely you're not getting emotional over the romance of a couple you don't even know," he says to me, still looking through his camera.

I just roll my eyes in reply.

Reaching the setup for the ceremony, I hang on to Dean's camera bag while he starts taking photos of the families in their seats. I spot RJ, looking very handsome, and Emma in the front row.

The setting is beautiful. The sun casts a golden glow on everyone in their formalwear, seated in the white rows of chairs decorated with colorful sprigs of pink and white flowers. The ocean sparkles behind the wedding arch. The gentle melody the guitar player on the right is strumming floats over everything with the evening beach breeze. If love were a place, this might well be it.

I wait on the sand, feeling unexpectedly moved. I haven't been to a wedding since I was too young to remember. When I was five, I was a flower girl in my uncle's wedding, and all I recall of that day are the photos we have—me in a deep-green dress, carrying white rose petals.

Maybe it's just this setting, so gorgeous it seems outside of real life, or maybe I'm just older now, but there's something magical about this. When the groom takes his place at the front and the guitarist switches to something slower and more romantic, everyone falls silent, their heads turning. From the tree line, the bride emerges, wearing a flower crown and smiling brilliantly.

I watch. Every second seems to shine like the light glittering on the water. I see the groom, a man I've never met and will never see again, have one of the greatest moments of his life as his soon-to-be wife walks down the aisle. I see her, fighting to keep her steps slow in the name of ceremony while her face says she wishes she could run to him.

I've only ever seen commitment as scary—something

that gives someone else the power to hurt you, to judge you and find you wanting. But here, caught up in the sheer love of this day, I feel none of the familiar fear.

What I do feel, watching the couple kiss for the first time as husband and wife, is the happy, jolting prickle of tears spilling down my cheeks.

I clap wholeheartedly with these people I don't even know, feeling connected to them just for having seen this. The sunset seems in on it somehow, reveling in its finery, flinging streaks of gold fire out over the ocean like how the flower girls sprinkled their petals on the sand.

When the bride and groom walk back down the aisle, beaming, Dean rejoins me. His brow is sweat-slicked, but he looks energized from the moment. His eager photographer's eyes flit to me, then to the scene, drinking in details—then double back to me, where this time they linger with soft curiosity.

"Kaylee Jordan," he says with incredulity I don't think he's putting on. "Are you crying?"

I sniff. "Only a little. It's a wedding. Everyone is crying." Defensively, I shrug, like I'm shaking off his observation.

My little show of carelessness clearly doesn't convince Dean, who grins delightedly. "Who would have thought a serial dater like yourself would be so sentimental?" he asks.

I stick my tongue out in reply. Laughing, he leaves me with his small victory and goes to get photos of the wedding party lining up near the water.

Watching them—this joined family, these people who are facing forever no matter the dark clouds or shining days—I hear Dean's question repeating in my head. The wind dries the tearstains on my cheeks, their cooling paths like reminders of what he pointed out. *Who would have thought a serial dater like yourself would be so sentimental?*

Not me.

I don't know what's coming over me.

Twenty-Five

UNFORTUNATELY, DEAN IS NEVER hotter than when he's taking photos in formalwear. I have less to do during the reception since the point is to capture candid moments—my job is essentially not to intrude.

I perform it excellently from the comfort of our table, largely obscured behind the buffet. The reception is on the club's sprawling veranda, where hedges separate us from the panorama of the water. In front of the buffet, guests' circular tables surround the dance floor. Emma and RJ wave to me when they pass by, but they're understandably busy, celebrating with their family.

It leaves me on my own to simply *watch* Dean do his thing. He looks to be in the midst of his own unique dance. While Earth, Wind & Fire transitions into Taylor Swift, Dean threads through the crowd, holding his camera up and snapping pics quickly, urging people to stand together. His competency only makes him more attractive.

I lose my sense of the minutes flying by. Time seems to vanish in this sphere of happiness. Only when the newlyweds slip away for a private moment does Dean finally collapse into the chair next to me at our table, looking exhausted and exhilarated. He hardly ate when I prepared him a plate an hour ago, and now his food is completely congealed. Noticing, I spring for the dessert table, which is stacked high with cupcakes.

I grab one for each of us. When I return to Dean with the dessert in hand, his eyes light up. Holding the moist cake delicately, I present him his, then bite into mine.

Dean shakes his head in ecstasy. "They could've paid me in these, honestly," he declares.

While part of me wants to wholeheartedly endorse this cupcake-based compensation scheme, it's not the first thing on my mind. Not the first thing I feel like I need Dean to hear. "You're doing an amazing job," I say sincerely. "Watching you . . . it's just really cool."

Even where we're sitting, far from the lights of the dance floor, it's impossible to miss the way Dean's cheeks flush. He looks a little bashful as he wipes frosting from his fingers. "Thanks. You've been a huge help, you know. I probably would have fainted during the cake cutting if you weren't insisting I drink water."

I shrug with false modesty. "You can always count on me to champion the virtues of hydration."

Dean finishes his cupcake. He leans back in his chair, splaying his legs out in front of him, and closes his eyes for a moment. With the music drifting over us, the smell of celebration hanging sweetly in the night, I can't help myself. I stare at him. I find myself focusing on the droplet of sweat ready to slink down the side of his face. The stray hair going rogue from his topknot. My eyes run down his body to where his shirt is starting to pull out of his waistband. I'm tempted to reach over and fix it for him, but I restrain myself.

His eyes still closed, Dean remains oblivious to my internal drama. "How are you holding up?" he asks.

"I'm fine." As soon as I say it, I'm sick of the word. I'm always *fine*, even when I'm not. Right now, I'm a lot of things, including aware of Dean's attractiveness. Unable to share this inconvenient fact, however, I settle for something I *can* say out loud. "I'm just glad to be out of the house for the day, actually," I tell him.

Dean cracks open an eye to look at me. "The family tension too much for you?" he asks.

"That and . . ." I hesitate, fighting the fearsome inertia of being fine. I push through. "My mom told me she's coming out of retirement."

Dean's eyes shoot open fully now. He sits up straight. "Whoa," he says, watching me intently, like surprise has electrified the exhaustion right out of him. "When did she say that?"

"On our hike yesterday. Obviously, it's not really about me, but it just changes how I thought my future would look." I finish speaking, my eyes on my feet.

I'm ashamed of my own feelings, terrified of saying them out loud, like my reservations will become more real, more difficult to ignore by admitting them to someone else.

They *are* real, though. They *are* difficult to ignore. Whether I speak them aloud or hide them away in my heart.

"It's absolutely okay to have complicated feelings about this. It *is* complicated," Dean says. His voice is so gentle I look up at him, finding compassion and understanding written in his features.

It's nearly unbearable how much relief his simple validation gives me. The emotion grows within me, swelling too big to contain. It emboldens me to keep going. "I . . . I guess I just need time to get used to the idea," I say, not shying from meeting his eyes.

He smiles the sort of soft smile that says, *I'm here for you.* "Of course you do. That's okay, Kaylee." He reaches out, putting a reassuring hand on mine on the table. "You don't have to be so . . . *okay* with everything instantaneously."

My skin feels like it's burning under his palm and the hidden meaning in his words. I *do* work to be okay—to be fine with everything. Comparisons to my mom, lost matches, breakups. Dean's and my failed romance. I was *okay* as soon as I had to be, while Dean . . . wasn't.

Still, I'm not sure it's as simple as that. I didn't just get over heartache—I *spared myself* heartache. I'm not sure I would prefer languishing in sadness. Not sure I could handle it, even if the alternative is paying for my okayness in constant pressure.

Like Dean can read the existential spiral in my eyes, he continues, squeezing my hand softly. "You're a good daughter, and your mom loves you more than anything. This will be all right."

I swallow, then nod with a smile. "Thanks for saying that. It helps."

Suddenly, I feel bare to Dean, to this whole party, to the night and the elements. It's like everyone on this beach can see through to my real self, not the self I carefully control and cultivate. My skin itches, my heart pounds, the vulnerability overwhelming me. I'm desperate to put my armor of perfection back on.

Just as panic is reaching down into my gut, the DJ changes the song. "Everyday" by Buddy Holly comes on. *Our* song. The song that was playing when we first kissed on Dean's birthday, the song he then made sure to put on every playlist for photoshoots and study nights.

Just hearing the simple, sweet melody, old feelings threaten to take hold of my heart. Tasting Dean's lips, laughing in his car together, smiling whenever I listened to this song while working out and missing him. Maybe it's because we're in the midst of this ridiculously fairy-tale wedding. Or maybe it's just because Dean has been perfect in every way. But I can't fight back the emotions, not the way I should.

He removes his hand, his eyes skirting mine. I don't know what feelings this song conjures for him. Is he remembering what I am? He must be. Does it leave him sad? Regretful? Whatever it is, I don't want this relic of our relationship to wreck an otherwise perfect evening. We can move past this. I'll prove it to him.

I stand up and take his hand, tugging him lightly. He doesn't move.

"Dance with me," I say, smiling.

He looks up at me, his expression startled, but not, I find with some small measure of reassurance, unwilling. While the song builds to the chorus and my dress flutters around my legs in the night breeze like it's anticipating dancing, I wait, not wanting to rush him. Eventually he gets to his feet and steps toward me.

He puts a hand on my hip. Not low enough to be romantic, but still, the memory of the last time he touched me there sends a shiver down my spine. We aren't on the dance floor. We're not surrounded by other guests. The sounds of their laughter drift over to us in the dark, distant yet calming, like we've stolen just this single moment for ourselves.

Lifting our linked hands above me, I spin for him, starting us off in a rhythm we've perfected. We may not have our hands in each other's hair, I may not feel his breath on my neck while he trails kisses down my chest, but we've moved together to this beat too many times to miss a step. When I straighten in front of him, I lift our hands once more, this time urging him to spin. He does so, his laughter ringing out under the clear sky.

When he comes back to my arms, he holds me closer than before. Closer than I know I should be. But I don't break our embrace. I sink into him, swaying with him, feeling light enough I could float into the warm night.

Even though I know every verse and refrain to this song by heart, the ending catches me by surprise. I'm not ready to give up this moment yet. The music changes, though, and our rhythm fades. Dean steps back from me.

I'm still grinning, my cheeks flushed with happiness, when I notice Dean's demeanor has shifted. He looks defensive, even timid.

"You can probably go home now," he says. There's something wrong with his voice, like the words are fighting themselves in his chest.

I blink at the sudden dismissal. We were having fun. Things were finally just like they used to be. Or they're close, and I could live with close.

The breeze dies, and the hem of my dress falls back to brush my ankles. Dean's shoulders have squared, the stiffness in his voice now working into his whole posture. He looks like a sketch of himself, sharp lines depicting hollow features. "I can handle the rest of the photos on my own," he continues in the same vacant way. "I think the party is winding down anyway."

"I don't mind," I say. Unlike him, I have experience in struggling to sound carefree. I use the skill now. "There's no need for you to get a Lyft. I'll stay with you until you're ready."

Dean doesn't reply immediately. Finally, he looks up from the grass, staring determinedly past me.

"I made plans with RJ," he says. "For . . . after."

His abrupt change suddenly makes perfect sense. It feels like the rare moments when someone lines up their shot some way I'm not expecting, and the next second the volleyball slams into my cheek or forehead. The confusion, the effort, the concern rush right out of me—I just want to leave here as fast as possible.

"Right. Good. Great. Yes, you should definitely do . . . that," I manage haltingly. I gather my phone, keys, sunglasses, everything in a hurry, not wanting to make this awkward. Or *more* awkward.

"Yeah. Sorry," Dean replies.

"No need to be sorry," I reassure him. "I'll just, um, go! Have a good rest of the night." Feeling the prickle of hurt waiting for me deep in my heart, I fight to ignore it. While my head runs familiar interrogations—whether I'm even entitled to hurt, whether hurting is past the perimeter of who I'm supposed to be—I am, once more, projecting *fine*.

I wave with what I hope is friendly cheer and walk swiftly off the grass, heading for the parking lot under the expanse of palm trees swaying in the night. I hammer reassurances into myself like punches. *This is the right thing. Dean needs to get over me. RJ will help.* I'm not lying to myself. This is exactly what I wanted.

Want, I remind myself sternly. What I *want*.

Twenty-Six

IT IS ENTIRELY ORDINARY to pace in one's bedroom past midnight. It is *not* the symptom of profound underlying confusion, nor of romantic discontent. It is just a very normal thing for someone to do when they can't get certain thoughts out of their head.

While the rest of the house sleeps, I crisscross the floor of my room, sometimes pausing to lean on my desk, from which the small blue lamp I've had here forever provides the room's only light, or to slouch with my elbows on my dresser, where photos in seashell frames hold the history of the Freeman-Yu–Jordan vacations.

I'm not jealous. I'm just . . . curious. What are Dean and RJ doing right now?

I can't help remembering the first time Dean kissed *me*. The images cycle in my head, one endless PowerPoint presentation I can't manage to quit out of. The kiss caught me by surprise. Of course I knew Dean had a crush on me, but I figured it was mostly for fun. Nothing he would ever choose to act on.

When I went with my parents over to his house for his birthday, I expected a night of pancakes for dinner—Dean's favorite since we were young—and an art house film. What I did *not* expect was what happened in the sweet interlude after our syrupy, incredible meal. While the parents drank wine in the kitchen and Dean's sisters were playing in Lucy's room, Dean and I ended up on the couch, swapping music recs. I asked him what he wished for when he blew out his candles.

He took a breath.

"This," he said.

He leaned in, slowly enough I had time to withdraw. I didn't. I didn't want to. Honestly, I respected the brazenness of it—to set himself up for possible rejection on his birthday? But while I hadn't meant for the kiss to be more than a kiss, when our lips touched, my stomach swooped. Effervescent need hummed through me. Before I knew it, we were making out on the couch and only fumbling apart when we heard footsteps.

I shake my head, wishing I could cast off the memory—or capture it harmlessly, contained like one of the photos on the dresser, not repeating endlessly in my head. I need distraction.

Leaving my room, I tiptoe into Lucy's. The lights are off, but I know better than to assume Lucy is asleep. I was thirteen once. Sure enough, when I nudge open her door, I find the blue light of her phone illuminating her face. She's sitting up in bed.

"Can I come in?" I ask.

Lucy eyes me like she's evaluating my request, then pulls out her headphones. "Why aren't you bothering Dean at this hour?"

While I walk in, she makes room for me on the bed. The gesture looks instinctual, which makes me smile. I nestle in under the covers with her, remembering all the sleepovers we had in this room when we were kids. Dean would get so jealous that the parents eventually had to ban sleepovers on vacation unless they were held in the living room with all the kids present.

"He's still at the wedding," I reply, hoping I sound casual, informational.

Lucy raises an eyebrow, seeing right past the facade. I should've known she would—once again, I remember being her age.

"It's eating you up, isn't it?" The posture she's putting on is adultish savvy surrounding unmistakable concern.

Her perceptive question isn't one I can handle right now. I deflect, knowing the move is cheap and needing to make it anyway. "Hey, how's volleyball? Are you excited for club this year?"

Lucy narrows her eyes. "Actually, I might quit. So which one of the hot siblings is Dean into?" she asks, returning to her original course with conversational footwork I have to give her credit for.

"You might *quit*?" My final syllable risks waking up the house. "Lucy, why?"

"It's the boy, right?" she shoots back. "They were talking about art museums and trendy restaurants for like an hour before you got home."

My stomach knots, the echo of what I realized yesterday returning insistently in my head. Of course Dean deserves to have a meaningful connection with a fellow artist. They could probably have something real, unlike us, who have nothing in common. This is good. It's good for Dean. It's good for whatever hope I have left of recovering our friendship.

In the silence of Lucy's bedroom, I wait for my reassurances to resonate. They never do. Feeling cowardly, I reach once more for diversion.

"Lucy, why do you want to quit volleyball?" I whisper into the dark of her room, gentler now. "You're so good. You're better than I was at your age."

The praise works, at least momentarily distracting Lucy from her interrogation of me. Her cheeks pinken with pride, and she smiles, curling her lips over her braces like she's hiding the expression.

"My mom says I shouldn't prioritize a sport over school, and it's really hard to do well at both," she says softly. She pauses, her smile starting to fade. "My grades slip during club season."

I nod understandingly. I've been there. In fact, I was just there this past year. While all my classmates are now more focused on school than ever—everyone hyperconscious of the importance of junior-year grades in college apps—I earned my lowest GPA in years. With the hours I spend in clinics, practice, training, and conditioning, I'm left with next to no time for sleep and homework. And if I don't sleep, then I don't have the energy to train. It's especially infuriating because I know I *could* get better grades if I had the time to get to all my homework or review every chapter before a test. But I don't. Ultimately, I've made my peace with it, because volleyball is my future, not my grade in biology.

"It's definitely not easy," I tell Lucy. The last thing I want is for her to think she's somehow lesser for having worse grades. Grades don't matter—unless they matter to her. "But quitting volleyball should be *your* choice. Is that what you want? Or is it what your mom wants?"

Lucy shrugs, then settles back into the pillows. We barely fit in this twin bed anymore, both of us so much bigger than the little girls who tried to keep each other awake to see the sunrise.

"I don't know. Honestly," she says. She leans her head on my shoulder. "It feels unfair I can only do high school one way, and no option is really *my* way. Like what if I want to do volleyball and science? Why do I have to also find time for history? It sucks to get bad grades. Even when it's a subject I hate, it's kind of hard not to care."

"Yeah. It is." A tiny piece of my heart cracks. I hate that Lucy, only thirteen, already feels such pressure to be perfect in everything. I wish I knew what I could say to make her feel better, but the truth is, I haven't figured it out for myself. I settle for leaning my head on hers, reminding her I'm here.

She shifts under the covers. "You can only sleep in here if you answer a question."

Evening my breathing, I pretend I'm already drifting off. Lucy isn't having it. She pokes me hard in the stomach, making me gasp and laugh.

"For real," she says sternly, ignoring my giggles, "why did you break up with Dean? You're obviously stressing about him."

I close my eyes. The weight of her question settling over me isn't like the cozy heaviness of these sheets. It's constricting, not comforting. In Lucy's quiet room, I wish I could somehow vanish into the dark and elude this persistent conversation. "It was just time," I say, hearing how insubstantial the reply is starting to sound. It's getting thinner and thinner each time I give it.

I put constant effort into willing myself to be and think a certain way, but it's not working. I'm exhausted, not from coordinating wedding photography on my feet for six hours. Exhausted deep down.

Either because my reason satisfies Lucy or, likelier, because she hears the struggle in its hollow ring, she doesn't press me. She slides down onto her pillow and nestles in next to me. The rhythm of her breathing is the last thing I hear before I escape the maze of my thoughts into sleep.

Twenty-Seven

WHEN I WALK BACK to my room in the morning, I notice Dean's door is closed. He came home.

The sight releases some of the tight tension in my chest I'm never without—my constant companion. My steps lighter, I get dressed for a workout, then head down the stairs into the morning-lit living room. I continue out into the yard, where the day is still warming in the prelude to summer heat. The sunlight is crisp, colorful, like the Malibu of magazines or Instagram in real life.

On the side of the house, I grab the plank of wood my mom bought from Lowe's a couple years ago. She painted an X in the middle, the excess paint leaving dried droplets running down from each line.

I lodge the plank under the deck, supported by one of the stilts, where it fits upright, then grab the volleyball bag. I start doing spike drills, slamming the ball into the X, enjoying the force of my swing. For the moment, I feel good.

I expect the thunking sound of the ball striking the wood will wake up Dean, with his room one story directly above my target tree, but he never pushes open his window to tell me off. As the sun rises higher in the sky, I switch to a leg-and-back workout, doing lunges up and down the patio and wall sits.

Still no Dean.

I want to barge into his room, but I resist. How late was he out last night for him to be sleeping in to this hour? The nagging question winds into my muscles, clenching them up with every searing lunge. I don't *want* this to preoccupy me so viciously. I don't *want* to be this curious.

I just can't stop.

Shaking out my strained limbs, I finally have to admit I can't keep doing lunges for as long as it takes Dean to wake up. I return upstairs to my room, where I change into my swimsuit.

Fifteen minutes later, I'm stretched out on the sand with a protein shake, hoping to swap my spandex tan lines for something more bikini-friendly. I FaceTime Brianna, who provides me with an excellent reprieve from the Dean question. While I know she would want to hear about what's going on with me, I . . . don't want to share what's winding me up. It's an instinct, or maybe just a habit. When I spend so much effort maintaining my shiny image, my facade, I can't help hiding problems or doubts from my friends. Even Bri.

Instead, when I direct conversation to her, she goes with it enthusiastically. She's started emailing her future college roommate and has lots to share about Margot from Houston.

Then we hang up.

Then I finish my smoothie.

Then, while the sun moves past the middle of the sky, I flip over onto my stomach, ignoring a million irritating questions.

Finally, when I'm nearly ready to head in, I see Dean emerging from the house.

I check my phone. It's past two—which means Dean probably got back closer to morning. While he walks down to the beach, I study him with embarrassing focus, gathering details like I'm inspecting crime scene photographs. His hair, I note, is disheveled. His eyes look sleepy.

"There you are," I say, only just managing to keep my voice light.

He lies down on his stomach on the sand next to me. "Barely," he replies. "What have you been up to?"

I eye him. *Is he really not going to tell me what happened?* I give him the very boring rundown of my morning, and when I finish, I wait for him to reciprocate.

He doesn't. Instead, he closes his eyes—which have dark circles under them, I catalog—to soak in the sun.

I simmer with irritation. I feel like I'm trapped once more in the paradox of this vacation I thought I'd pushed my way out of. In front of me, families swim in the deep blue water. Paddleboarders chat while rowing on the horizon. Someone's dog trots past me down the shoreline. This place is the epitome of relaxation, but not for me. I'm pissed off in paradise.

Using every ounce of patience in my body, I wrestle down my temper. "How was the rest of your night?" I grind out through my teeth.

Dean yawns. "Good," he says while grinning.

I wait for him to say more, but, impossibly, he just closes his eyes again, resting his head on his forearms like he's going to go back to sleep. I take a breath, feeling very close to flinging him into the sun. He knows exactly what he's doing, and I won't let it get under my skin. I've had girls scream in my face on the court. I can handle one hipster playing with me.

"You were out pretty late," I comment leadingly.

Dean just *mmmhs* in agreement.

Unbelievable. He's not going to tell me what happened unless I ask him outright. Which I absolutely refuse to do. The line has to be drawn somewhere.

When I say nothing, wrapped up in my little knot of refusal, Dean cracks one eye open. He looks at me, then laughs.

In the shoreline's heat, my cheeks flame even hotter. I'm done playing this game with him. I don't care how immensely he's enjoying himself. What's it to me what he did with RJ last night? Nothing.

I smile chipperly at him. "Do you have any plans for the rest of the day?" I ask.

Dean sits up, his eyes sparkling. "I'm going to Santa Monica." He pauses just long enough I know some other sandal is going to drop. "Emma and RJ are going to teach me how to surf," he continues.

I can't help studying him. He doesn't blush when he says RJ's name. The plan is with Emma, too, so what does *that* mean? *No*, I chastise myself. I don't care. I wouldn't mind if Dean's plans involved him and RJ finding their own private cove with the loveliest sunsets on earth.

"I'm doing what you said," Dean continues. "Accepting every invitation, right?"

While his secrecy was annoying enough, hearing him weaponize my own suggestion against me is a whole new level of unacceptable. I fight to maintain my plastered-on grin. "That's right," I say.

"I'd invite you, but you made your feelings pretty clear. On surfing," he says, placing the pause carefully.

I don't let my expression flicker. His taunt in the dressing room yesterday runs gratingly through my head. *I just hope you don't wait until it's too late and you've missed your chance to get back together.*

Still, Dean is underestimating his opponent if he thinks he can rattle me. Composure is practically my superpower. "Don't worry about it. Actually, can we carpool?" I ask. "I have plans in Santa Monica, too."

His eyes widen a fraction. I know he wants to ask what my plans are. He doesn't.

Which is good, because I'm 100 percent bullshitting.

"Of course," he replies.

"Great," I say cheerfully, resolving to figure out my "plans" as I go. Dean's stiff smile now matches my own.

A stalemate.

Twenty-Eight

THE FAMILIAR DRIVE INTO the city passes in an overly cheerful standoff. I obviously refuse to ask about the details of Dean's night, and Dean, clearly practicing his own self-restraint, won't ask about my mysterious, presently non-existent plans in the city.

Instead, with the glittering ocean flying past our window, we make conversation about the nothingest of nothings. The traffic, what our families will have for dinner tonight, the weather.

When we park in one of the Promenade's huge parking garages, I realize I've spent so much time *not* asking Dean about last night that I do in fact have no idea what I'm going to do for the next several hours.

Dean definitely reads the panic in my expression. He addresses me over the Jeep's roof. "You know, if your *plans* fall through, you can always join us. After surfing, we'll probably hang at their hotel. It's the Playa Del Mar," he informs me, sounding like he enjoys saying the name slowly and directly, making sure I remember.

My smile doesn't slip. "Thanks, but that won't be necessary."

Dean shrugs. We exit the garage onto the sidewalk corner, where palms and hedges share the street with crosswalks and parking meters. Dean heads toward wherever he's meeting Emma and RJ, glancing over his shoulder one more time with unrestrained interest.

I smirk, then face the street and my half-baked plan. I can't just stand here—if Dean looks back again he'll have proof I have nowhere to be.

I spin in the opposite direction Dean went and start walking into downtown Santa Monica. The Promenade isn't the only worthy destination in this part of the city—many of the cooler coffee shops can be found farther inland, or there's the famous pier. Playing carnival games by myself would be a little embarrassing, but there's no going wrong with the old-soda-shop-style ice cream parlor.

Despite the pearlescent shoreline just steps from here, much of this coastal city isn't very different from other downtowns. Wandering in search of something to do with myself, I pass city buses with lawyers' faces on the sides, hole-in-the-wall doughnut shops, and low apartment complexes. Only the hotels on nearly every street and the smell of the sea remind me where I'm walking.

Nothing draws me in, however. I hoped inspiration would've struck by now. But I won't admit defeat.

I focus up, pushing myself like when I've fumbled several points in a row. *What's my favorite part of Southern California?* The beach, probably. Except, if I sit on the beach, I run the risk of Dean spotting me on his way back from surfing, and I can't let him see me alone.

So . . . not the beach. It's fine. There's plenty else I can do. The important thing is what I'm *not* doing, which is wondering what Dean and RJ did last night. Because even if I'm enjoying spending time with Dean—even if I find him, okay, *attractive*—we can't get back together.

I read out the reasons why in my head like I'm rehearsing a speech for class. I can't yank him around according to my ever-changing whims. It isn't right. I need to consider his feelings. No matter if he's being a pill. No matter if he's using *my own advice* against me—

I stop on the street corner. *Of course.* How could I spend ten minutes ambling aimlessly around Santa Monica when I've spent years developing methods for getting over every kind of romantic hang-up?

The way to handle my present problem is suddenly incredibly obvious. I need to follow my own advice. Like focusing on my passion.

I spin on the sidewalk and double back, knowing exactly where I'm headed now. After twenty minutes of navigating the tourist-packed path down the bluffs, I reach my destination. Santa Monica's beach volleyball courts line the sand, nearly to the shore, with the pier's iconic Ferris wheel in the background. I can't imagine too many better places to play volleyball.

I walk slowly by the games in progress on every court,

catching pieces of them. LA is full of professional volleyball players and colleges with competitive teams. While the game play in front of me is impressive, it's within my reach. Inspiring, not intimidating. I have no problem imagining myself on these courts, holding my own. Earning my spot on this grass.

It feels like home.

Suddenly I'm incredibly glad I'm here. Not just because I have something to do while Dean is occupied, but because standing on these courts is slowly, gently easing the weight I've felt on my chest since my mom said she was coming out of retirement. It doesn't really matter if my mom is playing. My place here is *my own*, not hers to occupy. Even with the formidable Judy Jordan in the game, there's room for me.

When I reach the end of the row, I linger, watching the group of guys in front of me. They're close to my age, each with the windswept hair of frequent beach days. They're . . . I mean, hot. I give my eyes free rein to roam over their shirtless shoulders, their long legs, their wonderfully flexed stomach muscles.

After they score the game-ending point and walk off the court, I approach the tallest one while he drinks from his water bottle, volleyball tucked under one arm. I'm picking up momentum, enjoying the new confidence of my recent epiphany. It puts easy strength into my voice when I speak. "Great game," I say, holding my shoulders back. "Where do you play?"

The guy looks over at me. He does an appreciative double-take, and I don't think he's admiring only my volleyball-ready height and physique. "Hey," he says, somehow managing to make the single syllable sound like an invitation. "I'm a recruit. Going to play indoor for Princeton next year. You're Kaylee Jordan, right?" He smiles when he notices the surprise I must have let flit over my features. "I read your *Sports Illustrated* feature," he explains.

I straighten, pleased. Maybe it's immodest, but being recognized delights me. "Nice eye," I say. I hold my hand out, keeping my chest up just a little flirtatiously.

I see how his body language responds to mine, how he pulls back his shoulders like he's showing off. *This is good.* When I'm unsure of myself, I can fall back on the fun and flirty persona I adopt for Instagram.

He takes my hand, his fingers cool from the condensation on the water bottle he's drinking from. "I'm Everett," he says. *Nice. He even has a hot name.* "You want to play a match, or did you just come to watch?" he asks.

I grin. "Oh, I never just watch."

Everett tosses me the ball, flashing me the mirror of my smile.

I enjoy the leather's firm, familiar grip in my hands. The ball feels sturdy, anchoring me to myself. It's reassuring, the feeling of remembering *this* is who I am—the princess who makes it look easy. No matter how hard I work or how much I sacrifice.

Twenty-Nine

FEELING MORE LIKE MYSELF, I head from the courts toward the strip of hotels on the shoreline. Dean texted me to meet him there. They finished with surfing, and they're grabbing something to eat at Emma and RJ's hotel.

Before I left, I gave Everett my number because he asked, and I figured, why not? Princeton isn't impossibly far from Newport. It was the perfect reminder that the world is full of guys to meet for simple, no-strings flirtation—harmless, easy fun, like sliding into the warm ocean only feet from here.

Combined with walking onto those courts, without any mention of my mother, it renewed my confidence in myself, clearing the clouds from my overcast heart. I'm over Dean. Really. Which means I can comfortably handle seeing him with RJ.

I walk with my head held high onto the hotel restaurant's patio, which spills onto the beach, with unobstructed views of the stunning orange-and-pink sunset.

When I spot Dean, however, he's sitting alone.

This is fine, I counsel myself. I certainly don't *need* RJ here. I'm perfectly capable of sitting with only Dean. Watching the sunset from this perfect view. Not permitting my steps to falter, I walk up to his table, where I drop down into the open chair across from him.

He's holding up his camera to photograph the sky's colors. His expression engrossed, he doesn't stop when I sit.

"Where are Emma and RJ?" I ask in greeting. I gaze out over the space, searching for a sign of them. The patio is flagstone nicely complementing the stately cream-colored edifice with walls wrapped in high-winding bougainvillea. Cocktail glasses litter the tables of vacationers in every corner. In front of me sit half-finished drinks and a basket of picked-over fries, like I only just missed Emma and RJ.

"They had to go pack before dinner with their family tonight and their flight home tomorrow," Dean replies, lowering his camera to look at me.

None of the playful tug-of-war from our drive down here sparkles in his eyes. He's . . . sad.

Recognizing that makes me wilt a little. Whatever he and RJ had was enough to leave him feeling like this.

"Are you okay?" I ask, preparing myself for whatever his answer might be. I genuinely want to help—another important reason I want to make sure I'm over Dean, I guess. I don't just want to spare myself heartbreak. I want to be capable of comforting my friend when he needs it.

Dean's eyes return to the sunset. "I'm fine," he says. "Only a rebound, right?"

Finally, it's the confirmation I was waiting for all day. And

I . . . wish I didn't know. The thought of Dean and RJ hooking up doesn't feel like the success I imagined. I sit quietly in front of him, suddenly not wanting to ask a million follow-up questions.

Dean sets down his camera. "I'm going to need real food before the drive back." His voice sounds sturdier, as if he's already hard at work putting this rebound behind him.

I understand the purposefulness in his subject change. He doesn't want to dwell on RJ's fresh departure. And neither do I. I reach for the menu propped up by the ketchup.

"No," he preempts me. His expression is nearly impossible to read, like fine print with water spilled on the page. "I don't . . . Let's just go somewhere else. I mean, if you want to come with me, that is."

I hesitate, wrestling with this seemingly simple suggestion. Under most circumstances, dinner with Dean in Santa Monica would veer dangerously close to date territory, but he's practically heartbroken over someone else right now. I assume it's the reason he's proposing leaving this restaurant. He doesn't want to spend the evening hearing the echoes of his parting conversation with RJ or looking up expecting to see his crush's face.

Which . . . means he's over me.

"Yes, let's go. I'm starving," I say.

Wordlessly, Dean packs up his camera, looking like he's not finished fighting his way out of his head. I follow him through the old-fashioned splendor of the Playa Del Mar's lobby onto the walk-street, where he leads me to the highway-spanning concrete bridge from the beach up to the city. From the direction we're heading, I immediately know where we're going—a food hall we first tried last year, when things were decidedly flirtatious between us. I'd thought it was casual then, not the beginning of something that would end almost as soon as it started.

Now is not *the moment to remember flirting with Dean*, I reprimand myself. He's not revisiting our past. He's focused on RJ.

While we wait for the crosswalk, I decide to speak up. "It's okay to feel weird after a rebound," I venture.

Dean looks over, meeting my eyes with wary interest. In the wake of the sunset, the sky remains orange yellow, with deep blue starting to descend from overhead. The combination lights him from behind, cloaking his features in twilight-colored shadow I can't help thinking perfectly complements his grudging curiosity. It looks like—well, like one of the photos he might take.

The streetlight changes. We walk with the crowd into the crosswalk spanning Ocean Avenue.

"It's confusing sometimes," I explain gently. "Like you have all these feelings still under the surface from your last relationship, and it all redirects to this new person." I realize my misstep when Dean's face hardens. Clearly, I'm off the mark. "Or it can be the opposite," I supply, quickly course-correcting.

"How so?" Dean's voice is gruff, but I hear its intrigued undertow. He wants to know more.

We reach the opposite curb. While one side of Ocean is emerald lawns where palm trees point toward the stunning view of the ocean, the other quickly changes to the low concrete and brick combinations of storefronts and restaurants.

The food hall where we're heading is just off the Promenade, two blocks from here.

"Sometimes," I elaborate, "you can feel *less* with someone new and worry something is wrong with you. That you won't ever have that flutter in your chest with anyone else. Like, when I started dating Jeremy, I felt like I was working out the muscles of liking someone again. It took conscious effort in a way non-rebounds don't."

Dean's eyebrows lift in what I'm pretty sure isn't amusement. "I didn't realize you considered Jeremy a rebound," he says levelly, "since you were the one who broke up with me."

I frown in instinctive confusion. "Of course he was a rebound."

Dean meets my eyes. New understanding lights his expression like the edge of the sun in the first seconds of sunrise—first it isn't there, but then it is, sending rays out onto the water. I drop my gaze, uneasy about his sympathy. I don't deserve it, not after I broke his heart.

I push past him to open the door to the food hall. "Want to do the usual?" I ask with feigned cheer, ready to end our previous conversation.

"Sounds good," he replies, following me in. "I'll take the right side, you take the left."

"Sounds good," I repeat stiffly.

I dart off, walking to the counter nearest me. It's a familiar routine from when we would come here last summer, and I pick it up easily. We divide the industrial-hip, high-ceilinged space in half, each of us picking up one item from every stand on our respective side, before meeting at one of the empty tables in the center of the room.

The result is our own personal potluck. Dean returns with two small tacos and a spicy chicken tender on a piece of white bread. I contribute chicken shawarma and ramen. We settle in, swapping dishes back and forth to sample each item.

It doesn't feel at all like last year, when we kept up a constant stream of conversation about everything and nothing. Right now, I don't even trust myself to make eye contact with Dean. We sit in the non-silence of the gratingly enthusiastic dance music echoing in the room, under the orange streaks of the colored overhead lighting. The decorations feel fun when you're *having* fun, but when you're not, they feel like they're rubbing the fact in.

Dean speaks up suddenly. "So what's next?"

I look at him over my taco, which is suffering from structural integrity issues. "We . . . go back to the house?" I suggest.

He shakes his head while elegantly capturing the perfect bite of ramen. "No. What do I do next in your lesson plan? Your get-over-you program?"

I clear my throat of taco, surprised. "Oh, I don't know that you need any more help there." In my head I can't help adding, *Right? It's really over now.*

His eyes slide off mine, straying over the restaurant stands. "Say I did, though," he replies slowly. "What would you suggest is the next step?"

I honestly envy the unreadable control in his voice. While Dean is ordinarily my opposite in this regard—frank and unreserved when I'm performing perfection—he's impressively keeping something under the surface right now. Setting down my collapsing taco, I wipe my hands before replying. "Take some time to reflect on the things you love about yourself," I say, remembering my afternoon alone on the courts with complete strangers, how I was the fearless, fun girl I aspire to be.

In the midst of my reverie, Dean scoffs. "Seriously?"

I flatten my expression. "Don't mock my program. Yes, seriously."

Dean says nothing for a moment. While he nods slowly, I notice something sly in the grin starting to pull up the corners of his lips. "How about you start me out?" he asks. "Where should I begin?"

I eye him skeptically, sensing a trap. "You're a wonderful friend," I say diplomatically.

Dean frowns with enthusiasm. "That's all? You can do better than that."

I know what he's doing, but I'll play along. Maybe he needs to hear this from me after I dumped him. "When you let someone in, you're sort of overwhelmingly charming, and for a consummate hipster, you have an earnest zeal for so much that makes you impossible to resist," I inform him with simple honesty, like I'm presenting him for show-and-tell. "Your enviable style could put you in front of the camera as well as behind it, and you're a great photographer because you see beauty in everything."

Dean blinks. He's silent.

I feel my face burn. Maybe I overdid it. Maybe I should have held in some of my long, rambling run of compliments. Yet, deep down, I'm glad I didn't. It's all true, and I hope he sees it in himself.

"Your turn," I say weakly.

"I kissed RJ," Dean replies immediately.

My head snaps up. My mouth clenches shut. Hearing it out loud stings sourly.

"But then I stopped," he goes on.

I can barely get the word out. "Why?"

Dean's gaze sears into me. "Because I was still only thinking about you."

Stunned, I feel like I've stumbled on a missed step and instead of falling, I'm flying, high off the ground, endlessly soaring. Is there such thing as an *upward spiral*? I can no longer quite hold on to every unexpected swerve in this conversation. More than stunned, though, I gradually realize, I'm horribly, guiltily *relieved*.

I can't find any words. Dean stands up.

"Soft serve?" he asks pleasantly.

I nod.

"You might want to start thinking more about that next step in your program," Dean adds. "From the look on your face, I imagine we'll both be needing it."

He heads for the soft serve, leaving me to stare at his back, wrapped up in too many conflicting emotions to even figure out how I feel.

Thirty

MY VANILLA SOFT SERVE was small comfort in the end. While Dean drives us home, I ignore him, staring fixedly out the window instead, frantically working through how to handle this. I need to return us to the almost harmless, pretty-much friendship we'd managed to recover. What I *cannot* do is keep treating him like a toy I pick up whenever the mood suits me.

For his part, Dean says nothing. He looks unworried, the rhythm of his fingers drumming on the Jeep's steering wheel joining seamlessly with the hum of the road under us.

When we get to the house, I speak up before he can get out of the car. "New rule."

Dean relaxes into his seat, smiling, watching me like I'm going to sing for him or do close-up magic.

I charge on, unflustered. "We need a chaperone. At all times."

He raises an eyebrow. "Why's that, exactly?"

I ignore his insinuation, and how it stirs warmth in my stomach. I face him, grateful for the seclusion of the empty driveway in the peaceful evening. "I thought we could handle dinner out together because you were over me and on to RJ. But if you're not, then what we just did was too close to a date."

"So you're saying you had a good time, then?" Dean replies immediately.

I frown. "Yes. That's the problem. We need to be more careful."

Dean's smug expression slips a little, revealing some of his disarming earnestness. "I don't understand. Do you not want to spend time with me?" he asks.

"No," I say gently. "Having a chaperone will mean I *don't* have to stop spending time with you. It's just, breakups always run a high risk of relapse." I remember Patrick's frustratingly accurate assessment, how often couples who split up return to each other. The prediction didn't sound like hope—it sounded like a warning.

Dean studies me. The porch light combines with the moonlight illuminating his features in the loveliest way. "Okay," he finally says. "We can have a chaperone. *Since* you clearly don't trust yourself around me."

Rolling my eyes, I get out of the car. At least he's being amenable. If he wants to cope by teasing me, fine.

As we walk up to the porch, Dean speeds ahead of me to block the door. "But, Kaylee," he says, staring me down, "if we're both not over each other, then I don't know why we're even doing this."

I manage to meet his gaze. What I can't do is answer him. I can't let him know I *do* have reasons, very good ones. I can't confess I don't trust myself, can't bring myself to say he deserves better. I don't want to open up this conversation, give him room to debate me and poke holes in my fading self-restraint.

So instead, I reach right past him for the door, not showing how the fact we're only inches apart now makes me feel. I just need to get inside, where we can't have these conversations because we won't be alone. We'll have six very nosy, very opinionated chaperones surrounding us.

Except when Dean moves aside in surrender and I swing open the door, the kitchen is empty.

We step inside. The floorboards have the audacity to creak, showing off the house's silence. I walk quickly, nervously, into the living room to peer out the sliding glass doors, and— nothing. No one is outside. No one is here.

Dean, who I realize has followed me, lets out a loud, de-lighted laugh. I grumble to myself. *I'm trying to do the right thing, and I don't understand why the universe is making it so hard.*

Facing Dean, I can't ignore how the house feels conspic-uously empty. Every inch of the overhead light illuminating the rosy wood of the cupboards, the white-painted doorways, the coastal details of the furniture seems to say, *See how no-body's here but you two?*

Dean leans on the edge of the kitchen island, crossing one leg over the other, looking entirely at ease. "Whatever could we do with all this privacy?" he asks with flourish. His eyes bore into me, practically searing in their intensity—in their reminder of everything I'm really trying not to think of right now.

I'm honestly considering locking myself in the car when, miraculously, I hear voices approaching the front door. The families pile in, filling the doorway with wonderfully loud conversation, having obviously just walked back from dinner. As I rush to meet them, relieved, I don't miss the look Dean gives when I pass him. It says, *You were lucky this time.*

Ignoring him, I approach Jessie. "Hey, let's do something fun tonight," I say, packing enthusiasm into my voice and hoping it doesn't come off like the emotional water-treading it very much is. "Do you want me to paint your nails?" I offer.

"I can't tonight," she says matter-of-factly.

I laugh despite my rising panic. Her frank deferral was incredibly cute. "Can't fit me into your packed calendar? Do you have other plans?" I press her playfully.

Jessie glances up, grinning hugely. "We all do. It's game night." She marches past me, calling out to her brother. "Dean, it's your turn to pick the game. Pick a good one!"

Dean's gaze lands on me. "Oh, I will," he promises.

Thirty-One

GAME NIGHT IS A hallowed Malibu trip tradition. Every year, everyone joins in one of our rotation of elaborate, often unconventional games. No sit-outs. No complainers.

They're invariably one of my favorite memories of each vacation. Last year, Terry and I teamed up to put on a massive scavenger hunt that included buried "treasure" in the yard. The year before, Lucy taught us how to play Mafia, and we were up past midnight interrogating each other.

In the living room with everyone, I wait nervously for Dean's pick, preparing for the worst. His creativity will not be my friend tonight, I expect. Perhaps he'll pitch some devious form of truth or dare, in which I'll have to take on increasingly ridiculous dares just to avoid admitting my confused feelings. Or—

"We're going to play hide-and-seek," he says.

I relax. I literally feel the muscles in my shoulders unclench, lowering like two full inches. This is perfect. I can

hide from Dean just like I planned, only now it'll be sanc-
tioned by the game.

"Partner hide-and-seek," Dean elaborates.

My stomach drops. Up go my shoulders. I should have
known not to keep my back turned on Dean's ingenuity even
momentarily. It's like wading in the peaceful waters of the
ocean only to feel something slimy brush your leg.

"While hiding, you have to have constant contact with
your partner," Dean explains to the room, "so the challenge
will be finding somewhere big enough. I'll also play music
through the house to make it a little harder for the seekers.
The last team to be found picks the movie tonight—unless the
seekers find everyone in under twenty minutes. Then they're
the winners."

I sweep my gaze over the faces of our family members.
Maybe everyone will hate this idea, some wild hope in me says.
Maybe they'll revolt. It would be the first unanimous over-
turn in the tradition of Freeman-Yu–Jordan Malibu Game
Night. History in the making.

Unfortunately, everyone looks like they're eating up Dean's
inventive new game. Darren rubs his hands together, eyes lit
up. Jessie does the little-sister thing where she eagerly looks
to Lucy to confirm her elder shares her excitement.

My dad raises his hand, his expression focused like he's
taking this very seriously.

He waits for Dean to call on him before speaking. "Jessie
has an unfair advantage," he points out. "She's small enough
to fit anywhere."

While Lucy smirks, Dean considers this. "Fair point," he concedes. "Lucy and Jessie will be the seekers since they have a size advantage."

Dad nods, satisfied with Dean's quick, reasonable decision-making.

"John, you and my dad are a team," Dean says. "Mom, you're with Judy, and Kaylee"—his eyes snap to me, and suddenly what was under the calm water wasn't something slimy, it was a shark, circling carefully—"is with me," he finishes.

I cross my arms, scowling.

All Dean does is shrug and smile.

Everyone disperses while Dean sets up the house speakers. He plugs in his iPhone, and seconds later the opening melody of the Cure's "Friday I'm in Love" cascades into the room at the volume of a loud house party.

"You two have to wait three songs before seeking," he half shouts to his sisters. "I'll start my watch then."

Lucy nods. "It's always Lord of the Rings or some old romance with Sandra Bullock, but not this year," she says solemnly. "This is *Mamma Mia!*'s year. Just you wait."

She pulls Jessie outside, where they huddle like football players on the last down with only yards separating them from the end zone. The parents are already off, both sets dutifully linking elbows as they head through the house.

Dean holds out his hand for me. He looks dreadfully, absurdly, impossibly smug.

"This is *not* a chaperoned activity," I feel compelled to point out.

He shrugs in mock innocence, his eyes glittering like campfire light. "Hey, I made my game night pick before you leveled these new restrictions on me."

I roll my eyes, not buying it. Ignoring his hand, I put one of mine squarely on his shoulder to steer him from the room. While he unsurprisingly complies, I realize something. Just because I have to play Dean's game doesn't mean I have to *win*. He's not the only one who gets to be devious. I'll make sure we're found first.

Leading him up the stairs, I notice how the music muffles our footsteps. I have to hand it to Dean, the game *is* clever. Under my guidance, we head into Jessie's room, where I'm confident Jessie will know every single viable hiding place. Forced to slide my hand to Dean's elbow, I lean down to look under the bed.

"No way," Dean says, shaking his head. "You can't fit your long legs under there."

Swiftly, like it's nothing, he grabs my other hand in his.

I ignore the feeling of his palm on my skin. The dizzying shock of sense memory, the half-welcome collision of now and then.

"How about—" he starts, leading me to Jessie's closet. The space is weirdly narrow and deep, so we've put a dresser inside. "Help me move this," he says, gesturing to the dresser, "and we can hide behind it."

I feel my nose wrinkle. "That's way too good a spot. We'll be stuck in there together forever."

Dean sighs, looking like he expected my resistance. "If

we win," he says heavily, "I'll throw my support behind *Miss Congeniality*."

I chew my lip. I do love *Miss Congeniality*.

Right then the first song ends, and a new one begins. It's "Dancing Queen." Dean's eyes fill with fear.

"Lucy hacked my Spotify," he explains urgently. "Kaylee, she means business."

I understand his concern. This development is, to say the least, ominous. Truthfully, I like *Mamma Mia!* What I don't like is how it inspires Lucy and Jessie to play ABBA nonstop for the rest of the trip whenever we watch it.

"Fine," I relent.

We start pushing the dresser against the wall to give us enough space to slip behind it—all while keeping our hips pressed together. It's awkward work, trying to get leverage without losing contact with each other. But when the dresser starts to budge, causing my balance to slip and my hip to slide off his, Dean's hand finds my waist, firmly tugging me back to his side. I stagger into him, my hand easily finding his chest in the soundless echo of a hundred faraway embraces.

No. I shake the feeling off. This isn't an embrace. This is nothing.

"Take a Chance on Me" is playing now, echoing insistently through the hallways. It's not a chorus I find particularly in-spiring at the moment. More like a vague threat. I give the dresser a final hard shove, and it knocks against the wall.

There's just enough room for us to inch ourselves past. Relenting, I drop my hand to hold Dean's, though I barely manage to fit into the nook we've created while keeping our fingers entwined. On the other side, we set to moving the dresser back into place. When the song ends, Dean pauses to start his watch timer, per the rules of the game. With the clock counting, he resumes helping me with the furniture, the scraping of the dresser on the hardwood floor now covered under "Super Trouper."

Relocating the heavy piece of furniture is doubly difficult without the room to maneuver we had outside of our hiding space. When we finally finish the job, I'm breathing hard, sweat starting to trickle down my forehead.

Our new hiding spot is dusty, nothing but several square feet of empty closet with a downward-sloping ceiling that leaves us even less standing room. There's no need to worry about keeping in contact in here—it's literally impossible not to be touching Dean.

I slump down the wall to sit on the floor, only to realize there isn't enough room for him to sit, too. I look up, checking on impulse whether he's reached the same conclusion.

He definitely has. "You could sit on my lap?" he suggests with what sounds like complete sincerity.

"Horrible idea," I reply. "Awful. No." I scramble to my feet, wincing when I knock one elbow into the dresser. I have to crane my neck under the ceiling's incline. This crevice wasn't designed for people—certainly not for volleyball players.

"Then I guess we both stand," Dean says pleasantly.

I'm mid–eye roll when we hear footsteps pound up the

stairs and the sound of Jessie singing loudly off-key to the music. Someone enters the room we're in, flipping on the lights.

Dean and I go still. I hold my breath. Sandra Bullock discovering the power of friendship while subverting pageantry stereotypes is on the line. What's more, while I would never admit it to Dean, my competitive spark flares to life.

Outside our hiding space, there's rustling of the bed, the curtains. As we stand unmoving, someone comes over to the closet. Even past the echoes of ABBA, I can hear the footsteps stop. The sound of scrutiny.

I meet Dean's eyes. For one moment, we're caught in shared suspense, the emotion written everywhere in his expression—the wild, electric friction of hope meeting fear—until the footsteps retreat again.

Leaving us alone. Without a chaperone. In a dark, cramped space.

I'm very conscious of everywhere my body touches Dean's. My ankle, the side of my thigh, my wrist. Necessities of partner hide-and-seek converted into hushed hints of something else, unintelligible urging whispers. I fight determinedly to ignore them, to shut off the charged current they send through me.

"How great would this be for making out?" Dean asks.

I narrow my eyes. "Remember when you were mad at me? Let's revive those feelings."

"I was never mad," he replies. "Not really."

I study him, surprised. He certainly *seemed* mad. But

before I can question him further, my mom's voice breaks through the moment. "Stay strong, everyone!" she shouts over the music.

Lucy's peal of giggling follows. "One down, two to go," she cries out delightedly.

The music gets louder. It fills the space, cheerfully menacing, which I'm sure is the intent. *The Battle Hymn of the Freeman-Yu Sisters.* In our small space, I shift slightly, finding room to roll one side of my stiff neck. I'm reaching the point where I could draw the details of our hiding spot from memory, the grooves in the floor, the small scuffs on the white paint of the walls. Unlike the light seawater scent of the rest of the house, our nook is heavy with the sweet smell of old wood.

When the second floor is silent again except for ABBA, Dean speaks up. "Look, you broke my heart. It wasn't awesome, but I forgive you. We can try again now."

In the dark, I can only make out the lines of his face.

"You shouldn't want that," I say quietly.

Dean is silent for a few moments. Somehow even the din of the music seems to fade into his hesitation.

"Maybe not," he suddenly says. "But I do. I still want you, Kaylee. I'll always want you."

My whole body flushes. My mouth goes dry. When Dean shifts a little in our confined quarters, I feel it everywhere, like warm summer wind rolling over my skin.

I try to turn away, but it's impossible without risking pressing my butt into him. These feet of space separating the dresser from the wall, our secret hideout, suddenly feel like the whole world. The song changes once more, but this time, I barely register it over the pounding of my pulse. I tilt my head, and Dean straightens. Without seeing him, I know his mouth must be somewhere near my neck. If I moved just slightly, I would feel his jaw against my skin.

When I breathe in, the hard line of his stomach kisses mine. I shift, hoping to dispel the hot charge between us. While I don't know if it's possible to generate static electricity without motion, I'm pretty sure it's what we're doing now.

My hand brushes his waist. Then I feel his fingertips trail up my forearm.

My breath catches. *I can't. I can't let myself feel this way. I can't hurt him exactly the way I did before.* The thoughts blare in my head like screaming sirens, but somehow they echo like they're far in the distance. I feel myself leaning into his touch, and the way he smells floods over me. Wrenchingly familiar, entirely distinct. His hair, loose from the knot at the back of his head, brushes my cheek.

"Dean . . ." I exhale. "This . . ."

But when his lips are centimeters from mine, the lights in the room flip back on, and something collides hard with the dresser.

"Found them!" Jessie shouts excitedly. She bounces up and down, using the dresser to push herself higher to peer over the top.

I'm equal parts relieved and frustrated. The shock of remembering the rest of everything—the families, the vacation, the past months—is welcomely grounding, but I'm . . . still not sure I want to leave the intoxicating possibilities of our private little world. Even the fact I'm a little tempted unsettles me enough I have to push past Dean to shove the dresser to the side and stumble into the room.

Immediately, my flushed face is hit with cool air. "Kaylee, wait," I hear Dean say behind me.

I half turn reluctantly, finding him sliding past the dresser, following me. Something searching is dashed on his expression. I wrestle with what the sight does to me. "Chaperone, Dean. Chaperone," I remind him.

"Why do you need a chaperone?"

The question comes from Jessie, who I face to find is scrunching up her brows inquisitively. Her eyes go from me to Dean. She's sweaty like she's been running from corner to corner of the house, but she's lit up with the excitement of seeking.

"When we go on field trips, our teacher says we don't need to be with the chaperone if we stick with our buddy," she explains, hurrying over her sentences. "Buddy system. Just stick together."

Lucy pops her head into the room. When she sees us, she nods sharply like she's in charge of fortifying the house from zombies or something. "Good job, Jessie. Let's move on."

Grinning ear to ear, instantly distracted from disputing me on the merits of chaperoning, Jessie skips out of the room toward her sister. "They're being weird," she tells Lucy.

Lucy glances from me to Dean. The smugness she lets slip

onto her face leaves me with no doubt she knows *exactly* why my cheeks are so flushed.

"They're always weird," she replies succinctly to Jessie, who scurries out of the room in search of hiding fathers. Her eyes remaining on me, Lucy softens, looking sympathetic while still proud of herself. "The moms are in the kitchen making popcorn," she says.

"Thank you," I manage.

Dean is silent behind me. *Good,* I remind myself harshly. Walking out of the room, I glance over my shoulder to shoot him a reprimanding look—wishing I didn't glimpse the signal fires lingering in his eyes or still feel everywhere his skin was on mine.

Thirty-Two

IT IS, IN FACT, *Mamma Mia!*'s year.

The parents cozy into the couch cushions while Dean stakes out one corner, the savory smell of popcorn filling the house. Dean's sisters, who decimated us in the game, finding everyone in under ten minutes, type the movie title into the search bar with near-religious concentration.

Even though I know the cinematic selection will mean nonstop singing from them for days, I'm too rattled by what almost happened behind the dresser to care. I pick the floor seat in front of the chaise longue so no one can see how distracted I'm going to be while the movie plays.

Except the girls don't let anyone passively enjoy *Mamma Mia!* They insist on singing along to every song, even doing some of the choreography on the carpet in front of the TV. Watching them, I can't help smiling. When Jessie exuberantly clambers up onto the long end of the sectional to match Meryl jumping on her bed in "Dancing Queen," my eyes follow her and wind up locking with Dean's from his place in the couch corner.

I let them linger, no longer feeling so stressed. The girls' joy is infectious, and I can't help lightening up. Dean holds my gaze, sending me a whisper of a smile.

The families have gotten fully into the movie by the end, singing the choruses and cheering when Meryl Streep and Pierce Brosnan get married. I'm laughing with water in my eyes as my dad dances with Dean's mom during the final credits. All the tension I've felt among the parents is gone.

It doesn't just feel good. It feels *normal*. It feels like our vacation should.

This easy warmth of family and fun is just how I remember every Malibu trip in years past. Maybe it took everyone a couple days to recover from me and Dean, but we did. We've found our way here from the rocky place where we started. We didn't mess everything up. *I* didn't mess everything up.

Sitting on the floor, surrounded by spilled popcorn, I start to believe we'll all be okay. As long as I don't divide the families again.

As long as I stay away from Dean.

I call on the firm reminders I issue myself whenever I head into practice exhausted, or start studying with aching limbs, or itch to snap at someone's degrading comment on social media. *It doesn't matter what I want.* This is what everyone needs. It's the right decision. What almost happened in hide-and-seek needs to remain an almost. It needs to stay where it started, in some secret place.

When the credits finish, I help my parents clean up. My dad is overdramatically stretching like the exertion of dancing exhausted him, which amuses my mom, who shakes her head playfully at him. She hums "Mamma Mia" while vacuuming popcorn off the carpet.

I decide now is as good a time as any. I'm all about making the *right* choices tonight, instead of following whims and insecurities. It's the way to be happy.

"You know," I say to my mom, "if we go to the same tournaments next year it'll mean we can share hotel rooms. We could have our own movie nights. It'll be fun."

I don't pause or waver. It's like it's not entirely me speaking, more like some noble, correct decision I'm letting flow through me. *I'm okay with this.* I've made myself okay with this.

Mom shuts off the vacuum and faces me, grinning. "Justice for *The Lake House*."

I match her smile for smile. "Finally," I reply. The word is a promise. Not just to enjoy Keanu and Sandra's ambitious and dramatic 2006 film—to figure this out within myself, day by day. To keep being okay.

While she resumes vacuuming, I head up the stairs. On the landing, I pass Terry and shoot her a tentative smile. I'm still not sure how to act around Dean's mom since she aired all her opinions about Dean's and my relationship in the uniquely uncomfortable conversation everyone had at dinner a few days ago. Nevertheless, in the quiet of my room, I double down on my resolve. Wherever I stand with Terry, I'll figure it out.

When I'm plugging my phone into my charger, though, I hear knocking. Opening my door, I find Terry in the hall. "Hey, you okay?" she asks, her expression inquisitive, verging on concerned.

The question flusters me. I'm not sure why Terry would wonder if I'm okay—unless she overheard my conversation with my mom. It's an unsettling possibility, rolling over my handmade fire like wind. I don't want my feelings on my mom coming out of retirement pried into, not by myself or anyone else.

I plaster on a smile. "Actually," I say, "there was something I wanted to ask you."

Nodding understandingly, Terry walks in, shutting the door softly behind her. The hall outside is silent, the girls having retreated into their rooms, tired from *Mamma Mia!* movie night.

Self-consciously unsure what to do with my hands, I slide one into the pocket of my shorts. I take a breath, then hear myself force out what's on my mind. "Why didn't you want me to date Dean? Was I . . . not good enough in some way?"

I'm not resentful, not picking a fight. It's the opposite. I *certainly* don't want to find out why because I want to get back together with Dean. It's so I can improve whatever flaw Terry found in me, smooth out my rough edges until I shine.

Terry's expression falls in horror. Within the coral-blue walls of my room, surrounded by my familiar wood furniture, she suddenly looks cornered somehow. "Oh, honey, *no*," she says gently, with desperate emphasis. "Of course not."

When I sit down on my bed, she comes over to sit next to me.

"I just see how much pressure you take on," she continues, searching out my downcast eyes. "You make being the perfect daughter to perfect parents look easy when I know it's not. And Dean, well . . . he's so close to your family. I knew a relationship with him would have even more familial expectations placed on it. On you."

I manage to meet her gaze. It's none of the many reasons I'd been spinning out in my head while lying in bed at night. I'm not sure how this one makes me feel. Relieved, for sure. But a little uneasy, too. I can't quite put my finger on why.

In my silence, Terry elaborates. "I want you to have fun and not worry about doing what people expect from you."

"I don't just do what people expect," I reply quickly, lightly indignant, like her comment unlocked some defensive instinct in me. I know where it's coming from, deep down— how often I've reminded myself it's not enough just to *do* everything right. I have to look like it comes naturally, too. Immediately, I think of all my resolutions downstairs. *It's different*, I tell myself. Terry is making it sound like I only dated Dean because the idea of uniting the families is expected, or like I only play volleyball to make my mom happy.

But neither is true. Dating Dean, volleyball—they're things I do despite the pressures of my family.

Terry pauses graciously, no doubt hearing the flicker of fight in my response. "I'm only saying, you can make your own path, too," she goes on slowly, like she knows she's wading into deep water. "Not every year needs to look like California with us between volleyball tournaments. That's the life your parents chose."

"Well, I choose it, too," I snap. Instantly, my cheeks flame. I don't understand how Terry's consolation is managing to touch every nerve in me.

Terry smiles weakly, but I can tell she doesn't quite believe me. When she stands, I inexplicably feel like I've failed some sort of exam. "I'm glad," she says. "I just want you to be happy. I love you."

I soften. "I love you, too."

When Terry leaves, I start getting dressed for bed. I realize I should have followed my own guidance—knowing the *why* doesn't help. I'm just as confused and anxious as I was when I didn't know why Terry disapproved of me.

I slip under my covers, frustrated, wishing I could have had just one night where I felt like I fixed vacation.

Thirty-Three

I'M **BACK IN THE** dark nook behind the dresser. This time, there's no blaring music. The house is silent. Still, my heart is pounding in my ears. My hands feel hot.

I know Dean is with me, despite the fact that I can only make out his faintest contours. His presence pulls me like gravity, ever-present, impossible to fight. I dip my head a little—and then a little more. His words play in surround sound in my head. *I'll always want you.*

His lips find my neck, and I let myself collapse into him.

The realities of the world slip out of focus, swirling into heated collisions of feeling. I wind my hands into his loose hair while he trails kisses up my neck, along my jawline, to the corner of my mouth. The sensation electrifies me until he leaves the soft skin of my cheek, hesitating, promising. My lips part, waiting—

Pounding on my door startles me. I jerk awake, disoriented, morning sunlight shocking my eyes. I'm not in the dresser nook. It isn't dark. Dean definitely isn't kissing me.

I'm wrapped in my sheets, my room heavy with the stagnant warmth of sleep. My limbs still feel soft with desire, but reality settles over me fast. *I was dreaming.* Immediately, I'm furious with my subconscious.

When the pounding starts up again, I pull myself out of bed to open my door and find—

Dean. Real Dean. Shirtless and wearing trunks, his hair down like in my dream and skimming his exposed shoulders. My brain catches on the confused nerves and synapses still firing, telling me this is who was just holding me, whose lips were about to brush mine.

His eyebrows rise. "Whoa, are you okay?" he asks. "You're, like, really flushed."

"I'm, uh—" I push my hair behind one ear nervously, then get control of myself. "I'm fine," I say, mentally congratulating myself for sounding it.

"Why are you ignoring my texts, then?" His question offers the first hint he's pretending the way I am. While his voice is casual, I can hear inquisitiveness straining in it.

Glancing to my phone on the nightstand, I notice the time. I slept in way later than usual. "I was asleep."

Dean's eyes sweep over me, no doubt finding pillow creases on my cheek, my hair rumpled and wild. I see it happen—the dark light of intrigue enters his expression, lifting the corners of his mouth. His unfortunately very dream-worthy mouth.

"Good dream?" he asks, his voice heavy with implication.

Hot embarrassment shoots through me. I should've thought this out faster. I should've said my phone died while I was doing morning yoga or something. "What do you want?" I snap.

Dean grins, delighted by my evasion. "Can I come in?"

"No. Chaperone, remember?"

"Oh, right," Dean nods philosophically, leaning on the doorframe. "Why do we need a chaperone again?" I put a hand on the door, ready to close it on him. Undoubtedly sensing his opportunity fading, Dean continues more earnestly. "Jessie, Lucy, and I are going to the beach. You want to come with?"

"I'll pass," I reply immediately. I do not need to be spending more time with Dean right now. Definitely not shirtless Dean.

He eyes me. "What, you have plans?"

"It's none of your business," I say. "Now, go get a chaperone for this conversation or I'll have to ask you to leave."

"I'll go." Dean pushes off the doorframe, lifting his hands in surrender. He lingers in the hallway, his eyes staying on mine. "Jeez," he adds, "must have been some dream."

I slam the door on his gloating grin.

From the hallway, I can hear him laugh, but I'm too furious with myself to care. Rules written on neon signs flare to life in my head. I *cannot keep* flip-flopping on Dean. Why do I have to have this persistent crush on a nice boy like him? Why couldn't I want to jerk around an entitled jock-bro? Why do I have to fixate on the sensitive, sweet artist I've known my whole life? It's unfair, really.

What I need is a Dean detox. A cleanse. I'll only put healthy things into my system today, no conflicted feelings or unwelcome wants. No Dean. I'm going to focus on myself. Which means meditation, a balanced breakfast, a group call with Bri and Leah. Maybe I'll even muster a run on the beach.

Inspired to start right now, I reach for my phone to text Bri. When my screen lights up, I find the messages I missed from Dean. The stack of them looks somehow precarious, like plates of fine china piled high.

Hey, are you up?

Beach day?

Are you ignoring me because you almost kissed me last night?

You can finish what you started any time.

Swiping them all away, I find one more message from an unknown number. I open it to read and thank the universe for this good fortune. *Change of plans.* This is even better.

I grab a bathing suit from my drawer and text my mom, asking if I can have the car today to drive to the Beach Cities.

Thirty-Four

I REMAIN EXCEPTIONALLY PLEASED with myself for my new plan. The whole drive to Hermosa Beach, I keep the windows down, my music blasting. Past Santa Monica and Venice, Vista Del Mar sends me down the coastline in one straight shot, the water shimmering on my right side. When I park, I scan the long beach, where I spot him immediately, shirtless, playing popcorn with one of the guys I recognize from yesterday. At the sight of me, he grins.

His text invited me to play here with him and his friends. Of course, I dove for the chance like I would for a spike into the corner of the court.

On Hermosa's soft sand, I play against Everett, although volleyball isn't the only game on my mind. I allow myself to smirk and eye him on every point we exchange. Honestly, my whole heart isn't in it. *Yet*, I remind myself. It's just like I instructed Dean—sometimes it's okay to practice interest until it sweeps you up.

So I practice, hard. I block Everett's spikes, putting our bodies close. I point at him before serving. I dive for saves, knowing my butt looks great when I do.

And when the game is over and I've won, I shake Everett's hand, holding on a fraction too long. He smiles down at the contact while I desperately coax the flicker of a spark in my belly higher.

Everyone starts packing up for the day. Lingering on the sand, with the rolling turquoise tide of the water in the corner of my vision, I finally check my phone. Unsurprisingly, I have a text from Dean.

Hey, where did you go?

I start to reply, then stop myself. Dean and I aren't together. I don't owe him any explanations on how I spend my time.

"You heading out, too?"

Turning, I find Everett smiling, still shirtless, walking toward me with his flip-flops dangling loosely from one hand. Despite his puffed-up posture, his voice sounds somehow small on the emptying shore. It's obvious what reply he wants.

I smile, focusing on his sandy hair, the way his grin forms dimples, or something like them. Close enough.

"Wasn't planning on it," I say, clicking off my phone screen.

"Good." The small victory doesn't diminish Everett's showy smile in the least. He stops inches in front of me.

I slant my head just slightly, so the movement seems innocent. "What do you want to do next?" I ask. The flirting is coming easier, which is nice—and suddenly, I have a miniature epiphany. I've found my answer, the irritating source of my unwelcome feelings. I'm not crushing on Dean again. I'm missing *this*. Flirting. Romance.

With Everett's eyes sparkling down at me, I don't think that'll be a problem for long.

"We could sit on the beach," he suggests. His shrug is comically un-casual.

I lead the way, smiling like I'm keeping a secret. Of course, there's nothing secret here. It's obvious neither of us wants to *just* sit on the beach. We walk down to the ocean, our feet sinking into the damp sand with each soundless footstep. Like we don't want to spoil the shine of anticipation, we don't speak.

Enjoying the delicious daylight of Hermosa Beach comes easily. The long stretch of white sand sloping down from the walk-street storefronts of the cheerful coastal town is one of the most beautiful beaches I've ever seen. Farther from the center of the city and its colleges, Hermosa is less touristy, the sand playing host right now to only one other set of volleyball players while locals ride bikes on the paved beachside path.

Everett settles onto the sand, and I sit down next to him, making sure we're close enough for our legs to brush. It's perfect. Rom-com-worthy, like I'm in my own version of one of the Sandra Bullock movies we didn't get to watch last night. A beach make-out in front of the waves after a great game of volleyball with a very cute guy. It's exactly what I need. Exactly what will get my head straight.

Neither of us says anything, because saying something is *so* not the point right now.

I eye him invitingly, leaning back on my elbows, which sink in like the sand was expecting me. Everett's posture shifts with mine—he moves closer, bringing his head down to mine, our shoulders knocking gently into each other. My heart is pounding, just like it was last night with Dean.

Except it's nothing like it was last night with Dean.

I close my eyes, hoping I can shake off memories of skin on skin and the smell of sweet wood. I need to be *here*. The Hermosa sun. The roll of the waves. Everett. Just because this is different doesn't mean it's not what I want. I want this. I want this. I definitely want this.

"Hey, so, want to hook up?" Everett asks, his voice close to my face.

My eyes flit open, fixing on the boy in front of me. Everett. *Yes*, my mind shouts, sounding like cheers mixed with marching orders.

"No," I say morosely.

My answer surprises me, and doesn't. Sighing, I stand on what is no longer my rom-com shoreline. It's just sand, water, heat—just somewhere I've found myself for the day. I don't want to hook up with Everett. I don't want this.

I only want to want this.

"I have to go. I had a nice time today," I say out of necessity, aware of how bewildered Everett must be. I don't look down, not needing to watch the predictable currents of confusion or hurt or indignation or whatever swallow the dimples in his smile or the sunlit sparkle of his eyes.

Instead I turn around, pointing myself in the direction of the parking lot. Of home. Unhesitating, I storm off, starting to feel absolutely furious with myself.

Thirty-Five

I DRIVE HOME IN stony silence, my knuckles white on the steering wheel.

The perfect sky irritates me the whole way. I'm usually the hugest fan of California's weather, the cloudless blue, the warm breezes, the glitter of daylight on everything. Not right now. Not when this very moment, I feel like a hurricane.

It's late afternoon when I get back to the house. The front door rattles closed in my wake as I march through the living room, ignoring the concerned glance from Darren reading on the couch. My footsteps hit every stair heavily. I feel like if I'm not careful, I might knock this place down. Category-5 Kaylee.

When I get to my room, I slam the door. *How could I mess this up so badly?* I had the perfect opportunity to get over Dean and I flubbed it. Now I don't know what I'll do.

While I'm pacing, enduring the taunting tranquility of my pastel walls, my door whips open. It startles me. I spin to find Dean framed in the white rectangle of the doorway, looking alarmed.

"What's the matter with you?" The question flies out of him. "You bail on me all day and now you're slamming your door?" He comes into my room and closes the door, sealing us in.

I don't feel compelled to point out this violates our chaperone rule. I don't want a chaperone right now. I want to unleash the wild winds in my head so I'm not the only one swept up in them.

"I didn't *bail* on you," I say, emphasizing the repetition ferociously. "Because we didn't have plans today. I don't owe you any explanations for how I spend my time. We're not dating."

From the clouds over Dean's expression, I know I've managed to distribute some of my furious mood to him. The problem is, it doesn't make me feel better—not in the slightest.

"I *know* we're not dating," Dean returns, scowling. "But we're friends."

"Right. Friends," I seethe. I'm conscious of how unlike myself this is—the pretty, polished Kaylee I work on being every day feels unfathomably far from where the cyclone in my heart is carrying me. What's happening to me right now is leveling every wall of my facade, shattering every window, hurling open every door. I don't recognize the girl fuming in the middle of her cute bedroom, but I have no choice but to be her. "So since we're just *friends*," I go on, "then there's nothing wrong with me meeting up with a guy intending to hook up with him."

Emotions crash over Dean's face. Jealousy, hurt, anger. I let them roll over me. It feels like sinking into a warm pool on a hot day, doing nothing to abate the heat.

"Well, I hope you had a good time," he says curtly.

"I didn't!" I explode. "I couldn't even kiss him."

Dean stills. The lightning in his eyes freezes. The thunder in his expression goes silent. Over the charged space of the room, he watches me like he's reckoning with something, or deciding something, until some sort of resolution settles over him. He steps closer to me. "Yeah, it sucks being turned down. Not that you have much experience with it," he says.

I laugh. The sound is nearly frantic. "I wasn't turned down. I couldn't kiss him because I wanted to kiss someone else."

Dean's mouth gapes open.

He understands. I know he does. He says nothing.

"Don't stop now," I urge him. "Ask."

He watches me. We're not in the hurricane winds now. We're in the eye of the storm. "Who did you want to kiss?" he gets out, quieter.

I drop my gaze to the floor, shame engulfing me. I've truly failed now. My silence is confirmation enough, and it's the only confirmation I can bear to give.

My gaze still pointed downward, I see Dean's shoes come one step closer to me. He's wearing one of his favorite pairs of Japanese leather sneakers even on this eighty-degree Malibu day. It doesn't surprise me—which is infuriatingly significant.

"Has the feeling faded?" His voice is even softer now. I want to shy from its gentle caress, and I also don't.

I look up. His expression is like hope restrained.

"Unfortunately, it's only gotten stronger," I whisper.

It's reckless. It's impulsive. It is, however, the only thing I can make my mouth say.

He closes the final distance separating us, his arms around me, resting on the edges of my shoulder blades. His scent is everywhere, his proximity overwhelming. I feel like I'm home in a place I hardly recognize. It makes no sense, and it's intoxicating.

"I tried. I really did," I say weakly.

"I know you did." He smiles a little.

The sight pushes me over the edge.

I grab his face in my hands and pull his lips to mine. Suddenly, for the first time in what feels like forever, I'm kissing Dean Freeman-Yu.

It's . . . *everything*. Everywhere. Within me, enveloping me, inviting me—we're no longer surrounded by the whirl of our own personal storm. We *are* the storm. Soaring, spinning, ever higher. I deepen the kiss, feeling my fingers clench sweetly when Dean finds my rhythm. He remembers how I like to be kissed, giving me room to set the pace, not pushing in until I open to him. Which I do, pressing my body flush with his, folding into him when I feel his hand find the curve of my neck.

I don't let go of him, reveling in every feeling I convinced myself had faded. They roar to life in my chest, as strong as they were the day I told him I loved him.

The day before I broke up with him.

I step sharply out of his embrace. "I can't. We— This can't

happen," I say, forcing the words out like I'm sprinting over shards of glass. "I can't go back and forth on you. It's not fair."

Dean looks dazed. I understand his reaction perfectly well. I feel like we're falling, plummeting from the wondrous height of the kiss. We haven't hit the ground yet, but we will.

"How about you let me decide what's fair," he gets out.

I chew my lip, which is the wrong move. It reminds me of what my lips were just doing.

"I want this," Dean goes on. "Do my feelings not matter to you?"

"No, of course they do. But I'm trying to be responsible," I insist, frustrated by how far out of my control this is spiraling. In my voice I hear how I'm not just explaining myself to Dean. I'm drilling this into my mind, my soul. *I can do this in every other piece of my life. Be responsible. Be considerate. I just need to do it with Dean, too.* "I shouldn't jump into stuff because it feels good," I say.

Dean grins at my phrasing, which I should have expected. In other circumstances, I would roll my eyes. Right now I'm stuck hating how charming I find the flirtation.

Then the humor softens out of his features. "What if we don't jump?" he asks.

I furrow my brow, feeling inklings of relief. Disappointment, too. I mean, he could have fought me on it *a little.* "Right. So we stop kissing," I say.

"No!" His eyes wide, Dean looks comically frightened by this possibility. "Just . . . what if it's *only* kissing? No label. Does that help? More of a hop than a jump."

Unable to stop myself, I laugh a little. While I expect to protest immediately, I notice how some of the pressure lifts off me. I let the idea of what he's suggesting sink in. If it's not a relationship, I won't have to worry about breaking up with him again.

No consequences. No pressure.

It's . . . perfect.

"If we're not getting back together, then we're . . . what?" I ask hesitantly, hiding my eagerness.

"This." Drawing me back to him, he kisses me.

It feels easier now. I let the freedom steal through me, the uncomplicated joy of just . . . kissing him. He smiles into my mouth, like he can feel how this is working. I quiet the questions in my head—how long this can last, if this is wise, whether it really avoids a breakup.

I can't think while Dean is kissing me. So I don't.

Thirty-Six

WE LOSE TRACK OF time, the afternoon slipping into evening while we make out. Dean has surprising stamina and an incredible attention span. He moves slower than some of my exes, but I don't mind. Not at all. It's more like he relishes each step so much he doesn't want to rush.

I relish them with him. While the light changes in my room, the shadows lengthening, the blue of the walls seeming to turn hues of periwinkle in the late afternoon, I follow him— or lead, when I want—from each perfect minute to the next. I'm floating on currents of happiness with no destination.

We never had sex in the months we dated, but we got close a couple times. Right now Dean isn't pushing to pick up where we left off, which is nice. He's content to be back at the beginning, and so am I.

Less content is my stomach, which growls mid-kiss. Dean laughs, and my cheeks heat.

"Hey, I wasn't planning on a marathon make-out when I

got home," I say in my defense. "I didn't do any conditioning. Didn't even carbo-load."

Dean pushes himself up from the bed. His eyes sparkle like he knows we're only putting what just happened on pause.

"Let's fix that," he says, extending his hand to me as I get up.

The house is quiet when we emerge into the hallway. Glancing out the window, I see the parents playing paddleball on the sand. I nod to Dean, signaling our path is clear.

We head downstairs into the kitchen. Despite the vengeance of my hunger, I'm . . . happy. I feel myself practically floating down each step. It's not the heartwarming happiness of winning matches or getting good grades or making everyone proud, either—this joy is weightless, gravity-defyingly sweet, like cotton candy fog.

In the kitchen, I head straight for the fridge, where I reach for the first thing in front of me. Cubed watermelon from yesterday. I pull the whole bowl out.

When I close the fridge, I find Dean leaning over the kitchen island, his eyes fixed squarely on my butt.

He betrays no sheepishness at being caught staring. "What?" he shrugs, lifting his gaze to my face with deliberate laziness. "I'm just practicing the skills you taught me. Checking people out. Imagining how things could go . . ."

I chew my lip, not wanting to show him how charming I find his cleverness or how flattering his attention. Despite the effervescent joy pervading me, in this moment, playing coy feels more fun. I turn away once more.

"Carry on," I say.

Starting in on my watermelon, I can practically feel his eyes on me. I hear a rustling and smile to myself. When his hands gently but firmly find my hips, I spin around, finding myself pinned between him and the counter. It feels right and full of promise, like stepping outside on the first day of summer. Not the one on the calendar—the first day it *feels* like summer.

"Watermelon?" I offer, knowing it's not what he's here for.

He shakes his head. The simple gesture makes anticipation prickle in my red-stained lips. Dean leans down, kissing me, strands of his gorgeous hair falling loose to tickle my cheek, watermelon sweetness shared on our—

The screen door slams open.

Dean only just has time to fly to the opposite counter when Jessie appears in the kitchen. She stops sharp, and I know Dean wasn't fast enough.

"What're you doing?" she asks innocently.

Nervously, I meet Dean's eyes. "Having a snack," I say with casual composure. "Can I fix you something?"

Jessie's expression turns skeptical. "You weren't kissing, were you? Are you dating again? Wait, are you getting *married*?"

Dean flushes, half panic and half genuine exasperation. "Jessie, you weren't even born yet when I said Kaylee and I were getting married."

She shrugs. "Yeah, but everyone tells the story so much, I feel like I was. So are you?"

"No." I scoff. "We were just—playing a game."

It's a horrible explanation. Out of the corner of my eye, I

notice Dean's eyebrows rise. However, it miraculously seems to satisfy Jessie, or maybe she just doesn't really care. Either way, she grabs a juice from the fridge and then runs out, leaving a trail of sand on the hardwood.

I don't dare speak up until her scampering footsteps have receded into silence. "That was close."

Dean looks like he's fervently thinking the same thing. "Unless we want to deal with six outside opinions on this, we . . . might have to be more careful." He grinds out the final words, like the idea of not kissing me whenever he wants pains him physically.

Honestly, I very much sympathize. However, I'm glad we're on the same page when it comes to the parents. The reason for the whole no-strings situation with Dean is me *not* wanting to have to break up with him again. If our parents knew what we were doing, I'd have to explain to them when this ends, which in a way would be just as bad. "Definitely," I say. "I mean, this isn't a relationship anyway, so there's no reason to upset the family dynamic all over again. Our parents definitely don't need to know we're hooking up."

Dean's smile doesn't slip, but his eyes sparkle a little less. While I feel like I've hurt him in some way, I'm not entirely sure how. This was what he proposed, wasn't it?

"I just mean this is new," I go on, reaching for some pleasant spin to put on whatever misstep I've made. "And we don't know how it's going to work. You remember how weird they were when we started only hanging out again. I know I can't figure anything out if I'm having to deal with their judgment."

Dean nods slowly, like he understands, or he's trying to. "This is about us, so we're the only ones who need to know."

"Exactly," I exhale, relieved. When something returns to Dean's eyes—warmth if not sparkle—I step toward him, then stop myself before reaching for his hand. The effort requires curling watermelon-stained fingers into my palm. "How about I meet you back upstairs in five?" I ask, still conscious of the screen door's ominous presence.

"Deal," Dean replies immediately.

He wavers like he wants to go in for a quick kiss but also thinks better of it. Leaning on the edge of the counter, he looks as if he's fighting gravity.

While I watch Dean head upstairs, I can hear my dad cheering outside. It jars me for a second—an electric reminder of the new precariousness I've managed to instill into this vacation—until I quickly get the feeling under control. It'll be fine. I can manage secrecy with Dean.

I just have to block out my family's voices so I can enjoy whatever this is. For a little while, at least.

Thirty-Seven

I FEEL RIDICULOUS. I mean, I've spent most of my time with Dean since we arrived in California, and what's more, we *already* dated for *months*. We haven't just had our first kiss— more like our fifty-first. We're not flushed with the new glow of going from friends to something else. This warmth I feel is familiar.

Yet somehow, I feel like I can't get enough of him.

It's made the past forty-five minutes practically unbearable. We paused the afternoon's packed schedule of making out only because we decided it would be better to head down to dinner separately. Less conspicuous. So while Dean went to hang out with the parents in the kitchen, I languished in my room, desperately bored.

Until now. I speed my steps down the stairs, unreasonably excited to see him. Jumping the final step, I bound into the kitchen, where I find Lucy setting the table. Dean is standing by the fridge, pulling out refillable glass water bottles. I stop short, giving myself over to the wonderfully silly feeling of how the person you're into reduces the rest of the world to a hazy backdrop. Dean's loose white button-down, the dark sable waves of his hair, the perfect cut of his shorts—they're my entire field of vision.

Closing the fridge, he catches me staring. His face splits into a grin.

I smile back. I'm literally unable not to. I feel my face making the expression before I'm even conscious of what I'm doing. So much for being less conspicuous.

"Dean, move!" Jessie shouts.

He startles, looking down to find Jessie at his side, trying to open the fridge door. She shoots her eyebrows up, reveling in her bossiness. While I blush fiercely, Dean laughs and steps aside.

The dads bring forth their "famous" chili, a recipe they purportedly developed in college. The smell of spice fills the kitchen, the sunset glaring through the windows. Getting everything ready for dinner, Dean and I find ourselves circling each other in a dance. It's impromptu, yet perfectly choreographed. We fetch bowls, napkins, glasses—each time finding new excuses to brush arms or move each other aside with a gentle hand on the hip. It's nothing anyone would notice, except us, of course. I'm hyperaware of every glancing contact.

When we all sit down, cramming around the oval table like one large family, I choose the seat across from Dean. It's the right decision. Very, *very* right. Every time I look up to find his dark eyes on me, it sends a warm chill down my spine. When he rolls up his sleeves to shred cilantro over his bowl, I know it's not only the spicy food responsible for the sweat springing to my forehead. I'm done for.

"Kaylee, some support here?"

My mom's voice yanks me out of my stupor. In the corner of my vision, I notice Dean silently laughing at how I'm the one caught distracted now. I dart him a reprimanding glance while struggling to process the pieces of conversation I heard but didn't pay attention to. It feels like the few times I've gotten called on in class when I was spacing out or surreptitiously focused on my phone under my desk.

"Sorry, I, um." I swallow. *Get it together.* "What about Lucy's tournament schedule?" I manage, miraculously coherent.

From the funny expression on Mom's face, I know instantly I've filled in the wrong blanks. "I was asking," Mom starts with patience I'm very grateful for, "you to tell Lucy she's really good and she shouldn't quit the club team next year."

I latch on to the lifeline. "Right. Right. You *are* really good," I say to Lucy in earnest. "If you don't want to play anymore, though, that's okay."

When my relief at having reentered the conversation semi-successfully fades, I notice Lucy's reaction. She's chewing her lip. In her seat next to Dean, she suddenly looks small for five-foot-eight. "I do want to play, but . . ." Her eyes flit to her mom, who's sitting next to me. Terry doesn't look pleased with how this discussion is unfolding.

"Judy, don't pressure her. She's just a kid," Terry says, frowning.

"I'm not pressuring her. I'm encouraging her," my mom replies with good cheer. I recognize the resolute quality in her enthusiasm. It's her coaching voice, the one that's supported me in countless backyard drills. "She's exceptionally good, and I just think it would be sad to throw that away."

"There's more to life than volleyball," Terry shoots back.

My mom shrugs. Her carefreeness seems intentional. "Obviously I know that," she says, recklessly flippant.

I watch them, feeling those rock shelves underneath us pressing into each other again, the tension increasing with decades of subtle shifts. It's unnerving, feeling them shudder out here, on our shared retreat. Like realizing we're vacationing on our own private fault line.

The dads exchange glances, no doubt understanding what I have. Something has got to give. It's clear this conversation isn't really about Lucy. Quickly, seamlessly, we've managed to move into much deeper rifts. The speed of it is unnerving, suggesting its own questions—why now? Years after Terry gave up volleyball, why is this churning to the surface?

It makes me uneasy. Seasick on solid ground. While the Freeman-Yus feel like family, they're not. If Terry and my mom finally let this pressure erupt, would there be anything to bring them back together? We could easily end up in Malibu next year alone.

"I think we need to reinstate an old rule," my dad says, and I feel myself exhale.

"Yes." Darren quickly jumps in. "No volleyball talk while we're on vacation."

Terry smiles, but her eyes are still hard.

"Agreed," my mom says. Like she's forcing herself, she faces the dads with an imitation of levity. "The chili is great, guys."

When Dean's foot nudges mine under the table, I refuse to look at him. Not right now. My head is still stumbling over the unevenness of my endless questions. It's no longer the moms' quiet conflict I'm snagging on. It's what my dad said. Just how often was volleyball a source of contention between my mom and Terry for the dads to have to ban the topic on vacation?

"I remember one time Darren tried to make it on his own," Terry says, the humor in her voice sounding slightly less hollow.

Dad looks betrayed. "Darren, how could you?"

Everyone laughs, and all the tension dissipates, like smoke out an open window. It leaves me wondering whether I'm the only one who remembers it. I sincerely doubt it—yet when I scan the four parents' faces, I see every sharp edge has disappeared under the surface of good-natured, entirely ordinary smiles. The conversation moves on, smoothing over the new cracks in the ground. I'm no stranger to hiding stress under easygoing expressions, but if that's what they're doing, they've got serious skills.

"It was the week you two were broken up. I was lonely," Darren explains in his defense.

Lucy straightens, looking genuinely curious as well as

glad not to be the center of conversation. "You broke up?" she asks.

This isn't news to me. My parents love to needle each other for their infamous one-week breakup when my dad was in college. Like Lucy, however, I'm eager for dinner table discussion to move in other directions. I watch my mom, still not quite believing how quickly she's composed herself.

She just rolls her eyes, smiling like she's enjoying the story's familiar patterns. "We *barely* broke up."

Dad looks skeptical. "That's not the truth," he interjects. "You even used the words *I think we should break up.*"

"And took them back less than a week later," Mom returns, like she can't believe she's having to repeat this for the hundredth time. "Still, somehow you *had* to bring it up at our wedding."

Dad shrugs grandly, unbothered. "Well, you put me through hell for that week."

"You put all of us through hell," Terry says, joining in. "I remember you told me"—she rounds on my mom—"it wouldn't get in the way of our friend group, but of course it did. I didn't even talk to Darren for that week, except for when he emailed me to ask what I thought John put in the chili."

"Wait," I cut in, something squirming in me. "Why did none of you talk if it was just Mom and Dad who broke up?"

"We didn't want to pick sides," Terry explains with cheerful resignation, eyebrows rising like, *What could we do?* "So the whole thing turned into an awkward four-way standoff."

The squirming in my gut constricts fast, clenching my

stomach in its coils. Suddenly, I'm in no mood for famous chili. Dean, for his part, has his eyes now firmly fixed on his cornbread.

"Yes, yes. It was a giant catastrophe," Mom replies dryly. "I won't ever do it again."

"Better not," my dad says, smiling at her. Then his gaze shifts to me. "Now you know why we were nervous when you and Dean dated. But turns out we underestimated you. We're all so impressed by how maturely you've put your relationship behind you."

I'm on the very edge of standing up to leave—faking sick, or producing some flimsy excuse of Brianna calling me. Whatever will get me out of this smiling snake pit. Only years of composing myself, of fixing my expression in place with seamless little screws, keep me sitting here instead, returning my dad's carefree grin.

"Glad you noticed," I get out through the guilt squeezing my lungs. To avoid having to elaborate, I spoon way too much chili into my mouth. If my dad weren't overly confident in his recipe, he'd definitely see through my tactic. Instead, he only smiles, proud of his culinary prowess.

When I've succeeded on not choking on the excessive beans or crying from the heat of the jalapeños, conversation has mercifully moved on. I haven't, though. My stomach won't settle. Won't let me ignore the precarious implications of my parents' story. They broke up for *one week* and it split our families apart. It's nothing short of a miracle we all survived Dean's and my initial breakup. If they found out what Dean and I were doing now—

I resist the thought. Giving in to my attraction to Dean is reckless, selfish, shortsighted. None of which are qualities I see in myself. Am I really willing to wager *this*, my second family, over a couple dizzying make-out sessions?

Tentatively, I meet Dean's eyes across the table. Maybe reality will have smothered the fire he lights in me. I desperately hope it has. I want so badly to look at him and feel nothing but guilt and the resolve to be better.

He turns toward me. His eyes are kind, his brow relaxed. The corner of his lips twitches up in a secret smile for me only.

I don't feel guilt. I'm not filled with resolve.

All I feel are the same hatefully delicious shivers racing up and down my whole body.

Thirty-Eight

OVER THE NEXT WEEK, Dean and I take home the Olympic gold medal for hiding one's non-relationship from one's family.

We don't conceal ourselves completely. We're smarter than that. We hang out casually in front of our families, lulling them into a false sense of our friendship. When they walk in on us alone in the kitchen, it isn't newsworthy. When Dean makes me laugh at breakfast, it's nothing.

And when we take one of the cars nearly every day to beaches that *can't* be seen from our parents' bedrooms, no one is the wiser. We come home, sandy and sun-kissed, and we loudly announce our arrival. At night, we watch *Miss Congeniality*, the entire Lord of the Rings trilogy, and *Mamma Mia! Here We Go Again* with the families, who couldn't possibly guess that when everyone goes to sleep in a few hours, I'll silently slip into Dean's room. Sometimes we make out. Sometimes we do more. Sometimes we just hang out, curled together on his bed, watching movies with the sound low and the subtitles on.

It's our unspoken agreement—neither of us wants to stay apart from each other for very long. I love feeling it silently reinforced whenever our eyes lock over some innocent dinner conversation, or when we cross on the stairs, or our hands collide over Uno cards or Connect 4 pieces.

I've failed, of course. Unquestionably. I'm not someone who fails, but in getting Dean over me—not to mention getting over him myself, like I diligently started back home in Rhode Island—I've failed like I never have before.

But right now Dean is the exception I allow. Every time I reassure myself *we're not back together*, I wrap our fling in layers of safety. It'll fade out. I know it will. It'll slip below the horizon before it becomes another problem between the families.

One week into our non-relationship, I'm sitting up in bed, evading questions about Dean from my groupchat with Bri and Leah. They're rightly wondering whether our weeks of proximity have changed things, but—I don't want to explain. I don't want the pressure or the feeling of expectant eyes on this wonderful new thing.

So I'm deflecting, firing off questions of my own. *Have you met your teammates yet, Bri? How's your internship, Leah?* Really, I'm killing time like I've done for the past few nights, waiting until everyone goes to sleep for my chance to sneak into Dean's room. I won't pretend the suspense of our little reverse *Romeo and Juliet* situation doesn't increase the heat.

I check the clock. It's nearly midnight, which is usually

when Darren—the last to go to sleep—gets up from the couch and heads to bed. I cross the room to my door, tiptoeing to keep the hardwood from creaking. When I crack my door open just enough to peer down the hall, I see the lights are off.

Just like yesterday, just like the day before, I let myself enjoy the way my heartbeat quickens. Grinning, I turn off my lamp, then silently shut my door behind me and dart into Dean's room.

Except I don't find him.

He's probably just in the bathroom, I figure. I sit down on his bed to wait. The gray comforter is rumpled slightly, not the neat way Dean makes his bed every morning, which lends some support to my theory. I'm smiling to myself, remembering the first time I came in here on this vacation, how very differently it went. Shaking me from the memory, my phone buzzes in my hand.

I look down, blinking in momentary confusion. It's from Dean.

I'm outside.

Curious, I kneel on the window seat to peer out, where, sure enough, I see him. He's lit up by the moonlight, standing on the shore, holding his camera up to the sea.

The sight fills my lungs with giddiness. I don't grab shoes—I just spring as lightly and silently as I can down the stairs and out the back door.

The night is California cold, only chilly enough to wake

my skin up. The sky covers the ocean in one even cloak of darkness. I walk down the white stretch of sand, heading for the figure standing only feet from the water. The moonlight is otherworldly, lending pearly detail to everything. It's quiet out except for the sound of Dean's shutter, which drifts up the shoreline in a series of calm clicks as I approach.

"You know I could totally see you from the house, right?" I say to him when I'm close. There's no need to speak louder than library volume, not when my words carry perfectly in the hollow night.

He turns, his face lighting up as it always does when he sees me. "Look at the moon, though," he says like he's pleading his case. "It's stunning. I had to come photograph it."

His eyes return half-impatiently to the horizon, like he hasn't yet captured whatever essence of the scene pulled him out of the house in the middle of the night. Like he's itching to grab hold of its fragile beauty before it turns into tomorrow.

Smiling softly, I stand beside him and face the water. With the ocean rippling in front of me, waves gently rolling white foam toward shore, I try to see the evening the way Dean does, the way his photos will render every shimmering detail. The water is the night inverted, the stars stretching ever deeper under the surface. It's beautiful, but I know when I see Dean's shots, they'll have brought out something I didn't notice.

He has a gift. Seeing it in use reminds me of our conversation about passions and careers. "With everything that's happened," I venture softly, "we never really talked about how you felt photographing the wedding."

Dean lowers his camera. Even in the ethereal near-darkness, I catch the sly gleam in his eye. "By 'everything that's happened,' you're referring to how your mouth has been glued to mine for a week."

"Please." I scoff, hoping the night hides the flush in my cheeks from the mere reference to this week's extracurriculars. "Like it's such an inconvenience to you."

He laughs. "You are extremely inconvenient, and I wouldn't have it any other way," he replies.

His voice is like Pop Rocks—first sharply sizzling, then pure sweet. I could melt into the sand right here.

He trains his eye back on the ocean, like he didn't just threaten to liquefy me with highly concentrated flattery. "But about the wedding," he goes on. "It was fun. I'm not saying I'll never photograph anything professionally. But it didn't change my mind. I don't want photography to be my career. This"—he gestures to the empty beach and the two of us—"is how I want to take photos. No pressure. No expectations. Just me and my camera and my favorite inconvenience."

I grin, no longer hiding how charming I find everything he's said. His self-knowledge, his confidence, his flirting.

I realize he's like Terry, both of them choosing not to make their passion into a career.

Dinner the other night flits into my head, the moms' brittle back-and-forth over Lucy. Terry's decision to keep her passion out of her professional life has become a wedge between her and my mom. I refuse to let it become one between me and Dean. Just because we see this differently doesn't mean *we're* different. I know art and sports are often seen as opposites. Are they, though? Dean and I both have highly personal passions that come with unique risks and rewards.

"I understand," I say sincerely. "I may not see it the same way, but I know what you mean. Being an athlete means putting my body—myself, really—up for everyone's scrutiny. It's . . . not always an awesome feeling. Art is the same," I explain, watching the water. "While it might not be your body, it's personal to you. I get not wanting to share it with everyone."

When I finish speaking, I find Dean's no longer looking at the ocean. His eyes are on me, his camera held close to his heart.

"Yes," he says, his voice breathy. "Exactly. Do you . . . ever find it's too much?"

I snort. "Sure. Whenever people comment on my thighs or my body type."

I wrap my words in bluster, but it doesn't help. I don't know what hurts worse—strangers on the internet criticizing my shape or coaches and nutritionists warning me about my *problem areas*. When I continue, I bare what I'm feeling to the open night.

"I do wish I could keep my body and my sport separate. But ultimately . . ." I swallow, feeling the way my heart holds on to what I'm going to say next. The unshakable honesty of it. "This is *my* choice. I like letting people know me on social media. I like that I might inspire people, or even that I can just give someone the joy of watching a great game."

Dean turns his whole body to face me now, like what he

wants to say is important. The moonlight shining on him makes his skin glow, softening every line, illuminating every facet. It's impossibly lovely.

"I want you to know that I respect that about you so much," he says. His voice is low, heavy with sincerity.

I feel part of me grow shy from such intimate praise, but his words warm me too much for me to retreat. It's like slipping my feet into the hot sand of the day—first the searing of exposure, then the perfect comfort of underneath.

Reaching for the flicker of strength it lights in my chest, I face that vulnerable spot in me head-on. "Would you take some photos of me? Some that are only for me?" I ask, lifting my chin up. "Only for *us*. A piece of myself I won't share with anyone."

Dean's eyes remain fixed on me, his expression silently reverent. I wonder how I look under the stars. If the same otherworldly sheen lights the skin a million voices have sometimes made me question.

Slowly, he nods.

I give him a nervous half smile. Then, fully clothed, I walk into the ocean.

The long T-shirt I wear to bed floats up to the water's surface. The waves swirl the shirt's folds, the movement of the tide soaking me higher up my back. With the perfectly cool sea surrounding me, I'm weightless. I spin, enjoying the feeling of fabric and moonlight and water on my skin. I hear Dean walking into the ocean, the swish of his footsteps joining with the inconspicuous sound of his shutter starting to click.

Until it stops. I turn to face him, finding his eyes are on me, not on his camera's view. Like he can't look away from the sight in front of him.

I smile. A real smile. Not the close-lipped one I splash on social media. I don't need to see these photos. Knowing they're being taken, knowing this is being preserved, brings new magic to the moment.

Dean lifts his camera once more. I turn back toward the horizon, feeling radiant.

Eventually, he returns to the shore to wrap his camera in his hoodie and drop it off in the sand. From the water, I follow his every movement, not bothering to disguise my interest. He strides back into the ocean, still in his shorts and shirt. When he reaches me, I submerge myself deeper, letting my collar slip beneath the surface.

Under the water, he reaches for my leg and pulls me firmly toward him. I make a wordless, delighted noise, not caring how nakedly happy it is. Dean's movement carries me forward, my own personal riptide, and I wrap my legs around him.

He brings his mouth to mine. When we kiss, our clothes wet and sticking to our skin, it's perfect. We sway with each other in the sea, and a quiet realization surfaces from the depths of my heart.

Our promise of a non-relationship is shallower than this shoreline.

Thirty-Nine

THE FAMILIES DECIDE TO take a hike the next day. Dean and I bow out, ostensibly for different reasons. Me because I want to train, Dean because he wants to edit photos. Easy, ordinary explanations.

Dean wasn't lying. I definitely was. When the cars leave the driveway, we indulge in the privacy, lounging in Dean's bed while he pulls up the pictures of me from last night. I can't fully comprehend how different the girl in them is from the summery Kaylee Jordan of social media—how the pale light drew out my few freckles like the stars reflected on the water surrounding me, how the moonlight shimmered on my hair like mercury. I'm not sure whether I don't recognize this girl, or whether I do in ways I never have before.

Some of each, maybe.

Dean doesn't do much editing—he never does, I've noticed, preferring crisp realism over dramatic saturation. Still, his touches draw my eyes to new colors, to details I wouldn't have spotted otherwise. With each move he makes, I feel the photos coming closer to how the moments in them *felt*, not just how they looked.

I move to sit up behind him, resting my head on his shoulder while he works. It's quietly fascinating to watch how effortlessly he manipulates the images on his laptop. I feel overwhelmingly grateful I'm one of the people he's willing to share his art with.

"That's very distracting, you know," he murmurs, his eyes not leaving the screen.

I snake my arm around his stomach, feeling him shiver as my hand lowers. Smiling, I press my nose into his neck, making him groan.

He snaps his laptop closed suddenly, then pulls me down with him so we're lying with me propped up over him. My hair drapes down in waves, pooling on his shoulders. With the same quick hands he had on his camera's shutter last night, he deftly unties the front of the wrap dress I'm wearing. It falls open, revealing the bra I picked out specifically for this possibility.

His eyes roam over me while he pushes my hair behind my ear. With him staring up, the same wonder I saw in his eyes when I found him looking at the moon over the water, something flickers to life in me. The same overwhelming, impossible warmth I felt once before. Recognizing its return nearly steals my breath.

I curl my fingers around the collar of his shirt. Maybe— *maybe* if we keep this between us, if we keep it from our families, from expectations and spotlights and comparisons, this time I won't lose it.

It's like Dean's art. Does something beautiful *have* to be shared with everyone? Isn't there something more precious in privacy? In holding this piece of us back from the world? All I need is for Dean to feel it. No one else.

Dean's voice floats up to me softly, pulling me from my thoughts. "Why are we pretending this isn't real?"

Little shivers slink over my skin, not just from his near whisper—from the question itself. My answer slips out of me too fast for me to second-guess it. "I don't know."

It feels like defeat and victory all at once. Everything seems to stop, like the very rotation of the planet is pausing for this private moment in his room. I feel like even the waves in the ocean outside must be suspended midair instead of crashing.

"I think it is real," I continue on into the sunlit quiet.

Dean swallows, his eyes reaching, searching, daring to hope. As if he's ready to restart the world. "Then are we . . . ?"

I bring my mouth to his, on the verge of whispering *yes* against his lips. I feel safe here, like I did in front of his camera. Kissing him playfully, I line our bodies up and lower myself slowly. His hand skims down my side, pressing my hips harder to his, making my heart pound with the crashing of my imaginary waves. When his fingers glide to the skin of my thighs, I exhale, or Dean does, or we both do, one shared breath—

The door flies open.

I rip my mouth from Dean's. Everything happens fast, and yet I'm aware of every frenetic millisecond flying past us. Simultaneously, we whip our heads to the door, where Jessie is watching us, open-mouthed.

Delighted vindication flickers into Jessie's eyes. I feel my jaw start to drop just like hers.

"I knew it!" Jessie full-on shouts, turning her back on us. "They *are* getting married!"

I wouldn't be more shocked if Dean's room physically collapsed, the walls falling in. I don't breathe. My limbs won't cooperate. I'm frozen in place—in the worst possible position. With the moment dragging on, my thoughts catch on the utterly unimportant detail of how we didn't hear the car coming back so soon. Did they forget something? Did they—

It doesn't matter. They're here now.

Like groping for shipwreck driftwood, I search frantically for how we'll explain ourselves, right up until all four parents barge into the bedroom.

Forty

SCRAMBLING OFF OF DEAN is my first mistake. It leaves my dress hanging open, exposing my carefully chosen underwear to our parental onlookers.

With one glimpse, Darren immediately walks out of the room, while my dad violently slams his eyes shut. "Kaylee!" he shouts. I recognize very distantly that he's going for stern. The exclamation comes out closer to a yelp.

"Get out?" I shriek in reply.

"What's going on here?" Terry asks, pushing to the front. This only requires effort because *five other members* of our respective families have congregated in the hallway—Lucy having joined the crowd with Jessie, peering in like birdwatchers.

I fumble with my dress, finally resorting to just holding the front closed over my chest when my sweaty fingers can't manage the ties. "It's not what it looks like," I say. "It's nothing."

Dean's head swivels toward me, and immediately I know

I've wounded him. But we haven't even finished articulating what we are to each other yet—does he really expect me to tell our parents before I've told him? I close off the questions, forcing myself to shut down what the painful swirl in his eyes makes me feel. I'm in survival mode. Right now I'll say whatever I need to get everyone out of this room while I'm still half-dressed.

Fury lights up Terry's eyes, but it's not me to whom she directs her words. She rounds on my mom. "We never should have come. I *told* you this was a mistake. We shouldn't have put our kids in this position," she says, her voice like flattened steel.

My dad, eyes remaining firmly closed, waves his hand in Dean's and my general direction. "You can't honestly blame *us* for this."

"I blame all of us," Terry replies without hesitation. "We were too focused on ourselves, on our traditions, on our perfect foursome to make even a single sacrifice. We were being selfish." Her face is red, her hands shaking.

The force of her reaction is startling enough for me to momentarily forget my mortification. I've rarely ever seen *my* parents this mad, not to mention someone else's. While I'm obviously not too naive to forget parents are *people*, this is a harsh wake-up call.

Dean gets up and, with downright impressive presence of mind, manages to step past me, looking halfway composed. "Look, I know this is awkward, but we were being safe, so there's really no reason to be upset."

Hesitantly opening his eyes, my dad looks relieved to note the state of my dress. "I should *hope* you were being safe. How long has this been going on?" he asks.

I study Dean's face, watching stone close over his expression. "It doesn't matter," he says. "Kaylee and I aren't serious. Like she said, it's nothing."

Unable to control my reaction, I wince. He's not just repeating my words. He's rubbing them in, staining each syllable with new venom. While it makes me itch to explain myself, I can't—not here, in front of an audience.

"That's obviously not true, but it ends now," Terry demands.

"Terry, we can't seriously forbid Kaylee and Dean from being together if that's what they want," my mom says. Her face is the competitive mask I've seen in plenty of Olympics videos, her voice edged like Terry's. I'm honestly surprised to hear my mom support us, what with how often she discouraged me from dating Dean originally, but I get the sense this might be more about opposing Terry than defending us.

"*You* were the one who first raised concerns when they started dating, and you were right. We never should have let it happen," Terry fires back, facing my mom once more.

It's the ugly parallel of when I've seen them play each other on opposite sides of the volleyball net, exchanging judgments like spikes in this high-stakes parenting match. Lucy steers Jessie gently out of the doorway.

"When one of them inevitably gets hurt," Terry continues, "we'll either have to cut each other out of our lives completely or rip open their heartbreak every time we bring our families together. Just like we did to Dean when we agreed to come on this trip."

I straighten in surprise. I didn't know the Freeman-Yus coming to California this year was ever in question. The way my parents framed this vacation—their inviolable plan, with no room for questioning—made me feel unreasonable for even thinking Dean's and my breakup might matter. For not just smiling in service of what everyone else wanted.

"It was the wrong call. But now we need to put our kids first," Terry finishes firmly.

My mom bristles, color flooding her cheeks. "You think I don't put my kid first?" she snaps. "Why? Because I'm a professional athlete?"

I hardly dare to take a breath, afraid to even be noticed at this point. Until this trip I hadn't even known of the deep rift running underneath my mom's decades-old friendship with Terry. Now, right in front of us, they seem ready to split the chasm wide open. I'm scared of what will get sucked in. I'm scared of what will get spat out.

"You're not serious," Terry replies incredulously. "Judy, have you even spared a thought for how Kaylee feels about you coming out of retirement right when she's trying to make a name for herself?"

Mom blinks, thrown off by this turn in the conversation. "What are you talking about?"

"Come on," Terry begins, sounding disappointed. "You know how much Kaylee is already compared to you. Do you think this will help? Now it's not just your record she's pitted against. You could very well win spots and trophies that could have been hers."

My mom's response is immediate, her words coming faster. "You're not her mom. I am. She's fine with it."

Terry's eyes dart to me, something almost apologetic in them. "Kaylee would say anything to be enough for you. It doesn't mean what you're doing isn't hard for her. I may not be her mom, but even I can see that."

The words land like punches. I watch my mom's whole demeanor shift, her anger flickering. She looks—she looks like I felt when she told me she was coming out of retirement, stuck on the mountainside together. Like her whole idea of the future, our future, is realigning in one sharp flip. She searches my face, trying to read the truth of what Terry's said on my features. I want to speak up, but I don't know what to say. I don't want to take a side in this fight, don't want to make this worse.

My mom turns her attention back to Terry, new stiffness in her features. "Don't take your regret for walking away from your dream out on me," she says, her voice deathly low.

The whole room goes silent. My dad's face falls. I have the sudden urge to reach for Dean, like I know this could really be the end for our families.

Terry collects herself, her eyes going cold.

"Dean, pack up your things," she says slowly, still looking at my mom. "Then help your sisters. We're leaving."

As suddenly as she entered, she walks out.

Seconds later, my mom does the same.

Neither of them even acknowledges the ostensible reason for what's happening right now—us. In the empty silence, the wake of their swift exits, I feel the twisted reprise of what I did when it was just me and Dean. Like the world has stopped spinning, now for entirely different reasons.

I hear his voice over my shoulder, horribly hollow. "You should probably go, too," Dean says.

I want to reply, but my dad is still in the room, looking uncharacteristically not sure what to say next. No matter what, I refuse to discuss my splintering relationship status in front of him. When he walks out, gliding one nervous hand through his hair, there is nothing I can do but nod to Dean and follow my dad.

In the hallway, I softly shut the door behind me. The handle clicks loudly in the stillness of the house, leaving me feeling like I'm closing something off between me and Dean.

Forty-One

I WATCH FROM MY room while the Freeman-Yus load up their car. The idyllic scenery cuts in contrast to what's playing out—the hibiscus flowers out in front of the house looking garish next to the procession of parents hefting luggage into the trunk under the oblivious sun. Dean's sisters wait by the car door, looking lost in the driveway's greenery. Lucy hides her confusion guardedly. Jessie doesn't.

Dean hasn't joined them yet. I wait, expecting that surely he will come by my room and say *something* before going. With my door left cracked open, I listen with every passing second for sneakered footsteps in the hall.

But when he emerges from his room with his two duffel bags, he walks quickly to the stairs without stopping.

First, I'm hurt. Each of his footfalls on the steps lands like something heavy enough to leave bruises. We were really on the verge of something before the parents interrupted us— something real. I'm stuck, standing by my window, wrestling with my helplessness, fighting to melt my ice-locked limbs.

Then the anger steals in. While Dean's parents might be forcing him to leave, nobody forced him to respond the way he is right now. How could he be ready to throw this away because I didn't react flawlessly to family members walking in on me half-dressed? Couldn't he cut me just a little slack? Don't I deserve it?

No, of course I'm expected to be perfect.

I kick my door shut. *I don't care*, I instruct myself fiercely when I hear the sound of the Freeman-Yus' car leaving the driveway, dirt grinding under SUV wheels.

"Kaylee?"

My dad's voice comes muffled through my closed door. I groan, hand rising to the pre-migraine sensitivity pooling in my forehead. The last thing I want to do right now is discuss how *safe* Dean and I were.

"What?" I ask flatly.

"Can we talk?"

I exhale slowly. "Do we have to?" I grind out. "If this is about my sex life, I'd rather—"

The door opens slightly, revealing part of my dad's face. "That's none of my business," he replies. His dismissal of the idea hits me with immediate relief. "I want to apologize. Can I come in?"

Wordlessly, I nod. He walks in, his posture disarmingly humble—hands pressed palm to palm, contemplation etched on his face—and sits down at my desk.

"I'm sorry if all our comments about you and Dean made you feel like you had to hide your relationship from us," he says slowly. Despite my headache starting to fade, I watch him hesitantly, waiting for the other shoe. While my dad isn't domineering, John Jordan is not exactly the world's foremost practitioner of self-doubt. "I'm getting the sense you and Dean have been . . . whatever you are for a while now," he continues.

"Yeah. A week," I reply, still wary about the direction of this conversation.

"So we fucked up. I'm sorry," Dad says.

I feel my eyes widen. It's an unprecedented admission from him, head-spinning in how out of character it is. Watching him lean forward in my desk chair, staring into the center of my floor, hands resting on his knees, I don't reply.

He doesn't look like he expects me to. "You clearly like him, and everyone having an opinion on you two made you feel like you couldn't be honest about it," he goes on, roughness in his voice, like love mixed with regret.

"I mean, obviously we were right to hide it," I say, my remorse rising straight to the surface. "Terry and Mom are never going to speak again."

"You're not responsible for your mother's relationships, and I won't let you put that on yourself." He looks slightly surer of himself now, his voice confident and definitive.

It bothers me. He can say that because it *should* be true, but that doesn't make it true. "Oh, so you think if I call a family meeting and tell everyone Dean and I are hooking up, be *honest*, the Freeman-Yus will come back and everything will be fixed?"

Dad frowns. His eyes slant to the emptily gorgeous day outside my window. "I mean, maybe not *right* now," he says measuredly.

"The thing is, I get it." I charge on, recklessly chasing the ugly contradiction I'm feeling, half shame, half righteous indignation. "If I date Dean and dump him again, it'll just drive a bigger wedge between us all. It's like you said. I have to be responsible for my actions." I weigh emphasis on my final words, wishing I could communicate how heavily they lie on me.

"No." My dad shakes his head. "The only people whose feelings you have to consider are you and Dean."

I spare him a flat look. "Where was this philosophy at the beginning of the vacation?"

A hint of humor flits into the shadows in my dad's expression. He shrugs. "Yes, your father's not perfect. Revel in my mistakes."

I laugh, and it makes me feel better. My dad smiles like he's won something, which I guess he sort of has.

"That cat's already out of the bag anyway," he goes on. "If you and Dean want to be together, you should. Besides, I don't think interfamily relations could possibly be worse."

I open my mouth—then close it.

"You do want to be together, right?" he asks. He searches my face with real concern, catching me off guard. While I've never felt like my parents didn't care about what I wanted, the directness of the question still feels subtly unfamiliar.

I swallow, my nervous heart picking up speed. "I . . . think?"

Dad groans, undoubtedly enjoying himself now. "Well, what are you doing talking to me? The only person you can figure it out with is at the Shore View Hotel right now."

I blink. "How did you—"

"I may have heard Darren and Terry discuss it while they

packed." He stands up from my desk chair, stretching generously, looking pleased with his possession of secret knowledge.

I stare past him, chewing my lip, my mind racing. New possibilities meet me like the water rushing up the shore with each wave. We can pick up where we left off before we were interrupted. I'll tell him what I meant to. Like my dad said, the damage is done. I might as well give in to my worst impulses.

The more I lean in, the more I find myself loving the idea. I can be selfish. I can ask for Dean back even if it's not a good idea. I've already wrecked our families, and I'm hurting Dean regardless, right? Either I'm hurting him by diligently insisting I don't want a relationship—or I'm hurting him by letting us be together until we've run our course.

Why not do what feels good for once?

With this wonderful new recklessness firing through me, my eyes snap to my dad. "Can I—"

"Car keys are on the counter," he answers my unfinished question. I'm getting up when he goes on, his voice a little sterner. "Oh, and, Kaylee, I meant what I said. You're not responsible for everyone else's expectations."

Rather than reach for the doorknob, I pause. I hear the solemnity he's putting on his words—he wants me to listen. He wants to feel heard.

Even though I don't believe him, I nod.

Forty-Two

DEAN PROBABLY HATES THIS hotel.

The Shore View has none of the stucco stateliness of the Playa Del Mar, none of the natural splendor of Malibu. It's loud, large, and incredibly crowded. Edgy parents escort dripping children down the tiled hallways past the shops in the entryway, where guests cycle endlessly, picking up sunscreen or souvenirs. I don't need Dean's eye to know the hotel's design is not exactly creative—plastic houseplants pop out of low rectangular planters everywhere imaginable, while in the high-ceilinged lobby where I'm standing unframed photos of seashells decorate the turquoise walls.

Only the breathtaking Santa Monica ocean, the shore view of the hotel's name, past the outdoor pool deck saves the experience. I watch the shimmering currents, trying not to tap my foot on the gray stone.

When I texted Dean asking if we could talk, he told me he didn't have much privacy and his mom wasn't in the greatest mood for guests. He said he'd meet me here, in the lobby.

It isn't the best place for a heartfelt reconciliation. But this doesn't have to be perfect, I remind myself. It *isn't* perfect. Our families won't speak to each other, and this is ultimately a redo of a relationship that failed once and will surely fail again. It's far from perfect.

The elevator dings. Dean emerges, stress etched into his elegant features and hair bun in disarray. Even so, despite his haggardness, seeing him is like the ocean outside. One small, stunning relief in the midst of everything else.

He reaches me, hands in his pockets. "Hey," he says, sounding tired.

"Hey," I repeat, then start right in, not wanting to miss another chance. "I'm sorry I said we were nothing. We're not nothing. Or at least, I don't think we are."

He straightens, but I'm dismayed to see no spark of hope or excitement in his eyes. "I don't blame you for what you said in front of our parents. It was not an ideal situation," he offers, using the delicate understatement one reserves for complete fucking disasters. "It's . . . You know, this whole week, I've been accepting whatever you're willing to give me because that's how much I want to be with you. But—"

He takes a deep breath like he's searching for some resolve within himself. He still looks like the ocean, only now it's one with storm clouds covering the horizon, the restless chop of the waves tossing endlessly.

"But I think I'm worth more than that," he concludes.

"You are," I reply confidently. My hope flags—he is not delivering good news, I know from his posture, the defensive stiffness of his shoulders, the uneasy swirl in his eyes. Even so, I feel some spark of pride in what he's said. Wasn't this my goal the whole time? Wasn't trying to get him over me about helping him understand he's worth more?

He looks at me sharply, obviously finding no flattery in my words. I wait, my heartbeat pounding in my stomach. "Well, if we're—*not* nothing," he says, "I have a right to know why you broke up with me."

I slacken. I really thought we were past this. Hasn't he seen how meaningless it is?

When I say nothing, my mouth working uselessly, Dean shakes his head with dismayed impatience. "You can't tell me you don't know, because here you are saying we're not nothing," he goes on, his voice narrowing intensely like the sun through a magnifying glass. "What does that *mean*?"

Surrounded by the chorus of snapping flip-flops, rattling bellhop carts, elevator jingles, and ebullient guitar music, I can't believe he's insisting on having this conversation here. Now. "Dean, it wasn't about you," I start miserably.

He doesn't reply, just waiting. Saying silently, *I didn't ask what it* wasn't *about.*

I look around the lobby, aware how many people are close enough to hear. Not that they matter, but—everything in my life seems to have spectators. Returning my attention to Dean, I catch the emotion flickering in his unwavering gaze. There's no vindictiveness, not in the least. He's not pushing me to do penance or pass some test. He's desperate to know. He looks like I'm holding the key to some lock he's pulled on until his fingers bled.

I sigh.

Dean is my friend. He's my whatever-we-were.

I have to try.

"I . . . reach a point in every relationship where things start to tip from fun into serious and it's just . . . I feel like I can't breathe," I say. It is not easy. It's the first time I've spoken this out loud in full. "It happens with every guy I date. I'm scared he'll get committed, while I'll just want something fun. Something free. It's like I know constantly that if I stay in a relationship too long, the guy I'm with will expect more—expect me not to dump him, expect me to fall in love. *Expect, expect, expect.* Then when I do end it, I'll hurt them. I'll disappoint them."

When I glance up, Dean's gaze is sour. "So—you were scared I'd fall in love and you wouldn't."

I exhale hard. "No. With every other guy, yes. But not with you."

Dean says nothing. Some of the sting is leaving his expression.

"With you," I continue, pushing myself, choosing every word, "I was prepared for that to happen. I was ready for our fling to run its course. But . . . it didn't." I swallow. "And that was even more terrifying."

I find I can't face him for this part. This quiet confession I've hidden even from myself. I look to the sea sparkling outside.

"There are opinions on absolutely everything I do," I say. "I've made my peace with that, but I guess I don't want anyone to see me get my heart broken. To see me lose something.

Really lose something. They already see every time I miss a serve, lose a match, rank second instead of first. There are some imperfections I'd just rather not put a spotlight on. When I told you I loved you, I meant it, and by meaning it I knew one day, you, my family, your family—everyone might see me heartbroken."

Dean is listening closely now.

"I wasn't scared of you loving me," I say softly. "I was scared of loving you."

I fall silent, my pulse racing like I just sprinted across the court. Sweat beads on the back of my neck, but I stand tall, refusing to give in to my insecurity.

His expression finally softens. "Thank you for telling me that," he says sincerely.

"So . . ." I swallow. Forget reaching the other end of the court. I feel like I'm still sprinting while standing in place. "Does that mean we're good? We can go back to how we were before our families found us?"

"Back to how we were . . ." Dean repeats like he's puzzling out the phrase.

While he hesitates, impatience sears into me. The endlessly looping music on the speakers is starting to grate on my ears, like some mocking metaphor for how this conversation isn't moving forward.

Finally, he speaks. "I understand why you didn't want our families to know about us, but it wasn't just them you kept this from," he says with unbearable calm. "It was yourself, and I helped you do it because I was happy just to have you however I could. But I don't think I can do it anymore. Everything you just said, the way you've treated me this week—you're still scared of trying this for real."

The hotel music disappears. Not in real life—in my head. It's swallowed under the roar of waves of sudden fury.

I step forward, wrapping my voice in wire to keep myself whispering instead of shouting. Like what Dean said has flipped a hidden switch in me, I'm exploding inside. Only the fake pleasantry of this huge hotel lobby keeps me contained.

"Of course I'm scared," I hiss. "One of us will get our heart broken here. I don't want it to be you. I certainly don't want it to be me. Not just because it would hurt, either. Because I'd be a mess—and I *can't* be a mess."

Dean doesn't flinch. He doesn't step back. The light coming in the hotel windows catches his irises, making them flare gold. "Kaylee, you *did* break my heart. But I'm still here. I'm still standing. I'm the proof you need," he says, insistence pushing past his composure for the first time. "I'm proof you'd be okay, too."

I struggle to speak, not knowing how to explain or not courageous enough to do so. Doesn't he understand? I know in my heart, in my stomach, in every part of me, what's on the line here. If we ruin things with each other, I might never get this—*love*—right. Because Dean . . . Dean is the one for me.

So I stay silent, frozen with fear.

I see the moment it happens. Still without moving, Dean withdraws. He decides something, then closes himself up.

"As long as you've decided we'll end in heartbreak, this won't work. I'm . . . done," he says.

Water fills his eyes, but he doesn't let the feeling into his expression. In a numb part of me, I respect him for it.

"Congratulations," he goes on icily. "You did what you set out to do. I'm over you."

He turns before a tear can slip down his cheek. I watch him walk toward the elevators, wanting to go after him, to fix this, to reassure him. But what could I even say? I refuse to lie to him. In the end, this is the best possible outcome. Maybe we can come back from this. Maybe we can still be friends. We did it once before.

I repeat the reassurances to myself despite each one feeling like shards into my heart. Even I never knew positivity could be so painful.

Holding my head high, I walk out of the hotel, finally feeling the heartache I fought to avoid for so long.

Forty-Three

I POUND BALL AFTER ball on the sand, spiking each one with vicious precision into the X on the plank outside the house. My hand stings, and I know I can't keep this up much longer without risking an injury I'd regret. It's impulsive, even reckless.

For one more moment, however, I'm letting myself not care.

"You're going to break my board in half if you keep at that much longer," I hear my mom say.

I hit one last ball right into the X. It bounces hard off the wood, rattling the upright plank. Wiping stray strands of hair from my forehead, I turn, finding my mom has come out onto the deck. Immediately, I notice her eyes are slightly swollen, lasting evidence of her fight with Terry.

I swallow, not needing one more reminder of how okay everything isn't. In silent reply, I head to collect the volleyballs scattered on the shore. Sweat paints the sides of my face.

The sand is hot under my feet, the morning sky imposingly gorgeous. Overhead, the palm trees sway in their unbothered rhythm.

Watching me, my mom takes a seat on the wooden step leading down to the beach. She continues, her voice not quite level. "When I told my reps I might return to the sport, you know what they asked me?"

I clench my jaw, glad she can't see my face. I do *not* want to discuss this right now. I don't want to discuss my mom's career, and I definitely don't want to discuss the accusations Terry made in their fight about my feelings on the subject.

I return to my position in front of the plank, where I continue spiking, very pointedly saying nothing.

My silence doesn't deter my mom. "They asked me how I thought I stacked up to the last time I competed," she says, ignoring the sound of my shots slamming into the wood. "It was their first question. Without hesitation. They weren't trying to be harsh or critical—they just wanted to know what sort of path I should focus on. The moment I walk onto a court again, people will compare me to the younger woman who walked off an Olympic podium with a record-setting medal win," she continues. "And I'm . . . not her anymore."

Despite my vigorous effort not to listen, to put every figment of consciousness into the ferocious swing of my elbow, I notice even the scratching sound of her placing her coffee mug down on the step. My eyes remain on the X in front of me. I send the ball down hard, dead center.

"My body isn't the same. I'm out of practice mentally and

physically. No matter how much I work, I know I won't be the *Judy Jordan* everyone remembers." She says her name with something like the spiteful parody of sportscasters' enthusiasm. "I mean, my friend's thirteen-year-old daughter scored on me the other day."

She laughs, sounding incredulous—and, maybe, scared. I pause, just for a second, then serve my next shot.

"No matter what I achieve," my mom continues, "it will be *less*. I can't defy time and biology. I know I can't. And yet, it's all anyone will talk about. Sometimes I even catch myself thinking—what if I *could, though*? What if I work harder than ever and do the impossible and set new records?" She scoffs to herself. "But thinking that for just one moment will only make it hurt worse when everyone points out how far I've fallen. I . . . I wish sometimes I didn't have to live in my own shadow."

I've positioned the ball in my hand for my next spike, but her words stop me, locking my shoulders in place. I drop the ball to my side, then finally turn to face her. I guess I'd never considered it—that my mom would be dealing with the same comparisons I do.

Mom smiles weakly. She hugs her elbows, resting them on her knees. The contrast is striking, how small her powerful frame looks.

"It's terrifying," she says, "and it's nearly enough to make me back out of this. To quit. To let my career end on a high note and pretend I'm happy never playing the sport I love while I still can. But I've been thinking about what Terry said—"

"Mom, don't," I interrupt. "She was wrong. I *want* you to play again."

"I know you do," she reassures me softly. "But she was right that I hadn't considered how this will affect you. I'm sorry. If you're ever uncomfortable about anything, we'll talk about it. We'll go day by day."

"Day by day," I repeat.

"But Terry isn't your mom," she continues. "She doesn't know you like I do. Doesn't know how strong you are. Every day you face those comparisons, that shadow. I see it, Kaylee, I do. You don't let them scare you, though. You hold your head high and you walk onto the court and you do incredible things. *You* inspire *me* to do this again," she tells me, her eyes shining. "To not let anyone's expectations or opinions hold me back from what makes me happy."

I swallow down the sudden lump in my throat. It's like my heart understands what she's said in ways my mind doesn't quite yet, still putting together the impossible pieces. My mom has always been *my* inspiration, and to be an inspiration to her—to my hero—is nothing I could have expected.

"I hope you know I'm profoundly proud of you," she goes on. "Not just of your volleyball career, which is really incredible, but of who you are. The grace with which you carry yourself."

I sit down on the sand, facing my mom. Chewing my lip, I drape my arms over the volleyball I have in my lap. "I'm not sure I'm all that graceful," I say.

My mom laughs. She picks up her coffee, her shoulders looking lighter.

While I'm happy to see her lifted spirits, her reaction frustrates me a little. "I'm serious," I insist. "I think I really messed things up with Dean because I put so much pressure on myself. But I don't know how not to."

I look up, suddenly desperate for her to know how much I mean what I've just said. It's not the flailing, meaningless excuse of someone who doesn't really want to change. The slicing reminders in my head of the standards I need to live up to, the migraines, the pressure of being *everything to everyone*—I'm not sure how to separate them from myself, but I'm pretty sure I need to start.

Mom considers, her eyes shifting to the ever-stunning sapphire of the ocean. "You're afraid of losing," she comments.

I can't help half grinning. "I mean, yeah. Always."

"Kaylee, you're an amazing athlete with a huge career ahead of you, but one day you'll either walk away or you will lose. And you'll keep losing," she replies with soft seriousness. She isn't my coach or my competitor now. She's my mom.

"I know that," I say quickly.

"And yet you're doing it anyway." The stare she's giving me now is unwavering. "You're going into something with your whole heart despite knowing one day, maybe today, maybe in twenty years, you'll lose. You will not meet every expectation forever."

I drop my gaze to the ball in my lap. The seams in the leather, the scuffs of repeated impact. Could it really be so simple? What she's saying makes strange, perfect sense—I love winning, but winning isn't why I love volleyball. I didn't choose this sport because I thought I would win every match or even be better than my mom. I play because I love every day on the sand, even when I fall short.

Looking up, I find my mom starting to stand, stretching to her full height on the stairs. "Mom," I say, wobbling past the thickness in my throat. "Thank you."

She smiles. "Glad I still have some things I can teach you." Eyebrows rising slightly, she nods in the direction of the beat-up plank. "Your form with those kills was intimidating."

Pleased, I grin. When she heads inside, cradling her coffee in the protective way parents do, I roll the volleyball off my lap. Standing, I grab my phone off the sand. I follow Mom up the steps to the deck, where I recline in the hammock overlooking the ocean.

In my camera roll I find the photo Dean took of my mom blocking my spike. Despite what I'm proud of in this photo—the power of my stance, the way the image evokes me facing my mom's legacy head-on—there's no mistaking what's happening here. I'm not about to score. I'm about to get wrecked.

Which is the point.

Deciding to break my social media hiatus, I slide over to Instagram, where I select the photo and credit Dean. Beneath it I write one single line of caption. *Pretty much how I felt after getting dumped by the guy I'm in love with.* When this goes up, everyone's going to know. My friends will text me. My followers will comment. They'll see the side of me I've tried to convince myself doesn't exist.

I hit post, my heart pounding. My whole life I've chased

what it would look like if perfect were a person. I'm *not* perfect, though. Nothing is. Not my role models, not the things I love. We make messes. We have fights. We embarrass ourselves. We lose. I'm no exception to the frightening, freeing reality that imperfection is everywhere.

I'm learning to be okay with it—I'm going to have to be.

Forty-Four

I SPEND THE NEXT day on my own, rejuvenating myself. It's ironic, I realize. The whole point of vacation is to relax, to recharge, to reset—to escape pressure for some reconnective personal time—yet the turbulent past few days have felt not like ones *of* vacation, but ones I needed vacation *from*.

Today, I throw myself into the chance. With the pearly sand under my feet, the Technicolor teal of the water in my eyeline, I focus on some much-needed Kaylee Time. I float in the cool ocean. I run on the beach, even sort of enjoying myself, or maybe just enjoying the distraction. I talk to Brianna and share the whole story with her, including being dumped in the lobby of a crowded hotel.

Despite posting my photo, I hear nothing from Dean. Still, I feel okay. Yes, I'm heartbroken and everyone knows it, but I'm also okay.

I am, however, bored by five p.m. I'm lounging in the living room with my mom, who's reading at the kitchen counter. No one is mentioning the weird loneliness of the nearly empty house. Over last night's dinner and this morning's breakfast, nothing. I wonder how long we'll go on pretending this is normal. I fear eventually it will *become* normal.

Not wanting to contemplate that possibility, I go get my computer and bring it down to the sofa. Reaching for one of my favorite coping mechanisms, I start typing in one search from my familiar repertoire—my mom's old games.

I haven't hit enter yet when I stop. I close the window.

Instead of immersing myself in the videos I know so well, I decide to watch my own. My dad has filmed all my tournaments, and I open the videos from last summer from the cloud where my family keeps photos. Even just the freeze-frame of myself in uniform, waiting on the court in between points, kicks vicious instincts to life in me. Watching my own games is usually when I'm the most critical of myself. It's deliberate, methodical—I find my flaws, write them down, and develop a training regimen to improve them. Often, those flaws look like all the ways I'm still falling short of my mom.

Right now I don't compare myself. Or, I do. Just not to my mom. Instead, I compare myself to myself. I remember how I felt on the court in my dad's shaky iPhone video, the decisions I made, the skills I used, and make note of every way I've improved since last summer.

Suddenly, pride blooms in my chest. The Kaylee of a year ago in this tournament wouldn't have placed anywhere near second in the national rankings. While the video plays, while my mom pages through her magazine nearby, I don't see my flaws. I see the work I've put in and how far I've come. Second place is incredible.

Nestled into the couch cushions, I find I'm grinning at my computer screen. I'm proud of myself even though I'm not first, even though I can be competitive and jealous, even though I'm heartbroken. It's okay not to be perfect, not to be polished. It's okay not to be everything. It's okay to be hurting even when you're proud. It's okay not to be fine.

Because I'm not fine. Today, waiting desperately to hear something from Dean, I've been doing the same thing I've done so many days of my life. I've told myself I'm fine in hopes of making it true.

If I can let myself not be everything, then I can let myself hurt, too. So I do. I let the not-fine in, like ice water spilled into the cracks in my chest. I hurt because of Dean, but not only because of Dean. Because the Freeman-Yus aren't here. Because my mom is pretending *she's* fine despite being in a huge fight with her best friend of twenty-five years.

Tired of this new normal, I close the video I'm watching. I head to YouTube, where I search for one of the few TV specials made about my mom's life, the one that hunted down old footage of when she played in high school with Terry.

I know the exact minute marker to find from having watched this video countless times and crank the volume up as loud as it will go.

It works immediately. Her voice cuts in from the counter. "Kaylee, why are you watching that?"

I turn around, perching the computer on the back of the couch so she can see the screen. The timing is perfect. The video is just reaching my favorite part, when they win the match and my mom goes barreling into Terry's arms. While cheering erupts from my computer's speakers, I fix my focus on my mom's expression, expecting sadness to stain her features, like I've just shattered her favorite framed photograph. Instead, she only watches, her expression placid.

I press her—I have to. "Are you really going to let your fight with Terry end a friendship like this?" I ask.

Mom gradually looks to me, like she's hearing me in slow motion. "We're not ending a friendship," she says as if it's obvious.

I feel my eyebrows rise, my incredulity matching hers. "Um, you haven't even spoken to Terry since they left. You know, you have to talk to people to be friends with them." The video playing while I'm speaking innocently fills the spaces in between my words.

She rolls her eyes, looking not unlike the teenager on my computer screen. "You think this is the first time we've gone a couple days without speaking after a fight?" she asks. Spinning the barstool seat around, she faces me completely. "Believe me, we've fought like this and worse before."

I can't help blinking in surprise. I never imagined my perfect mother was even capable of fights like this. It's not that I didn't believe my dad when he said Mom and Terry's blowup wasn't about me, but hearing this lets me release the last shard of guilt I'd been holding on to. Not only is it freeing, it's . . . sort of inspiring. If Olympian—not to mention respectable adult—Judy Jordan is allowed to be messy, then so am I.

Mom laughs, evidently seeing the astonishment written

on my features. "It's possible she and I have been more dis-creet in the past," she says.

I let myself crack a sarcastic grin. "More discreet than shouting at each other while I'm in Dean's bed trying to get dressed?"

I laugh with her, and it feels good to acknowledge that awful moment like it's nothing more than a punch line.

She comes over to lean on the back of the couch, watch-ing the footage. Her lips pull into a smile I'm pretty sure she isn't even aware of. "You should have seen the fight we had after this game," she says fondly, with nothing like forebod-ing in her voice. It's more like she's gossiping.

I lean closer, watching the video as if the screen is pulling me. My mom and her friend, exchanging smiles, high-fiving, looking incredibly young and yet just like themselves. "What was it about?" I ask, finally forfeiting my search for clues on the exhausted faces of the women I respect most in the world.

"I think it had something to do with her making a plan to go see a movie with her boyfriend instead of me," Mom says.

When I smile, she shrugs, unselfconscious.

"She's my oldest friend, and just like relationships, friend-ships are never perfect," she goes on. "Putting pressure on them to be perfect only ensures they won't survive. It's not easy being an adult and seeing someone you love and respect make opposite choices from you. It doesn't mean either of us is wrong—it just requires not comparing. Which sometimes we're better at than other times."

I nod, understanding, or starting to. It's suddenly, intensely reassuring, like your feet swiping the seafloor when you'd just started to feel out of your depth. What my mom is saying isn't unlike Dean's and my discussion about making our passions into our careers. He doesn't judge me for doing so, and I don't judge him for not.

I hear the front door opening, then the plastic-bag rustle of my dad returning with dinner. I close out of the video.

"We'll get over it," my mom reassures me. "Don't you worry."

Smiling, I start to stand.

"Speaking of that . . ."

I spin at the sound of the voice and find—Darren, in the kitchen with my dad. He looks determined, even to the point of impatience, his hands shoved firmly into the pockets of his chinos. My dad, for his part, is poorly hiding how pleased he is with this development.

"Darren," my mom says, jokingly scandalized. "You've crossed enemy lines."

He grins, reminding me where Dean gets the amber sparkle I sometimes catch in his eyes. "John and I are officially colluding," he declares, with put-on drama to match my mom's. "We want our vacation back."

"We haven't even gotten to watch all three Hobbit movies yet. This has to end," my dad adds.

"When you put it like that, maybe the fight could last a little longer," I suggest.

My dad scowls. Darren looks momentarily aghast. It's really not hard to imagine them as college roommates.

"I've come with insider information. Everyone is

miserable at the hotel," Darren says. "We have to intervene," he goes on. "Even Dean and Terry aren't talking, which means that Jessie isn't talking to me because she expects me to fix things. Lucy is just using this time to play ABBA at all hours of the day and night." Imploringly, he fixes his eyes on my mom. "Please, Judy."

Mom laughs, but her arms are crossed. "Why do I have to reach out? She's the one who left." Despite how she's keeping her voice light, there's no mistaking the edge in her words. Maybe it's one I recognize from how I've felt this summer. Two people are in pain, but everybody is only caring for one of them.

"Because you let her leave. You know she has too much pride to just turn around and come back," he says.

"True," Mom admits.

Darren claps his hands together, and my dad fist-pumps the air.

"If you wanted to stage a completely coincidental, unpremeditated run-in, we're all going to the beach tomorrow because Dean is taking a surfing lesson in Santa Monica at nine in the morning," Darren says. "Seems entirely likely that you might also be in Santa Monica at that time . . ."

"Wait, did you say Dean is surfing?" I ask.

Darren nods.

I face my mom. "We have to go," I say.

Mom sighs. It doesn't fool me. I see the new flicker of hope in her eyes, the sunrise glow of relief at the prospect of the end of this fight approaching.

"Well," she finally says. "All right. But if Terry is pissed"—she looks warningly at Darren—"I fully plan to throw you under the bus, D."

"She won't be pissed and you know it," Darren replies.

My mom's smile softens. "Yeah. I do."

I let my eyes drift from them as plans start to formulate in my head. I know exactly what I have to do. It's what Dean deserves, and what I should have given him sooner.

Forty-Five

THE SKY ISN'T CLEAR when we walk onto the sand in Santa Monica the next morning. It's not overcast, either, with only a couple picturesque wisps of clouds touching down on the golden horizon. It's perfect, sort of. Honest in ways empty sunny skies wouldn't be.

This early, the beach isn't crowded. The snatches of conversation from the other people here meld with the swishing of the ocean and the sound of bicycles on the street into one soft soundtrack for the morning.

None of it does anything to relax me. I'm wound up with nervous energy like it's a tournament day. The parallel is strikingly spot-on, I realize while I head with my family down the shore. I'm going to leave it all on the court, all my hope, all my nerves, all my effort, and it could very well end in heartbreak.

Again.

But love means risking heartbreak over and over, and

I'm ready for it. I square my shoulders, clenching my nerves down.

In the early light, I search the beach for the Freeman-Yus. My parents' heads swivel, clearly doing the same. While it's not packed here the way it'll be in just a few hours, it's not empty. We peer past umbrellas, scour beach chairs, and sweep our eyes over sunbathers lying on towels. Mom's stony expression gives absolutely nothing away, her jaw locked.

It doesn't fool me. I know she wouldn't be here unless she loved Terry. In one more way, I guess, we're sharing the same struggles. On the line for the ones we love.

"Aunt Judy!"

In the end, we're not the ones to find the Freeman-Yus. Jessie finds us first. She sprints over in an explosion of sand and jumps into my mom's arms. Mom is ready for her—she hoists Jessie up, even though she's gotten too big for it.

"Does this mean we can come back home?" Jessie asks rapturously from her precarious position hanging off my mom's hip.

Mom holds her close. "I hope so," she says, smiling down at her. "Where's your mom, bug?"

Jessie points to towels near the water, where, sure enough, Terry already sees us. With her arms crossed and something pointed in her stiff demeanor, her posture says everything. Darren is standing behind her, looking very much like he doesn't want to be noticed right now, and Lucy lingers next to them, clearly wanting to run over too but trying to be the big kid.

Dean is nowhere in sight. Which isn't a problem, I remind

myself, fighting my flagging hope even while my restless eyes keep roaming the beach. He's probably just in the water. I can still reach him.

My mom sets Jessie down but holds on to her hand as we walk over to Terry. We're some distance from them, leaving enough time for quiet to descend over our group. Like even Jessie knows there's some nerve-shaking charge in the conversation to come.

"What a surprise running into you here," Mom says cheekily when we reach them.

Terry scoffs and turns to Darren, who quickly looks the other way. "Traitor," she says, but there's no bite to her voice.

Sighing, she turns back to her friend.

"Well, we might as well start making up," Terry says.

Her voice sounds like she's opening an argument, but her words make my mom smile, like they've done this before. Which—of course they have. They've fought *and* they've made up, and their relationship will never be perfect, but it'll be worth it anyway.

Darren obviously notices the same thing I have. It's not just relief I see wash over him—he's happy for them. "Hey, girls, how about we get some ice cream?" he asks softly, like he's scared enthusiasm might disturb the fragile reconciliation.

"This early?" Lucy asks incredulously.

"Are you trying to talk me out of it?" Darren replies.

Lucy straightens. "No."

"Ice cream sounds great," my dad says. "I'll join you. Kaylee?"

I shake my head. While I recognize the gracefulness in the excuse they've spun on the spot, I'm here for my own reason—one surpassing even mint-chocolate-chip ice cream for breakfast on my list of priorities. The dads and the girls walk off up the sand while Terry sits back down on her towel and motions for my mom to join her.

I watch them a moment more. They don't speak, not yet. I know they will. Leaving them with what only they can unravel, I march up toward the surf rentals stand at the edge of the sand.

The flimsy white tent looks like it was set up this morning, wonderfully unlike the polished hotels across the street. The guy behind the makeshift counter sweating into his Quicksilver T-shirt is watching the ocean, his sunglasses reflecting the scattered clouds in the luminous sky. He smiles when I walk up.

"Hi," I say, "I'd like to rent a surfboard."

With the water flying past underneath the foam sword of my surfboard, I paddle with my eyes fixed on the horizon, finding my rhythm easily.

I'm obviously planning on stopping short of the iridescent line where the ocean meets the sky. Out past the breakers, the surf class is coming closer with every stroke I paddle. They're sitting on their boards where the water is placid while smaller groups of two and three take their turns swimming forward into the surf.

I reach the pummeling waves quickly. Or, really, they

reach *me*. While whitewash slams me in the face repeatedly, I quickly learn I have no idea how to navigate the eight-foot-long surfboard under me. I come out of each collision spitting seawater, wiping the stinging salt from my eyes, only to face the next pummeling curl of spray.

If anyone is watching me—which, I'm in full view of just about everyone on the beach—they won't find me particularly graceful or athletic. Every time I'm able to ride over a wave before it breaks, I flop heavily back down on the other side hard enough I feel like my chest will bruise. It's incredibly unimpressive.

Finally, face sticky with salt water, hair coming loose from my ponytail, I make it past the breaking waves. The class is close now, in full view, with no walls of water separating me from why I'm here.

I pick him out immediately. He's straddling his surfboard on one edge of the group, looking self-assured the way he always does. The water has set the sun to shining off his slicked dark hair, like the light is meant just for him. I notice his waterproof camera is secured around his wrist—promising photos I can't wait to see.

When Dean spots me, he actually does a double take. The waves are still loud, but I'm pretty sure he laughs then—yes. He's smiling, amused as I struggle the rest of the way to the class.

My aching chest takes it as a good sign while I paddle over to the instructor, a cool-looking older woman with beach-blond hair and a yellow rash guard.

"Hi, sorry I'm late," I say, or more like pant. "I paid down at the tent, and they said I could just paddle out and join."

The woman nods. "Fine with me," she replies, gesturing for me to join the rest of the group.

I paddle across the entire class, feeling everyone's eyes on me. On my disheveled hair, on how I wobble over the uneven water, on the paddling stroke I'm suddenly very self-conscious of. Suffice it to say, I do *not* feel like a world-class athlete right now.

I focus on Dean. Thankfully, I manage to reach him without much more ungainly paddling.

"What are you doing here?" he asks when I pull up next to him. His voice is low, for only me to hear. The surprise having faded from his expression, he looks playfully puzzled now.

I sit up, straddling the board and letting my legs dangle in the open water. I'm shaky for several seconds until I level out, proud of myself for not capsizing. "Did you see I posted your photo?" I ask Dean, hiding my nervousness.

"I did," he says.

Floating on the water, I wait for him to say more. He doesn't, only eyes my surfboard dubiously. *So much for my start to this conversation.* I'd hoped when I got out here this would go like paddling over the open ocean, evenly, without resistance. Instead, I'm starting to guess it might feel more like facing the waves.

I press on, undeterred. "Well, I have more to say to you."

We let ourselves drift a couple feet away from the class as everyone lines up to have their shot at the swell. "And you figured surfing class was the perfect moment to do so?" he replies.

I scowl. "*Not* perfect," I say. "Which is the point. I kind of have a whole theme going on."

Dean's eyes sparkle. "A theme," he repeats. "Wait, is there symbolism, too? Is the surfboard a motif? Oh, or the ocean?" He gazes past me, searching the glittering water for poeticism.

Exasperated, I rub my forehead. "Oh my god, no wonder I broke up with you once. Can you just let me get through what I have to say?"

He holds up his hands in surrender, laughing, which makes me laugh a little. My eyes snag on his—and linger for a long moment, long enough the lurching under us seems to cease. It's just *us*, suspended in impossibly familiar connection.

I have to look down at the water lapping over my surfboard to recall the talking points I'd prepared. Like I'm lining up my serve on the volleyball court, I concentrate on exactly what I want to tell him. "My whole life I've pushed myself to be perfect. But I've realized, in order to win anything, you have to risk losing," I say. "Or, in this case, having your heart broken."

Dean's eyebrows rise. "Well, we wouldn't want that, would we?" he cuts in dryly.

"What did we say about interruptions?" I reprimand him. When he nods demurely, I go on. "Like I said, I push myself to be perfect. Theme, see?"

He smiles, sincere now instead of sarcastic. "It's well done, really," he concedes.

I straighten up proudly, feeling stabler on my board. "Thank you. When I said I loved you, I knew I meant it. *Really* meant it. Which was the whole problem. I didn't know if I could be with you while the fear of losing you followed me everywhere. I'd screw everything up, because I wasn't perfect, because I was scared."

Exhaling unevenly, I stop. Dean, I notice gratefully, isn't staring. He just listens, his gaze returned to the horizon.

"Pressure to be perfect follows me everywhere. *Everywhere,*" I say. When Dean's eyes return to me with concern, I continue. "I'm working on it. But I didn't think I could be perfect with you, which meant I would lose you. Then everyone would see how shattered I was."

Dean nods. He looks like he understands. The clarity gives him no reassurance or hope—he just looks sad.

I'm not done, though. I shake out my wet hair with one hand, hoping the movement will dislodge the words I need. "*If* you let me into your life again—I'm still not sure I'll do everything right," I say. "But I'm willing to make a fool of myself trying. Clearly."

I gesture to the surf class around us. Right on cue, one of the other students falls in the middle of riding his wave, exactly like I did in my only previous surfing lesson.

"I'm ready to fail, but I'm still going for gold," I declare. Then my eyes slide to Dean.

He tilts his head, considering, hiding whatever my declaration is making him feel.

"Very *thematic,*" he replies.

The smile spreading on my face wobbles like the surfboard under me. Before Dean can say more, before I can find out what his verdict will be, the instructor motions us forward to catch a wave.

"Kaylee, you really don't have to do this part," Dean says. "Your gesture is already very clear."

I blow a stray strand of hair from my face. "Please. I'm all in," I reply, looking meaningfully at him for a moment before lying back down to paddle forward.

When I come up next to the instructor, she's surveying the swells. "Remember, when the wave is approaching, paddle, paddle, paddle until you feel the current carry you," she says. "We're just working on catching the wave right, so don't worry about standing up unless you want."

I head into the open water. Moments later, I hear paddling behind me. Pulling my attention from the gradual movement of the water, I find Dean next to me. His half smile says, *Ready?* I know he understands the grin I return. We face the open sea, waiting.

The swells rise gently, nothing big or scary. I immediately pick out my wave—then turn around and start to paddle furiously. As the water swallows my heels, I feel the rush under me, pulling me forward. It's sudden, powerful, inescapable.

The wave lifts me up. I surge forward, heart pounding. In seconds it'll crash, spitting me out of its foam, and—

My decision is split-second. *Might as well leave it all on the court, right?*

I pop up, my elbows and knees moving in one half-coordinated spurt. For two breathtaking seconds, I'm standing, riding the wave like it's solid ground under my feet.

Then my foot slips. Just slightly. My balance sways and—

I tip off to the right side, face-planting spectacularly in the water.

The wave crashes over me, churning me under, pulling my bathing suit and my hair. I can't help it—I open my eyes. The watery vision momentarily stops my flailing. I see nothing but dazzling blue and swirls of sand. It's stunning. The sounds of the world are gone. All I hear is the roar of the waves.

When I feel my lungs starting to sear, I kick my legs into motion, half regretting leaving this surreal, submerged world. Reaching the surface, I plunge up, sucking in air.

Wiping the water from my eyes, I find Dean flying past me, standing up like he definitely didn't need this surf class after his lesson with Emma and RJ. He's—holding his camera, snapping photos. Of me. While he fires off clicks of the shutter, he's laughing so hard his eyes are crinkling.

When he starts to lose his footing, instead of waiting to eat it, he gracefully falls backward into the sea-foam.

Grabbing my board, I line myself up to paddle into the waves, heading for the calmer waters. When he surfaces, Dean turns to do the same. The next wave rises in front of me, leaving me completely unprepared, rushing right into my face. I spit seawater, coughing my laughter, then wipe my eyes to find Dean.

Instead of imitating my exercise in gracelessness, Dean points himself right into the wave curling over him—but then dips effortlessly under the oncoming tide. He emerges on the other side looking perfectly in control. *Of course he does.*

Impressed by his technique for not getting completely decked, I keep determinedly paddling, getting closer to the tranquil deeper water. In front of the wave facing me now, I follow exactly what Dean did.

Incredibly, the wave hurtles over me, the water churning wonderfully past my heels.

When I emerge, I find he's beaming at me.

The rush in my chest is something no measure of surfing in the world could ever match. Past the swells now, I abandon my board, which trails behind me, tethered to my ankle, and swim to where Dean is waiting. When I reach him, I prop my elbows on his board across from him. Our faces are close, with only one foot of foam and fiberglass separating us.

"Dean," I say. "I have a question."

"Yes?"

"How would you feel about getting back together?"

Dean doesn't look startled or hesitant. He just smiles. He's—ugh—swelteringly handsome. "I don't know, Kaylee," he says with playful poise. "How would *you* feel?"

"I think I made a huge mistake by breaking up with you."

He nods once, still looking like he knows the lines to this scene. "Go on, please. Would you care to elaborate on your regrets? How big a mistake, exactly?"

"Colossal," I inform him. "I broke up with the guy I'm in love with."

Finally, his self-assurance falters. He's caught off guard.

"This has been the most stressful, most confusing summer of my life, but spending it with you, I've been lucky enough to realize something. Summer is for starting over," I say. "I love you. You're my favorite ex, my best friend, the ultimate hide-and-seek partner, the only photographer who's ever really seen me, and—I'm hoping—my boyfriend again."

With the ocean reaching out in every direction, I suddenly feel like we're the only people out here. The vastness of the water seems to shrink the world down to the two of us. No onlookers, no expectations. Only the gentle rocking of the waves, endless until the sandy stripe of the shore in the distance.

"Finally," Dean says.

He leans forward, closing the inches over his board.

When he reaches for my chin, I move forward to meet him. I start to go under, figuratively, losing myself in Dean. He tastes like salt. He smells like the ocean. He feels like home.

Forty-Six

I DON'T BAIL ON the rest of the lesson. Okay, I won't be pursuing an Olympic career in surfing, and I do get water up my nose more than once from wiping out, but it's sort of fun. Dean cheers loudly for me every time I stand up, drawing curious looks from the other class members.

When it's over, we carry our boards back to the tent. The sand is crowded now, patchworked with colorful umbrellas and swimsuits. The Santa Monica Pier is packed with visitors, the fairground lights of the Ferris wheel spinning slowly in the daylight. While we wait in line, Dean looks through the photos he took, chuckling to himself.

"Well, I think I found my perfect photo," he says.

Instantly dubious, I glance over. On his screen, I'm not surprised to find, is me. It's the moment I lost my footing on my first wave. My mouth is open in a startled frown, and I'm flinging my arm out awkwardly like I'm hoping to break my fall into the water.

Objectively, it's a hilarious photo. Subjectively, it's sort of my worst nightmare.

While my cheeks flame pink, I stare Dean down. "I must really love you if I'm not breaking up with you on the spot for even possessing this photo," I inform him.

He kisses my forehead, then clicks to the next image. "This is the one I meant," he says.

Even on the small screen, the photo steals my breath. It's after I fell, when I broke the surface. I'm smiling the sort of smile it's impossible to fake, even for me, despite my practice. The sun glistens on my wet skin. My hair is not slicked away from my face like in shampoo commercials. Instead, seawater sticks uncooperative strands to my cheekbones.

It doesn't matter. What this photo captures is precious. I don't look perfect—I look happy.

I swallow. Finding my voice isn't easy right now. "It's a wonderful shot, but you've taken so many wonderful photos. Why is this the one?" I ask softly.

"Well," Dean murmurs, "first you look unbelievably gorgeous. But really . . ." He pauses, like the same speechlessness I felt has stolen over him. "Some photos are like events," he explains. "Others are memories. This one is a feeling. It's how I felt in this moment. Indescribably happy because I knew we were really going to do this. We were going to be together."

I pull my eyes from the photo to look at him, despite the way his photographic vision draws me in like the currents of the waves. He's still studying his screen, quiet pride on his features. There's some sand on his temple, and his hair is twisted and coming loose from his hair tie. I feel the ache in my cheeks without even purposefully smiling. The emotion has me in its hold, unstoppable. I know I look ridiculous, and I don't care.

The line moves up. "So what now?" I ask, just because I have to say something instead of staring at him with hearts in my eyes. "Are you done with photography now that you have the perfect photo?"

Dean is also smiling. He's my joy reflected, like sunlight off the surface of the water.

"No," he says, shaking his head. "There are more perfects out there."

He reaches for my hand, and we step forward together.

Except for the several seconds needed to return our surfboards, my hand never leaves Dean's. We walk away from the tent, our fingers entwined like mine were meant to fit with his.

With the sand under my feet, Dean by my side, I'm starting to wonder if perfect isn't just something I can push myself to be. Maybe, sometimes, it's something the world gives to me, in little moments like this one. The ocean sparkles on our right. The sounds of the city echo on our left. Neither of us speaks, our smiles softer but steadier now. Surer.

We walk toward our families. When we get close, Dean starts to pull his hand from mine, but I hold on.

"I'm ready to tell them if you are," I say.

He doesn't hesitate. In reply, he squeezes my hand. We continue on, preparing for a range of reactions.

The moms are seated, looking worn out. It's striking how different the visual is from the documentary footage I watched with my mom, where they were physically spent, walking off the volleyball court with sweat in their hair. Emotional exhaustion lines their faces now. Still—the tension between them seems to be gone while they listen to Lucy and Jessie describe in detail all the ice-cream samples they tried from the Pier's soda shop creamery.

It's my dad who notices us first, his eyes narrowing in immediately on our clasped hands. He raises an eyebrow.

I nod, answering his unasked question, then clear my throat to get everyone's attention.

Our families fall silent, even Jessie. The moms turn toward us, surprise making intrigue flicker into their features in ways odes to mint chocolate chip evidently could not. Darren starts to smile.

"So we know this is complicated for everyone present," I say, my voice not wavering. "But I will remind you we've already broken up twice, so it's not like things can get any messier. Dean and I are back together."

"Again," Dean adds cheerfully.

Terry's eyes linger on me like she's searching my face for how I'm feeling. Meeting her gaze, I let myself smile. It's hard to fathom how different the feeling is from *making* myself smile. I'm here, venturing into this with Dean once more because I'm choosing to. Not because of any expectations.

Clearly satisfied, she grins and shares a look with my mom. It's the sort of rare glance where I really remember how before they were our moms, they were the closest of friends.

"Well, that's terrific," Dad finally says. "Please, though. We've had enough drama on this trip. Can you at least wait until we're home before you break up again?"

I pretend to weigh his request heavily. "I think we can agree to that."

"I'd give us eight weeks this round, easy," Dean joins in.

Turning to him, I nod like I'm sharing his estimation. "Right. Then back together in two more?"

"Oh, undoubtedly."

The group is watching our little comedy show with open disbelief now. Terry shifts on her towel.

"I'm just worried how this will affect the movie night alliances," she says.

I feel my chest swell with light because it's starting to set in now. The families supporting us makes this real in some new way. Even if they get dragged into whatever happens between Dean and me, we'll find a way to fix it. Like we did today.

"Wait," Jessie speaks up dramatically. "So you *are* getting married? It's just like Dean said!"

While Dean's face turns sunburn red, I laugh into his shoulder, my body shaking against his.

EPILOGUE

One Year Later

I'M IN MY ROOM in Malibu, packing. Down the hall, Lucy is softly playing ABBA.

I smile, nodding my head along despite myself. While so much has changed in the past year, so much has stayed the same. Like the Freeman-Yu–Jordan vacation, in which I've spent the past seven days repeating my favorite lazy routines. It's comforting, as serenely predictable as the ceaseless rhythm of the ocean. Even though tomorrow I move in to my dorm for USC summer training, I know this will remain.

I'm looking forward to playing in college, despite it not being my original plan. When my mom returned to the sport with a stunning year of competition, I let myself consider other routes to what I wanted. Not because I felt like my mom was in the way of my dream, but because she showed me how success isn't defined by a timeline.

I love beach volleyball, and I'm still planning to go pro. Even so, I'm also excited to play on a college team. I have options, and I want to explore them while I chart my course as an athlete.

My course. Not the one my mom put down decades ago.

Gentle knocking on my doorframe pulls me from my packing. I turn to find Dean in the hallway, watching me with the slanted smile I'll never get enough of. Half devotion, half promise. He's supported me in every choice, every challenge, every celebration of this past year, not to mention sweetening every hidden moment when it was just us. No matter whether everything was perfect or whether it very much wasn't, he's been there. He's the streak of light setting the diamond facets of my life to sparkling.

"Come outside with me for a minute," he says.

I smile, walking over to take his hand. One wonderful change in this trip has been holding hands in front of our families, cuddling up on the couch for movie nights, and every other way we haven't had to hide. On our way down the stairs, we nod to Terry, who's heading up to bed.

"Not too late, you two," she says. "Kaylee has an exhausting day ahead of her."

"Promise," I reply.

The parents, after a minor adjustment window, have handled our relationship well—although when you've known your boyfriend's parents since you were a kid, they can get a little too comfortable teasing you. While I haven't noticed our moms fight the way they did last year, I know their relationship is not without friction. No relationship is. It's nothing they can't handle. When Lucy quit volleyball, my mom wisely was nothing but supportive. Now we go to Lucy's robotics club competitions, where my mom one time cheered vigorously enough she needed to be reprimanded by the referee.

I head with Dean through the living room. "Do you think they'll let us share a room next year?" I ask while he opens the back door.

He eyes me, smiling with wry skepticism. "Probably not. The traditions pull pretty hard around here. We've been watching the same movies for like the past ten years."

We step out into the clear night. "Speaking of," I say, "as my boyfriend, you really should defect from the fellowship. Join me on Team Sandy."

He laughs. "Kaylee, your dad would never forgive me. And . . . I don't know. Our traditions aren't the worst. They've kept our families together this long."

Without him needing to say, I know where we're going. Reaching the edge of the deck stairs, I slide my feet into the sand. "I guess it's for the best," I reply. "You'll be spending every night in my sweet athletic dorm this year. I'll probably be sick of sharing a twin bed with you by next summer."

He scoffs. "You, sick of me? Sounds unlikely." His eyes sparkle like the stars in the dark sky overhead.

I love how easily we joke about our bumpy history. How promises don't feel like words I have to live up to, but words I *want* to live up to. It wasn't our explicit plan to go to college together like our parents did. Understandably, however, when Dean decided on USC's renowned film school, I was very, very pleased.

He pulls us to a stop at the water's edge. The moon shines dazzlingly overhead. On the open ocean, the ripples of the water part the moonlight into uncountable strands, each one disappearing in split seconds, only to reemerge elsewhere. Different, yet never really changing. It's incredibly romantic.

"Happy anniversary of the last time we broke up," Dean says.

I shove him lightly, making him step into the water. "I'm pretty sure you're doing the anniversary thing wrong."

He shrugs. "Maybe, but I love our imperfections," he says. "I love *you*, Kaylee. I'm glad we went a whole year without breaking up. Wouldn't you say it's worth celebrating?"

I soften, reaching for his hand again. "I love you, too," I say, then straighten like inspiration is striking me. "Honestly, it *is* impressive. I'm really quite proud of myself. I mean, *me*, date someone for an entire year? Unbelievable."

Dean nods dramatically like he's *oh so impressed*. "Indeed. What a feat for volleyball star Kaylee Jordan. You know, if you ever did break your streak, it's good you gave me the tools to get over you."

I know he's joking, but just in case, I pull him into a long kiss. It's moonlit magic, like every kiss we share. Incredibly, I feel like I'm standing up on my surfboard whenever our lips meet. Except, somehow, I'm pretty sure I'll never fall off.

When we part, I walk into the water, Dean's hand in mine. Wordlessly, he follows me in until we're up to our chests. Swaying in the gentle sea, I wrap my arms around him.

"Well," I say, "there's no way I'm getting over you."

Acknowledgments

We never could have imagined when we were writing *Always Never Yours*, unagented and dreaming of having a book published, that it would lead to this, our sixth YA novel on shelves. We are deeply honored by and incredibly grateful to everyone who helped us get here.

Katie Shea Boutillier, our agent extraordinaire, where would we be without you? Thank you for championing us at every stage of publishing. We had no idea just how great a team we would make when we took our first call together back in 2016, but with every year you set the bar higher and higher. Thank you for the many phone calls, the emails and texts, and for reading who knows how many random pitches we've sent your way. We remain #TeamKatie always.

Thank you to Dana Leydig, our editor for all six of our YA novels. It has been a true gift to work with you on Megan, Cameron, Juniper and Fitz, Alison, Siena, and now Kaylee. Every discussion and edit letter inspires us, drawing out the story in ways we had envisioned and also in ways we had not. Thank you for being not only such a thoughtful editor and collaborator but also a friend. We've enjoyed every minute.

Penguin Young Readers and Viking Children's has been such a lovely home for our YA. Since day one we have been honored to be part of the Penguin family. We feel indebted to the thought and care of our copyeditors and proofreaders, Krista Ahlberg, Peter Kranitz, Sola Akinlana, and Lauren Riebs, and our production editor, Abigail Powers. Thank you to Felicity Vallence, James Akinaka, Alex Garber, Shannon Spann, and everyone behind Penguin Teen. You spread joy to both readers and authors alike and have created an irreplaceable bookish community.

A huge thank-you to our publicist, Tessa Meischeid. You have always been a true joy to work with. We will forever be grateful for your genuine enthusiasm and hard work. One of the coolest things about publishing is getting to collaborate with people like you.

Thank you to Monique Aimee for the most stunning illustration and to Theresa Evangelista and Kaitlin Yang for designing the perfect Malibu cover. Your contribution to our book only inspires us further. And to Kate Renner for the lovely interior.

We never would have reached book number six without our friends. To Bridget Morrissey—you know. But even though we reflect daily on the blessings of the time line that brought us together, it's worth saying here again. Thank you for being the kind of friend who could (and does) inspire novels, for making us laugh when we're ready to fling ourselves into the sun, for being there for us whenever we need. To Maura Milan, thank you for asking the questions that push every story we write further, and for always being willing to see an action movie or trade a video game.

Thank you to Bree Barton, Simone DeBlasio, Kristin Dwyer, Rebekah Faubion, Harper Glenn, Kalie Holford, Isabel Ibañez, Derek Milman, Diya Mishra, Kayla Olson, Farrah Penn, Aminah Mae Safi, Gretchen Schreiber, Robby Weber, and Brian Murray Williams. Meeting you all has been one of the great joys of publishing.

A special thank-you to Kellen Kartub for having the wedding that inspired this whole novel, and to Gabrielle Gold for being our best friend through everything. To our families, you inspire us daily. We love you.

Finally, our readers. To everyone who's every DMed us or tagged us in a post or approached us at an event—you are the best part of the journey. We wouldn't be here without you, and it's for you we write.

REAL ROMANCE FROM

A REAL COUPLE!